LAST TO DIE

DOUG SINCLAIR

Storm

To request permissions, contact the publisher at rights@stormpublishing.co

Ebook ISBN: 978-1-80508-508-9
Paperback ISBN: 978-1-80508-509-6

Cover design: Blacksheep
Cover images: Shutterstock

Published by Storm Publishing.
For further information, visit:
www.stormpublishing.co

ALSO BY DOUG SINCLAIR

DS Malkie McCulloch Series

Blood Runs Deep

For Barney. I'm still trying to make every day count, mate.

through the grubby double-glazing, deaf old cow. But he was skint and the shakes were starting again. His granny always warned him about his drinking, lectured him daily about the evils of alcohol over the rim of a sherry glass. That was before she died of emphysema from forty woodbines a day. Right now, he wished to hell he'd listened to the old girl.

He'd finally met someone who actually seemed to fancy him, but Jackie hated his drinking, said it reminded her too much of her own dad. So, Billy had made a life-changing decision. One last job, because Fisher was paying too much to say no, even for a dirty job like this one. Maybe just a couple more drinks afterwards to celebrate, then he'd tell Fisher no more, and start on a mission to clean himself up. He intended to charm Jackie's little white socks off. For the first time in his life he was prepared to put some effort into a girl. Wine and dine would have to be more like fish and chips in the moonlight by the River Almond, but where he and Jackie came from, that counted as romantic.

He stopped under a streetlight to check the address scribbled on the back of his hand. Fisher said not to use his phone, so he had to stop at a bus shelter to check a 'You are here' map.

He found her address. It was a shambles, the garden overgrown, weeds crowding either side of a patchy gravel path that led to a manky uPVC door. There were four small windows in a crescent at the top, two of them broken and filled in with plywood and gaffer tape.

He eased the gate open, which was tricky because it hung from just one hinge and scraped on the path. He could just about see through the front window, draped with grubby net curtains, and saw no movement, no sign he'd blown it already. He left the gate open in case he needed a swift exit.

Gravel crunched under his trainers, but he doubted she'd hear him over the racket from the TV.

He reached the window. The old woman sat, slumped low,

ONE

Billy thumbed the edge of his gleaming, brand new, illegal-as-hell combat knife and grinned, then swore as it bit him and drew a crimson bead. He sucked it, squeezed it in a manky tissue from his pocket, but the bleed refused to stop.

Bad sign? Maybe give this one a miss? Maybe a bit ambitious for him, his first actual murder?

She's seventy-three years old, Fisher had said. Easy money.

Still, his thumb stung like a bastard now. Bad sign, that.

He'd been told to keep it simple, make it look like a burglary gone bad. Then there was that stupid message he was to make sure she heard before she died. What the hell did '*sleeping dogs*' even mean? He expected to feel a right idiot repeating it, but you don't disobey a man like Fisher. Not when he asked for something like this. What the hell had the man got himself messed up in?

Billy hadn't wanted to work tonight, but Fisher had offered him a huge wodge of cash. Billy didn't admit to Fisher that this kind of job was a big step up from his previous jobs, and he was nervous. Plus, he was missing the rugby – Scotland at home against England, for fuck's sake. He could hear it blaring even in a high-backed chair in front of a log-effect gas fire, just like the one his granny had. He felt a brief pang of discomfort at what he was about to do to an unsuspecting old woman, but the cash Fisher was offering was too good to pass up.

Her TV backed onto the window so he couldn't see the screen, and the walls flickered and jumped with its lights. Odds-on the old cow was watching the bloody rugby herself. He checked his watch – if he killed her quick, he might catch the last fifteen minutes. She looked well out of it, still no sign she'd heard him, so he leaned closer.

Fisher had been telling the truth – she looked ancient. With her head flopped back and her mouth open and slack, she looked like a wee kid asleep in a grown-up's chair. Her short grey hair stuck up on one side where she'd been lying on it. One hand rested on the arm of the chair, her joints knotty, her fingers thin and bony. He couldn't guess why an old cow like her would deserve a death like Fisher had ordered. Now that the time had come, his earlier bravado deserted him, and he felt a pang of nausea at the thought of ending a life for the first time. But he couldn't afford not to finish the job, now he'd committed to it.

He moved to the front door. Locked, but always worth a try. Long years of robbing the elderly had taught him never to underestimate the stupidity of your typical pensioner. A concrete plant pot stood by the door, overflowing with weeds and fly-by litter. He crouched down and lifted. The bloody thing was heavier than it looked, but he raised it enough to slide his fingers under.

No key. No problem.

He checked the window one more time. No change in position. If anything, her face looked even slacker.

He slid his blade into the gap in the doorframe and waited. At the first roar of the crowd from the TV – had to be a try getting scored – he levered the blade and pushed the door in.

Rotten wood crumbled and fell to the filthy doormat at his feet. One more look through the window showed she hadn't moved.

Inside, the hallway was dark except for a wedge of flickering TV light through the living-room doorway. He placed his feet with care, the floor lost in darkness. He made it to the end without tripping over anything and peered inside the room.

The door opened directly behind her chair, which was handy. With no lights on he wouldn't cast a shadow. And if he couldn't see her over the chair-back, she wouldn't see him if she woke too soon.

A steaming mug of cocoa and a plate of biscuits sat on a side table beside her chair. Something about that bothered him, nagged at his mind but wouldn't come into clear view. Guilt? No. This wasn't his granny, this was just some miserable stranger whose rotten little life looked at a dead end, anyway. And besides, Jackie was worth what he'd agreed to do, tonight. Just once, first and last time. Then never again, he promised Jackie in his mind. He swallowed, told himself to grow a pair. If Fisher could see him right now – scared of one old woman...

He glanced at the TV. Yep – the rugby. Scotland ahead with only twenty minutes to go. He had minutes, no more.

He fingered the hilt of his blade, took comfort from its cold, brutal simplicity. He got it off a mate who got it off the internet. Canadian Special Forces, he said. Black stainless steel, with a sexy white logo. A Rat, it was called. He liked that. It made him feel dangerous, kind of sinister. You had to go in equipped: only an amateur used kitchen knives.

The Scotland fans roared rabid encouragement at him.

He licked his lips, tasted bile, the prospect of violence, his fear of stepping over a massive and ugly line. He leaned forward and reached over the chair-back to grab a fistful of her thin, grey hair, his blade ready to slam into her miserable, scrawny guts as soon as he'd delivered that stupid message.

The chair was empty.

He heard her behind him – which was bloody insane but who else could it be? Cold fingers grabbed his right wrist, gave it a brutal twist behind his back, and lifted the knife from his paralysed fingers. Something struck both his legs from behind and he went down. His chin slammed on the back of the chair and his teeth smashed together. She yanked his wrist halfway up his back and he felt like his arm was breaking in three places.

He screamed but choked it off when his own knife appeared in front of his face, then slid down to rest against his throat.

The pressure on his wrist eased, but the edge of the blade bit harder. He winced at a sharp scratch and felt his own blood trickle down his neck.

He whimpered. What the fuck had Fisher got him into?

'Hush now, son,' said a gravelly voice in his ear.

As ice ran down his spine and thoughts of fish and chips with Jackie flashed across his terrified mind, he caught a faint smell. Something like his granny used to wear. He remembered her pet name for him: Silly Billy. Because he was always letting other kids get him into trouble.

Why had he never listened to her?

TWO

Malkie's resolve nearly buckled but he stood his ground. Why did she always have to do this at shift-end?

His DI, Susan Thompson, had kicked meaner arses than his up and down the CID room, despite barely reaching five foot six in heels. She even put a DCI back in his box once. At a morning briefing, no less.

'Barclay bloody had it coming, and you know it.'

'Maybe. Possibly. But your name's on a complaint. Again. Did you really think refusing to show your warrant card would stop a man in his position identifying you? Are you really that big an arsehole? Or do you just not care about one more black mark on an otherwise bloody awful record?'

Thompson turned away, took a deep breath, sat behind her desk. She straightened her blouse, her professional appearance easier to control than her temper.

He glared at her, sullen, but she stared back, and he broke first.

'Bastard had it coming. He knew how dangerous it was, that shite his guys were selling to those pensioners, but he made sure none of it could ever come back to him, didn't he?' he muttered, but the fight had left him.

She met him halfway. 'Yes, he did. But you've got nothing actionable, so you leave him the hell alone. Right?'

'Nae justice.'

She glared back now, and he knew when to leave well enough alone, when a battle was lost. He continued to sulk but sat down, and kept his mouth shut. It wasn't her fault the Criminal Justice System was going down the pan and she'd be as pissed off about it as he was.

She opened a file on her desk and studied two pages. She tutted and sighed her way through the statement on the first, then gave up before reading the second.

'Christ, Malkie. What does it take to get through to you? You're good at the job, when you keep your gob under control. Why do you insist on going in a huff and blowing away all your good work every time some bastard gets off? We all know it happens too bloody often. As long as we keep the averages up, that's the best we can hope for.'

Her tone moderated as she talked, and she now looked slightly less intent on tearing a strip off him. They had been close as cadets back in Tulliallan, but it irritated him that she seemed to think they were still buddies. She was management now, a DI, the same grade he used to be and hated, but she hadn't turned – yet – into a fully corporatised Police Scotland automaton. He often joked that he'd soon need to file a written request in triplicate before taking a dump. It didn't get the laughs it used to; maybe he needed some new material.

'Malkie. Bloody pay attention.'

He roused himself from his thoughts, forced himself back into the room.

Thompson. Arse-kicking. Pay attention, man.

'Sorry, ma'am. Were we finished here?' She'd hate the *ma'am*, but his foul mood overrode his better judgment. He was lashing out, furious about Barclay but taking it out on Thompson, and she would know it.

She tried to wither him with one of her infamous looks but gave up. They went back too far.

'For God's sake, Malkie. I know it kills you more than most when someone like Barclay gets off, but think about your pension, if you can't give a toss about your reputation. No one else will have you if you screw up again. Gavin McLeish let you transfer to my team after his previous off-the-books investigation went arse over tit, but he's watching you now, waiting for just one cock-up. You do realise that, don't you? And I'm guessing you're still paying your dad's mortgage on top of your own?'

He nodded. He wouldn't take this from anyone else except her or Steph, but he knew her well enough not to doubt her sentiment.

'Aye, and he still doesn't know.'

She smiled, with no agenda. 'Then stop mouthing off at lowlifes when they slip through. For your dad's sake if not your own.'

And there it was.

Self-recrimination swamped him. Tommy, his dad had lost a wife of fifty years when Malkie lost his mum, and whatever chance the old man had at any scrap of future happiness now languished in Malkie's fallible hands. In the months since his mother's death, he'd never managed to piece together a single solid and irrefutable memory to justify his need for penance, to remind him of whatever miserable error he'd made the night their house burned down with her inside.

'Malkie. Stop that.'

He allowed her a small smile, acknowledgment that she knew him better than he'd ever be happy about.

'You'd better book another appointment with that counsellor. Even if I can talk Whittaker out of a full disciplinary, you're still looking at six sessions, minimum, to get your box ticked again.'

He'd prefer a simple booting, but she was bang on, and he needed to protect his pension more than ever now.

She obviously took some satisfaction from straightening his face out. 'Now piss off, Malcolm. I'm sick of the sight of you.'

'Yes, Susan. Thank you, Susan.'

He stood and stretched, felt his shirt pull free from his belt, held the pose until Thompson caught an eyeful of his sun-starved paunch. He was fonder of her than he'd ever admit, but he did enjoy pushing her buttons.

She smiled, like a cat at a fat, old pigeon. 'And by the way...'

He braced himself; this couldn't end well.

She flapped the file at him. 'You're off the Barclay case for now. You've screwed that pooch all you're going to. Next no-brainer shout that comes in, you're it.'

He stared back, his eyes dead. He refused to give her whatever reaction she'd been hoping for. Her smile disappeared.

Small victories, mate. Small victories.

As he turned to go, a beep sounded from her PC.

I know that sound, that's a new shout coming in. Dammit.

'Hang on, Malkie.'

She read her screen for a few seconds, then typed a few words, clicked her mouse a few times, then beamed at him.

'Stabbing. Craigshill. Probably a drugs deal gone bad. Piece of piss. All yours, you lucky man.'

'But it's nearly shift-end. Give it to Ballantyne.'

'She's fully loaded. You're it. Stop whining and go get 'em, Deputy Dawg.'

Her grin annoyed him more than he'd ever admit to her.

THREE

Fisher redialled. The wee shite had called when he'd reached Craigshill, as instructed, and confirmed he was good to go and his burner was fully charged. But now Billy wasn't picking up.

He'd told the lad to wait; he wanted one final attempt to talk his employer out of this stupidity, but she'd told him in her typical icy fashion to follow orders or he'd be next. She hadn't changed in the thirty years since he'd last heard from her. Fisher had never known her name; she'd recruited him via a mate of his from school who joined the Force when Fisher headed down the opposite side of the law. After that initial introduction, he'd always received work directly from her, but only ever by telephone, and names were never mentioned. The jobs back then weren't regular, but they were always lucrative, always more cash than he could ever say no to. When she'd eventually gone quiet all those years ago and he'd moved on to less ugly work, he'd hoped never to hear about her again. Why she wanted something this stupid done now, after so long, he couldn't begin to guess. He'd taken the job mainly because she'd offered him a stupid amount of cash and assured him it was the last time he'd hear from her, but also because he remembered some of the uglier jobs she'd had him do. Now, he was on her radar again, and that couldn't end well. His heart hammered in his chest. If he let her down – or worse, exposed her to any risk – he'd be on a mortuary table before the week was out. Heart attack or a drunken fall down the stairs of a high-street close. He'd been the one doing her cleaning up often enough to know she was capable of anything, and turning on anyone, and he also knew he'd never been the only man she dished out such jobs to.

He reached for his jacket and car keys, dialled one more time, got no answer again, and headed for the door. He had to get that phone. Burner 2, Billy Fuckin' Idiot Irvine. Fisher couldn't be identified from it, but the Pigs might be able to trace the call to his own burner, and from that to the location of every mast it had connected to. How could he have been so stupid, forgotten so much? Never call, even on a burner, from anywhere within a mile of your own patch.

The police would wonder why Billy no-mates chose to rob a cottage fifteen miles away from his own council flat, but that in itself wouldn't lead anywhere back to Fisher. Unless... *The fucking burner phone.* If Billy had taken the phone into her house despite having been told a dozen times not to, it would hold the photo he'd sent the wee idiot to ID the old woman. If nothing else, that would prove Billy had been there for a reason, that it wasn't a run-of-the-mill robbery-gone-wrong.

Worse, he had to hope the moron hadn't written down his instructions. He cast his mind back to yesterday, giving Billy his orders down the phone. He'd told Fisher to wait a sec while he found something to write on, hadn't he?

Could this get any worse?

Two minutes later he was on the road to Craigshill. If he didn't find the job done when he got there or if he couldn't clear up whatever mess Billy had made, he might be next on her list.

What the hell did she need done that could matter this much, after so long?

FOUR

Why did she have to dig it all up again? Hasn't she hurt me enough? Hurt all of us enough? Didn't she do enough damage the first time around? I tried to protect her, that night and for weeks afterwards, but I could only do so much, couldn't I? I had more than myself to think about. She's raking it all up but she was as much to blame as me for what happened to that poor girl. What we did to her.

And why after so long? We had no choice back then; trying to explain everything to anyone who mattered would have done so much more harm than good. It should have been kept between us, just the five of us. Together. It makes no sense, to turn on us, after so long. And now she's started something none of us can finish.

I know what the package means, the one she sent me. But what does she think it could achieve? She's never been the most direct of people, always enjoyed winding the rest of us up with her stupid cryptic half-comments. Always thought she was smarter than us, that was her problem.

Now she's decided to wake up some bitter old wounds and people are going to get hurt. And die. Have already died. Because she couldn't let it all lie. The damage done decades ago couldn't be undone. Surely she must realise that?

Why couldn't she let it go?

FIVE

Malkie took his time getting to the crime scene in the Almond Park, on the south side of the Craigshill neighbourhood of Livingston. His stomach turned over, his frayed nerves dreading whatever ugliness awaited his professional attention. Had he returned to work too soon after his mother's death? Was it obvious to everyone except him?

Stop thinking like that. Forward, man. Forward.

He told himself the sick lump of dread in his stomach was because he hated seeing bodies before they were bundled into a bag. He could get all he needed from the photographs, later; the police techies were very thorough. Even lurid colour prints always seemed somehow less real. He knew he was supposed to view the scene before anything was moved, in case he had a Columbo moment and spotted the single, tiny out-of-place item that would later blow the case wide open, but real life wasn't like 1970s Los Angeles.

He pulled up behind a patrol car by the roadside and killed the engine. In the late evening dark, and surrounded by a wide, flat expanse of public park, the crime scene circus looked like Cape Canaveral by night. Lights burned at four corners of the locus, taped off with red and white tape, flapping in the breeze. The evidence tent shone, blinding under powerful arc lamps, steaming in the rain which was just starting to die off. He was sure you'd be able to see the bloody things from the moon.

He pulled his overcoat up under his chin, got out of the car, groaned as cold night air washed around his neck anyway. He started across the grass but had gone only a few yards when he felt the unmistakeable sensation of shit under his foot. He stopped dead and lifted the soiled shoe. He couldn't see much, but the odour that rose off it told him all he needed to know.

'Oh fuck, no.' He loved dogs, always had, but he wished to hell you could teach them – or more accurately, their owners – some bloody manners.

He ground the sole of his shoe on the grass then continued on. He took his time. He could see the SOCOs were still fussing around inside the tent, and he wasn't about to allow them the pleasure of witnessing his discomfort. Most of the local teams knew he was squeamish, and most of them were still on his Christmas card list, but there were always a few who might be on-call tonight and waiting, eager, in the tent for his arrival and for their entertainment to begin.

As he approached the tape, a Uniform turned around and held up a hand.

'Stop there, mate. Tape's there for a reason.'

PC Eddie Wilson, Scotland's greatest hope if the International Olympics Committee ever started an Arsehole of the Year competition.

'No kidding, eejit.'

'Didn't recognise you in the dark.' 'Sir' followed, as an afterthought.

Malkie didn't thank him for lifting the tape, just stooped and stepped under, left Wilson to fill in his rain-soaked scene attendance sheet.

Before he could walk on, Wilson scored one on him. 'Shoe

covers. Sir.' And handed him a plastic pack. Malkie fitted the shoe covers then slapped the empty plastic bag on the Uniform's chest until he took it.

The SOCO tent stood fifty feet from a band of trees that ran along the bank of the River Almond where it flowed east through the park of the same name. He examined the ground surrounding the evidence tent. As often was the case, he saw absolutely nothing of interest, but it killed a couple of minutes. He couldn't see any photographers, and hoped they'd been and gone already.

He leaned close to the opening on the side of the tent.

'DS McCulloch in attendance. What we got?'

A masked pink face popped out, rimmed by the elasticated paper hood of her SOCO onesie. Malkie groaned. She looked barely old enough to be out of uni, let alone trained up and on active duty. He tried to recall how long ago he left his Uniform days behind and realised he had no idea.

'Evening, sir. Young guy, stabbed in the neck. You can have the body in a minute.'

Malkie cracked a sarcastic grin back at her. 'Lovely. Can't wait.'

Malkie turned away to see PC Wilson staring at him, and looking less than impressed. Malkie stared straight back, dared him to comment. The Uniform looked away, but not without making sure Malkie caught a slight sneer and a disapproving shake of his head.

Malkie could report the little shit for insubordination, but he knew word would get round the station and he'd end up the arsehole again.

Fuck him. Sticks and stones and all that shite.

He turned around to find a PC standing a foot away beside him.

'Fuck's sake, woman. Nearly shit myself.'

'Sorry, sir. PC Misha Howarth, sir. We have a witness,

thought you might want to talk to him now, while the SOCOs finish up.'

'Aye, good call. Where is he?'

She indicated a bench further along the bank, under the wide spreading branches of an ancient-looking tree. A man sat on it, hunched forward, staring at his shoes, his hands shoved deep into his jacket pockets. It wasn't particularly cold, so Malkie figured he was not handling the evening's events too well. Some people would have curled up on the ground and sucked their thumbs if they could, after an experience like this.

He reminded himself that this was an innocent bloke, caught up in something he might lose sleep over for weeks.

'What's his name?' he asked PC Howarth.

She took a few seconds to consult her notebook. 'Thomas Riley, sir. Owns a local restaurant. Was out for his bedtime walk.'

'What time did you ID him?'

She checked her notes again. '23:10, sir.'

Malkie checked his own watch. She blinked at him, no idea what he wanted.

'And you'd already forgotten his name. Well done, Constable. Keep up the good work.'

He couldn't help himself, but knew he was being shitty. She scowled at him as he passed her.

She spoke up again, in a tone suggesting she'd rather have her teeth pulled. 'Sir?'

He stopped, sighed, turned back to her with a long-suffering look. 'Yes, Constable?'

'I found a trail of blood spots leading across the grass towards the houses up on Pentland Park.' She pointed towards the back of a long row of terraced houses a hundred yards away across the grass. 'We started to follow it, but the SOCOs arrived before we got very far.'

Malkie waited. She didn't offer any more. Malkie took a

breath. He'd rattled her, knew he could have that effect on people, knew it was unfair of him.

'Well, now you're here, I need to start trying to cordon it off. Victim had to have staggered down towards the river from there so I need to preserve any evidence as quickly as I can. Obviously.'

'Aye, obviously.'

He sounded petulant, even to his own ears. 'Ach, ignore me. Misha, did you say? Shitty night, not your fault. Do what you can, aye? DS Lang should be on her way. As soon as she arrives, I'll send PC Wilson to help you.'

She smiled, but it was rueful. 'Do you have to?'

He grinned. 'Second thoughts, I'm supposed to be finishing my shift, so I assume you two just started? Thought so. Let's put him on scene protection all night.'

She smiled and turned to go.

Malkie approached the poor sod sitting on the bench who looked to be concentrating on not throwing up.

'Mr Riley?'

The man looked terrible. Malkie had seen witnesses react in all sorts of ways to the kinds of damage people were capable of doing to their fellow citizens. He himself got depressed and slept badly. Thomas Riley looked like he might react the same way.

Malkie sat down, turned slightly towards him. He kept his knees together, clutched his jacket in both hands, resting on his lap, and tried to appear as unthreatening as possible. The tree branches over their heads deflected most of the rain but occasional fat drops found their way through.

Riley lifted his head as Malkie approached. The man's eyes were dry, but his skin looked clammy and grey.

'Do you feel up to answering a few questions, Mr Riley?'

'Yes, sure. I'd like to get away as soon as you can let me?'

'Yeah, of course. Can I call you Tom?' He pulled his notebook and pen from his inside pocket and turned to a new page.

'That's fine.'

'One of the constables should have told you we'll need you to attend your local station tomorrow morning and make a formal statement. Will you be OK with that?'

'Yes, of course, but I can't really tell you much. I saw the old lady first—'

'Sorry – old lady?'

Riley looked at him, must have caught the irritation in his voice. PC Howarth had failed to mention this piece of information, but he had been taking his mood out on her at the time. He smiled at Riley, twirled his finger, indicated he should carry on.

'Yes. I was walking home along the river, and I saw her standing...' He paused to lick his lips and take a breath then pointed towards the evidence tent without looking. 'Over there, by the bench. She was just staring down at the poor guy. I called out to her, asked her if she was OK. There was something about the way she was standing there, so still, just staring.'

Malkie said nothing, just smiled his best encouraging smile, and Riley continued.

'She didn't hear me at first, probably too shocked by... Anyway, when she did hear me, she rushed up to me and told me she thought the guy was hurt. I checked him out, and – well, you saw for yourself. There was no way he was OK, not with that bloody gash in his neck.'

Malkie wasn't about to inform a witness that he'd not yet looked for himself.

'I couldn't bring myself to check for a pulse. There was just so much blood. I watched him for a couple of seconds, but I didn't see him breathing. I went over to the water because I was going to be sick, then I went back to check on the old dear. She was gone.'

'Gone?'

'Disappeared. It's two hundred yards in every direction away from the river, flat grass, not even any big trees or bushes, but I couldn't see her anywhere. It was dark, but you'd think I'd have seen her against all those streetlights on the road, wouldn't you?'

Riley was starting to look a bit fried, and Malkie decided he'd had enough for one night.

'Did one of the constables ask you for some ID, Mr Riley?'

'Yes. Why?' He looked alarmed.

'Just for the records, that's all. We need your details so we can contact you for your statement, that's all.'

'Right. Of course.' He relaxed.

'You go home and try to get some sleep. We'll be in touch. Thanks for hanging around for us.'

Riley stood, took one last look at the taped-off evidence tent, then turned around and walked in the opposite direction.

Malkie sat back and pondered. There shouldn't be any need to chase up Riley's mention of an old lady, but how the hell could a seventy-something old woman leg it so quickly? It was possible Riley was grossly underestimating the amount of time he took to lose his dinner into the river, but he'd need to have turned away for at least a couple of minutes to not have seen her wander off.

He shook his head. He was doing it again.

You're not Columbo. Work the case, fill in the forms, tick the boxes.

Somewhere, some shell-suited moron would be spending a few tenners on a couple of bottles of Buckie and some fags. He wouldn't feel a scrap of remorse, wouldn't lose a wink of sleep, and he'd probably parade around his gaff, bragging to his other fuckwit mates about how 'he done that one'.

Maybe one of his mates would dob him in if the case made it onto *Crimewatch*. If there was a reward for information leading to, etc.

But Malkie knew this case might never see the inside of a courtroom. Tom Riley hadn't said anything about anyone else, so his statement wasn't going to do any real good. He could only relate what the SOCOs were going to report in far greater detail, anyway.

The elderly woman had probably just wet herself and scurried off home to her cats and a pot of tea. Couldn't blame the old bird, really. He'd get a full description off of Riley in the morning, and he'd make sure the door-to-door guys asked everyone if they knew of any old ladies missing from next door.

The SOCOs appeared and started manhandling the body out of the tent. Malkie waited until they'd carted him off, before returning to the Uniforms. He had to admit, he felt for them sometimes. They'd be here all night, keeping the vultures and the ghouls away. He walked up to PC Misha. She stiffened and pulled her notebook out again.

'Mr Riley mentioned something about an old lady. Did you get anything from him about her?'

'No, sir. We only had a few minutes with him before the forensic guys arrived, then we had to tape off the area, then—'

'OK, OK.' He waved her protestations down. 'Just keep an eye out in case she's still wandering around here somewhere, OK?' He smiled at her. 'Sorry I have to dump you in this.'

He walked straight past PC Wilson without a word.

As he wandered back across the grass, he couldn't let go of Riley's claim that he had turned his back for only a few seconds. But even with what little they already had it couldn't look any more straightforward. If the coroner found drugs in the stiff, then the guy had gotten shivved trying to restock his stash. Then again, his wallet was nowhere to be found, so it might have been a simple mugging.

Malkie was halfway back to his car when a ridiculous thought occurred to him, and he couldn't help but smile.

He imagined a grey-haired old biddy in a cardigan and

sensible shoes pulling out her knitting needles and sticking them in some poor bloke's neck. Maybe she was a crack-fiend, and her pension hadn't come through. Maybe she was a dealer and was supplying half the geriatrics in town with imported skag.

It was sick, he knew, but hell – you had to laugh, didn't you?

He remembered PC Howarth telling him about the blood spots and turned around. The path was only yards away. Might as well have a look.

He found her walking slowly, studying the ground, stopping every so often to peer into the grass on either side.

As Malkie approached PC Misha Howarth, she looked up and grinned at him. 'We're gonna need a bigger crime scene, sir,' she said, in what sounded like a crap attempt at an American accent.

'Sorry?'

Her smile evaporated. 'Nothing, sir. Sorry, sir.'

'Stop calling me sir. Boss or Malkie. Not sir. You seen anything yet?'

She returned to studying the ground. 'Looks like he kept going off the path, then coming back onto it. I'm guessing he was already close to losing consciousness.'

'Aye, good call.' He stepped over and had a look himself. Her appraisal of the blood spatter looked reasonable. He straightened up, looked her in the eye, and smiled. Barely.

'I'll wait here. You go and grab one of the SOCOs, send them over here, OK? They'll be looking anyway, but they'll need to see this as a priority.'

As she walked away, Malkie spotted a car idling at the park entrance. Probably someone had noticed the ambulance arrive. The residents would be fascinated when they woke up the next morning to find a SOCO tent pitched on their favourite green space. He started towards the car, and it drove off at speed. Not just a nosy passing resident, then. Possibly a journalist, tipped off by some PC for fifty notes.

Or someone more directly connected to the proceedings.

He'd already had warnings for wasting police resources on tenuous theories, most of which turned out to be Grade A bollocks. He couldn't start a car chase based on one of his stupid hunches. Thompson was – probably correctly – likely to think this a simple gang-fight or a mugging, so she'd go through him like a bloody locomotive if some innocent punter reported him for harassment.

He had never been very good at keeping his mouth in check and was already in a foul mood tonight.

Malkie weighed up the situation. If the driver had anything to do with the stabbing, would they really have the balls to drive up and watch the body being carted off? They would have to be a moron or psychotic. No, likely just some rubbernecker hoping for a glimpse of something juicy to talk about in the pub.

He followed the blood-spot trail towards the back of the terrace of houses, slowly, to allow a SOCO to catch him up.

But he still had a feeling about that car. Something wasn't right.

SIX

Fisher parked up on the main street and swore some more. He'd seen the blue flashing lights some distance away, before he'd reached the park, and knew he was further in it than he'd thought. The optimist in him had told him to wait and see; maybe someone had seen Billy staggering away and had called it in, but it didn't necessarily mean they'd found the little shit.

He saw a forensics tent, too big for a few drops of blood on the grass. If he assumed it was the old dear in there, why wasn't Billy answering his damned phone? He couldn't afford to dial Burner 2 again, in case, against all odds, Billy occupied that tent. He slammed his phone down on the passenger seat, his mind tumbling.

He spotted a man studying the ground towards the left side of the park. He'd met enough coppers in his time, suffered enough kickings for resisting arrest. Every one of them had walked around as if they were the ultimate authorities on everything.

An ambulance drove past him and into the park. No blues and twos. No hurry. Which suggested if it was the old woman inside the SOCO tent she was beyond help and the paramedics saw no reason to hurry.

After several long minutes, a trolley was wheeled into the SOCO tent, then back into the ambulance, with a body bag clearly visible on top.

What the hell was his next move? Assuming the old woman was dead, where the hell was Billy? He had to find the little moron and make sure he'd followed at least some of his instructions and left the burner phone at home.

That was one problem. His employer was the other. Billy was supposed to have killed her in her own home and made it look like a burglary gone bad. Instead, the target had been found in the middle of a park, nowhere near her home.

Had Billy only wounded her and she'd staggered to the park? If so, he came right back to the question of where Billy was.

Too many questions. He needed to see her house for himself, if the coppers hadn't found it yet.

He saw the copper looking his way, so he drove off and headed for her address.

He couldn't shake an uncomfortable feeling that matters were spiralling away from him.

SEVEN

Malkie reached the edge of the parkland where the path led into a street, and still heard no sign of any SOCO joining him to assist. The trail led past three of the terraced properties, the blood more visible on the tarmac of the pavement than it had been on grass. He noted how the flow became more copious, which told him the victim had been stabbed here then staggered down to the park. The trail led through a garden gate to a front door. The door stood ajar, the lock forced, the wooden frame chewed.

He needed backup. He quick-dialled Steph Lang, his long-suffering, and long-suffered DC.

'I'm on my way. Five minutes.'

'OK. Good. I've got a feeling something's about to kick off.'

'Stay out of trouble, old man. Say "Yes, Steph."'

'Yes, Steph. Quick, please.' He hung up.

Just then, he spotted a shadow cross the light burning in one of the upstairs rooms. He craned his neck out to look up, just in time to see an old woman peek out then pull the curtains shut.

He heard a noise from inside the hallway, just visible

through the open door. He had no choice but to risk peeking into the house.

He pushed open the front door and peered inside. An old lady appeared from a staircase on the right, one sleeve of her blouse stained with blood. She held a small suitcase in one hand.

A man appeared in what looked like the kitchen doorway. He looked almost as old as she did but he also looked fit, like he could handle himself. He held some kind of multitool with a three-inch blade extended, his eyes on the woman and promising violence.

The woman hadn't seen him, distracted by a scruff like Malkie stepping through her front door. Malkie made a snap judgment call. Old lady, harmless, victim. Tall, well-built man, skulking around, armed. He threw the door open and made a move for the two. He yelled 'Kitchen!' and pointed behind her.

The woman's next action would live in Malkie's memory forever after. She looked confused but didn't waste time deciding which of the two men standing at either end of her hallway was the greater threat.

She dropped the suitcase at her feet, grabbed a vase from a side table and hurled it straight at Malkie. He raised one arm to fend it off, but her aim was perfect. It hit him in the forehead, and he went down like a sack of potatoes.

Malkie staggered back against a wall and watched a seventy-something-year-old woman duck under the swing of the younger and much larger man. His other hand, the one with the multitool, slammed into her from the other side but Malkie couldn't see if the blade connected. She thrust the heel of one hand up under his jaw. As his head snapped back, she reached around him with her other hand, grabbed a coffee mug from somewhere inside the kitchen doorway, and brought it down on the back of his head with a noise Malkie hoped he would never be on the receiving end of.

Malkie fought to stay conscious but knew he was fighting a losing battle. He dropped to one knee and struggled not to throw up.

He fell backwards, flat onto the floor. As he fought to stay conscious, he saw the elderly woman standing over him and staring down, one hand clutching her side where he now saw blood seeping through her fingers. She looked like ice wouldn't melt in her mouth, as if nothing particularly unusual had happened.

She rummaged in his pockets, found his warrant card. 'Well...' She read the card. 'Detective Sergeant McCulloch. It looks like I've started something, doesn't it?' She smiled then turned to walk away.

He wasn't sure he could have fucked this up any worse if he'd tried. If she didn't hurt him, that bastard in the kitchen might, and if he didn't, Thompson would crucify him anyway.

He lifted his head, opened his mouth to ask if she was hurt, then passed out.

EIGHT

Fisher awoke on the kitchen floor. Before he could think about finding the old woman, he heard a groan from the hallway and saw the copper shift slightly. He didn't have much time. He saw a CID warrant card lying on his chest and took a photo.

A dash upstairs confirmed his worst fear: she'd scarpered, already.

He'd thought she looked familiar and so wanted to search her home, find some clue as to who she was, why he'd been told to kill her, and where she'd learned to handle herself like that. He checked the copper again, saw him lift his hand to his head. He could hit him again, make time to do a proper search, but he knew two Uniforms stood just a couple of hundred yards away in the park and had no idea if the copper had called for them.

He had no choice but to make a hasty exit.

He didn't see the old woman anywhere between the house and his car, which surprised him. She'd looked barely capable of running for a bus, let alone clearing the end of the lane behind the houses, and he was sure he'd managed to cut her. The stupid cow who'd given him the job had some explaining to do. Hiring Billy for this job had turned out to be sending a proverbial teenage sheep to an abattoir, and he wanted to know why. The bloody woman had sent him in blind. There was a past here, and the old woman obviously hadn't been a seamstress in her younger years.

He would find the old woman and he would clean this mess up, but only after he'd had a hard conversation with the woman who'd dragged him into this.

He got into his car and dialled her number. She answered in seconds, as if she'd been waiting for his call.

'Who is that woman, the target? Tell me now, or...' He couldn't finish, wasn't up to a full-blown threat to her. The stories he'd heard about her all those years ago had rattled even the hard bastard he used to be.

'You don't need to know. Is the job done?'

Fisher could get no words out. Could this have gone any more wrong? How would she react?

'My man is dead. Your harmless old biddy killed him. How do you explain that?'

Nothing from her for long, long seconds, then a sigh. 'What the hell do you mean?'

Fisher flinched. He'd rarely heard her lose control of that ice-queen tone of hers, but she was losing it big time now.

'I mean dead. It's a pretty unequivocal statement.' As soon as he said it, he feared he'd gone too far. He'd never dared unleash attitude on her before.

Silence from the other end of the phone threatened to turn his newly found backbone to jelly again, but with what he believed her plans to be, she couldn't afford to consider him quite so indispensable now, could she?

When she spoke again, her voice confirmed his thoughts. She was very obviously pissed off, but the fact that she didn't hang up immediately told him she needed him.

'I'm not going to discuss this over the phone. Where are you?'

He knew this was going to reignite her, but he had to get this working relationship on an equitable basis.

'I'm still in Craigshill. Trying to clean this mess up.'

He could hear her composing herself, found himself enjoying the simple fact that for the first time in forty-five years, he'd rendered her speechless.

When she did speak again, her voice was neutral, controlled. 'You find her. You find her and you kill her. Is that clear? You have no idea what a shitstorm you're in danger of causing. Find her, or I send someone to find you.'

'Who is she? She's had training. You tell me who she is or I come and find you.' He couldn't believe he was saying these words. To her. He shook but hoped he managed to keep the tremor from his voice.

'I told you. You don't need to know.'

'I can't find her if I don't know who she is, you stupid fucking woman. Who is she?'

'One more comment like that from you, Fisher, and I'll be cutting your precious retirement very fucking short indeed. I'm now going to have to call in someone a hell of a lot more reliable to clean up your mess. Possibly you, too.'

Fisher's temper maxed out. 'Not acceptable.'

He almost felt ice form on his phone.

'What did you just say to me?'

Fisher swallowed. He was deeper in shit now than he could ever remember being before, but trying to back out now was futile. Time for a change in their relationship.

'You've never agreed to meet me and I admit I have no idea who you are, but that can change. I know someone who might know who you are. So, McArthur Glen shopping centre, Annie's Coffee Shop. Ten o'clock, tomorrow. Or I escalate.' He hung up, then gasped as a massive anxiety attack tightened chains around his chest. His left arm spasmed with a tingling so intense he cried out.

Would she meet him? How desperate was she and how convincing had he been?

He needed to drive home sharpish, pick up some things, park up somewhere remote, sleep in the car. Somewhere even she couldn't find him before morning.

NINE

Malkie had the worst headache he could ever remember when he finally came round.

He'd regained consciousness alone and lying on a floor covered in spots of blood, some of it now smeared on the back of his coat. Evidence, ruined.

He counted himself lucky to be alive, considering the vase-lobbing old lady and the big bastard who had left him out cold but unharmed, but then it had hit him exactly how deep he was in it.

After countless warnings from management about going off on one without backup, he had done just that. Again. Worse, he'd compromised a crime scene. He was in for yet another kicking from Thompson and would be the laughingstock of his department and several others when word got around, his reputation already a thing of legend.

If it got out he'd been felled by flying crockery from the hand of someone's granny, he'd be surprised if he ever managed to crawl out from under that one.

First thing he needed to do was to make sure he really was alone. He staggered to his feet, his head pounding and swimming. He found a lump forming on his forehead already. He made it to the foot of the stairs without throwing up and stopped to steady himself. After a few seconds he could see straight, saw the trail of blood lead into what had to be a lounge at the front of the house. He left that well alone, started up the stairs instead. In the front bedroom he found drawers and cupboards opened, and clothing spilling out of them and across the bed.

The obvious interpretation so far was that some lowlife had tried to burgle the old dear's home, found her in the house, and somehow she had scored a lucky hit on him.

He recalled Tom Riley's story about the strange old bird in the park. Granted, a town like this was chock-full of pensioners, but – like Malkie's bump on the forehead – two grey-haired spinsters in one night, both connected in some way with the stiff in the park, was too much of a coincidence to swallow.

So, she had done a runner. Just before Malkie had gone under, she had looked like she was dealing quite adeptly with the other bloke, so had she got the better of both of them or had he taken her? Although that bloke had tried to stab her.

If this was bigger than a simple burglary, then an unprecedented amount of shit would be dumped on him later if it emerged that he'd known something and kept it to himself.

He sat down heavily on the doorstep to wait. Steph arrived minutes later, pushed open the front door, examined him and the hallway. She closed her eyes, threw her head back. 'Why am I surprised?' She turned and walked back out into the front garden.

It took him an age to follow her.

'Before you start on me, there was nothing else I could do, this time. I followed the trail of blood and hoped you'd arrive before I found anything unpleasant. I ended up here, saw an old woman at an upstairs window. I barely pushed the front door – which was already open, before you ask – when I saw her appear downstairs about to be attacked by some bloke in her kitchen. I yelled her a warning but the silly woman threw a vase at me, got me right on the forehead.'

He waited. Steph stared at him. She folded her arms, studied him. As he started to think she was delaying his pain on purpose, she spoke.

'Aye, OK. I get that, but Thompson is still going to tear you a new arsehole. You know that, right? That's her job.'

Malkie sighed. 'Aye, I know. But I'd love to ask her what she would have done in the circumstances.'

Steph flashed him another look. 'I'd avoid that line of defence if I were you, Malkie?'

'Suppose you're right. Are the SOCOs heading this way any time soon?'

'Half hour or so, I think. Have you looked around?' She cast her gaze down the hallway and into the kitchen.

'I checked the kitchen. Back door was open but I saw no one in the back garden or in the lane, so I checked upstairs. No old lady, scarpered. She was holding a small suitcase when she came downstairs.'

'I wonder if she was leaving because she knew the attack was coming, or did she pack after her intruder was stabbed? Her apparent intruder. But you said the bloke in the kitchen was twice her size?'

Malkie heaved a long, heavy, tired sigh. 'What a fucking mess.'

TEN

The McArthur Glen and Almondvale shopping centres and adjacent retail parks formed the beating heart of retail therapy in Livingston.

Fisher arrived by bus, but other than a baseball cap and keeping his face down, he didn't bother with the other nonsense that TV people loved: he wore no disguise, didn't slink from doorway to doorway checking behind himself every hundred yards. He performed no sudden about-turns and he didn't wear sunglasses. In Scotland, in February, sunglasses made you stand out in a crowd, rather than blend in.

What he did do was arrive a full two hours early and sit in a burger bar on the opposite side of the atrium from Annie's Coffee Shop. He fidgeted with his phone, nervous. After so many years of her being nothing more than a faceless and menacing unknown, he couldn't quite believe he was about to meet her. If she turned up.

He recalled stories he'd heard about her on the criminal grapevine, her reputation spreading beyond just the jobs he got from her. Cold, sadistic, paranoid, a woman you gave no cause to believe you were a danger to or you'd end up being no danger to anyone ever again. All he'd ever heard on the phone was icy calm, supreme self-control, until last night. Now, he was dying to meet her, put a face to the horror story. He doubted any of them had ever met her, or even had the slightest clue who she was.

He studied a woman at the next table to his. Burgundy shell-suit, vape pen in her mouth, moaning at a brat in an equally tasteful tracksuit. He wondered how she'd react to finding out the balding, middle-aged man at the next table had snuffed out more people than she had vodka shooters every Saturday night. He did acknowledge, in the spirit of not judging a book by its cover, that she might not get off her face on vodka shooters every weekend. She might be a lager-tops girl.

He had to marvel at how small he imagined her world must be. Enough lizard-brain smarts to stay one step ahead of the benefits agencies, and a wide enough vocabulary to complain bitterly about what she was entitled to if 'they' ever tried to deny 'her rights'. A massive TV and satellite dish, roll-ups and cheap lager and four takeaways a week. He thought he could form a pretty good impression of the limits of her life.

He envied her in a way. Much as he sometimes wondered how it would feel to be a bird, or a dog, to go about life thinking only of what lay immediately ahead, never to dwell on what had gone before. The kind of existence he'd just imagined for Miss Burgundy Shell-Suit might be enough for her, all she needed. He felt confident assuming she never sat guzzling her watered-down, extra-large Diet Coke, wondering if she'd get to wake up in her own bed again.

His phone rang. He jumped in his seat and regretted it. Her name on the display.

'Calm down. It's just little old me, and I'm seriously fucking displeased to have to meet you.'

Fisher scanned the wide, high atrium of the shopping centre, but he had no idea who to look for. She clearly meant to keep it that way, but he chanced his luck, anyway. 'Where are you?'

'Did you actually think I'd meet you face to face, Fisher? I'm disappointed.'

'I had to try. I've been so looking forward to making your acquaintance properly, as it were.'

'You're as bad a liar as you ever were. So, to business. Tell me why I should let you carry on breathing, you having proved yourself an incompetent failure in your old age.'

Fisher dropped his hand to the table harder than he meant, drew the eager attention of Miss Shell-Suit and her brat. 'Maybe if I'd been in full possession of all the facts before—'

'Oh, stop bleating, man. What happened?'

Fisher choked down an urge to scream obscenities down the phone at her. 'First. I want to know who the old woman is.'

'Who is the man you gave the job to?'

He considered pushing for an answer to his question before giving anything back but had to admit he was the one who had fucked up.

'Nobody. An amateur. I thought it was an easy job. If I had known the old woman was dangerous...' He stumbled, didn't like to remind her that he had been outsmarted by a pensioner. 'I would have sent someone more experienced.'

'I told you specifically to send someone competent.'

'Yes, but you didn't tell me the fucking woman has had training, did you?' Miss Shell-Suit turned her full attention on him, already enjoying the shouting but eager for further entertainment. 'Who. Is. She?'

'Refresh my memory. When you worked for me, were you in the habit of thinking for yourself?'

Fisher couldn't believe what he was hearing. He leaned forward across the table, his rising anger unable to find an outlet. He wanted to surge to his feet, walk away, deny her the advantage of watching him from wherever she was undoubtably observing him. But he forced himself to relax, needed to hide as much as he could the fraying of his nerve.

'We. Are not. Those people. Anymore.'

He hoped that just once she would listen to someone. If she didn't, she might take him down with her, and he was damned sure he still had some things he wanted to do with his life.

'I'm a businessman now. Whatever you are, even if you're still the same... person you used to be, *I'm* not, and I have a long, boring retirement planned.'

She listened, but still said nothing.

'You might have scared the shit out of me back then, but things have changed. I can't go around cleaning your mess up like before. I can't even walk down a street without appearing on a dozen cameras. And if something goes tits up do you really think our previous working relationship will stay private? Can you really be that stupid?'

He'd gone too far again but was past caring. A week ago, he'd been bored and counting the months to his sixty-fifth. He'd stashed enough away to live comfortably for the rest of his days and only took this job at her insistence and her promise a of stupid amount of money. She had called him, and now he was up to his bloody neck in it again. Worse, he'd learned he couldn't handle himself like he used to.

She spoke at last. 'This one time only, I will tell you everything you need to know, and then you'll do your job without further question. Understand?'

He waited.

'Her name is Lillian Crosbie, and she's done something that forces me to have her taken care of and you will do it. Quickly and cleanly and correctly. Now you know all you need to know. Can I assume you'll complete the job, this time?'

Ice laced her voice, a promise of imminent – and permanent – early retirement, but the attitude and the arrogance of the woman pushed him beyond common sense.

'If this comes back to me, I'm taking you down with me.'

She refused, or failed, to give him the satisfaction of reacting. 'If this comes back to you, you won't get a chance to bring it back to me. Are we clear? Now, I trust there's no longer the slightest chance of any further misunderstanding?'

'Can you sleep with one eye open? Better learn fucking quick. Now, are *we* clear?'

'Language, Fisher. There are children...' She stopped in mid-sentence and hung up.

His fury boiled over. He had to resist an urge to slam his phone down on the table, refused to allow himself to lose control.

A thought tickled at his mind. His table was at the back of the cafe. Miss Shell-Suit and her brat sat in an alcove, the kid seated against the wall. Only a limited section of the atrium offered a view past his table into their alcove. He traced that line of sight, scanned the atrium, saw no one hurrying away, no one exhibiting any evidence of urgency to flee the location. He stood, crossed to the huge glass sliding doors that led to the car park, and there she was.

Jeans and a black wool overcoat, handbag hanging from her shoulder. She ran away from him across the car park, fumbled in her handbag and produced a bunch of keys. Fisher ducked behind a van and watched her through the vehicle's rear window. She leaned over the steering wheel, her forehead on her hands, and heaved in several long, deep breaths. After a glance back towards the atrium doors, she straightened in her seat and started the car.

As she drove away, he memorised her number plate without thinking.

He sat down on a concrete planter, and had to admit he was at a loss. He'd hoped to get a look, maybe even a photo, of her face, but he hadn't needed to see her from the front to know she wasn't looking nearly as sure of herself as he'd come to expect from her.

Between Lillian Crosbie handling him so adeptly the previous night and this cold, vicious blast from the past, never identified but feared by so many, he had to wonder which of the two women might yet be the end of him.

ELEVEN

The early morning sun blasted through Thompson's office window, and Malkie had to squint at her. After leaving the crime scene in Almond Park, he'd only managed to grab three hours in bed at the cabin he shared with his dad, and what sleep he did get was fragmented, broken into fitful episodes of the same dreams that kept him from sleep most nights since it happened. Since the night he allowed his mum to die as the family home burned to the ground. The dreams never revealed to him *how* he'd contributed to her death, but he clung to a stubborn conviction that something he'd done, or hadn't done, had to lie at the heart of the events of that night, and until – if – he learned otherwise, he knew they would grant him no respite.

He'd known a kicking from Thompson would be inevitable, so with any decent sleep eluding him he'd been at the office bang on time at eight o'clock for the first time in weeks. She hadn't mentioned the previous evening during morning briefing, and McLeish had been absent, attending some other opportunity for a potential step up the greasy pole. So, she had saved his arse-kicking for in private, even though the whole CID room now watched through the glass walls of her office.

The remainder of his current team for this case – Steph, DC Rab Lundy and DC Louisa Gooch – had been dispatched to their desks to follow up door-to-door interview notes and various other mundane jobs that made up the bulk of the exciting cut-and-thrust of modern police work. Malkie would join them after this, his latest in a long, long series of management bootings.

'What the fuck did you think you were playing at, you bloody clown?'

'I thought if I—'

'Did it slip your mind that there were two Uniforms just yards away, bored out of their skulls?'

'I thought I might—'

'And don't get me started on crime scene integrity. You did do that class at—'

'Bloody take a breath and I'll tell you.'

The ensuing silence was worse than her rantings. He stared at her, his blood still high, but realisation dawning on him: he'd just used what the policy makers called *unprofessional language* to a senior officer, and loudly enough for the rest of the CID room to hear every word, even through the closed door.

Just when he thought he couldn't fuck up any worse, he always did.

Thompson stared at him. Her fingers drummed on her trousers as she fought to control her temper. She sat behind her desk, folded her arms and stared him out for the second time in twenty-four hours.

He broke first, deciding it the prudent course of action.

'I thought—'

She unfolded her arms and slapped her hands down on the desk, leaning forwards, her eyes blazing. He cut her off with one upraised hand.

'I thought...' He paused, daring her to interrupt again. She closed her mouth, again, her lips tight, thin, and white. 'I thought if I waited for backup, the guy might hurt the old lady and do a runner. I didn't know what the score was. I think it fair to assume he's linked to the body in the park. I thought it more important not to lose him and to protect an innocent citizen. I believe our job description says something about that.'

He sat back, held his hands out to indicate she was now at liberty to lay into him again.

She waited a few seconds, then sat back too, her posture deflating slightly.

'Billy Irvine.'

'The dead guy?'

'The deceased. SOCOs ID'd him from a bank card in his pocket. His phone was a burner, which is not unheard of, but suggests more than just a housebreaking on his mind.'

Malkie waited. He'd known her long enough to recognise when she'd given up on him again. He didn't want to pour petrol on a fire that might be about to burn itself out anyway.

She sat forward again and pulled a manila folder from her in-tray. She opened the front cover and handed him a sheet of paper. A printout of young Billy Irvine's police record. Nearly a full page of minor offences, ranging from shoplifting to house burglary, which could have led to an obvious conclusion – he'd got himself stabbed by some homeowner who'd woken to find him in their house – if it hadn't been for the second man.

Most house burglaries were committed by idiots desperate for drug or drink money, or wasters too lazy to go out and earn their cash like decent people. They didn't usually arrange backup.

'This guy, Billy. He's nothing special. I see volume but nothing ambitious here.'

Thompson stared back at him, gave a distinct impression she was waiting for him to arrive at the same conclusion she already had.

'This other guy – the one I saw the old woman go for – it's a good bet he sent Billy there in the first place. And that means it was that specific house Billy was supposed to hit.'

Thompson nodded, still noncommittal.

'So, the old woman was the target. Not her purse or her TV.'

Thompson sat back, a look of satisfaction on her face that Malkie found patronising.

'What the hell were two dodgy-looking men doing going after a harmless pensioner? Why the special attention? And where the hell did he take her? I assume he took her because there's no way she could have got the better of both of us.'

He could swear he saw a glimmer of a smile on Thompson's face, but he soldiered on.

'So, the usual, then. More door-to-doors, keep an eye out for the old girl? What about *Crimewatch*? Did we find a decent photo?'

'SOCOs found one photo in the whole house. Man and woman in some seaside town, the quality suggests it's old. It was being used as a bookmark in an equally knackered old paperback. It had the words "Time and Silence" written on the back and was signed "Love, Ben". The photo, I mean, not the book.'

'What was the book?'

Thompson consulted her screen. 'Some thriller. Robert Ludlum or something like that. Looked second-hand.'

Malkie stood and turned to go.

Thompson wasn't finished with him. 'By the way.'

He paused in the doorway.

'Two o'clock tomorrow.'

Malkie shrugged, knew what she meant but made her spell it out.

Thompson looked up from Billy's file and smiled sweetly, which confirmed he wasn't about to have a great day.

'Timothy Crichton. Two o'clock. Tomorrow. He had a late cancellation, lucky you. Enjoy.'

Malkie couldn't help himself. He closed his eyes and groaned.

'Susan, I don't need—'

She cut him off with a casual wave of one hand. 'One more word and I make you go back to the shrink on the preferred suppliers list. And we both know how well you and she got on, don't we?'

Malkie considered taking the rest of the day off sick but knew he would only be delaying the inevitable. Besides, Timothy was the lesser of two pains in the arse.

On his way out of Thompson's office, he bumped into DC Louisa Gooch on her way in.

'Watch it, Gucci. What's the rush.'

She looked at him for a second, then looked past him to Thompson.

'We've identified the old lady, ma'am. Door-to-doors missed a couple of neighbours and one called us this morning, said he knew her name. You won't believe this – she's one of us. Or used to be.'

She checked the sheet in her hands. 'She used to be PC Lillian Crosbie.'

TWELVE

Fisher worked through the day. Seeing her run away, looking rattled, hadn't helped ease his fear of her.

He'd kept detailed notes of every scrap of intel he ever gleaned, from when he started working for her, through to the drying up of his private employment opportunities in the nineties. Newspaper clippings, handwritten notes now faded and near-illegible, photographs he learned to develop himself. He hadn't opened the box in forty-five years.

After the chaos of the previous evening, he found himself completely at a loss as to how to proceed, and to explain why the old woman constituted a threat serious enough to drag him into this ridiculous scheme.

Long years of following instructions without question had bred in him a habit of collecting all possible data on every target he was ever told to scare or torture or worse. Any job involving high-profile targets which might cause dangerous ripples tended to get assigned to him. To be done quietly and efficiently, while she made sure she was somewhere tens of miles away in front of unimpeachable witnesses.

Which meant last night's shambles was something that

might make waves. Ignorant of the risk she'd not seen fit to share with him, he'd recruited Billy, a nobody Fisher knew would mug his own sister for booze money. He couldn't have known that Crosbie was capable of taking Billy out, as appeared to have happened. She was no lame old geriatric.

The way the old woman had handled herself when she found herself caught between himself and that copper had smacked of formal training. Typical self-defence classes didn't include sections on the use of airborne crockery as a lethal weapon. Ordinary people trying to defend themselves was usually a comic affair, with lots of wild swings, half-hearted slaps and badly aimed kicks. The old woman had ducked neatly under his arm and sucker-punched him. Not in the gut where most amateurs would have aimed, but square under the jaw, which rattled him enough to give her vital seconds to land a knock-out blow to his head with more crockery. She had taken all of three seconds to perform the whole manoeuvre. His pride hurt almost as much as his head.

He opened his box of notes and started to work through the files he had spent so many hard years accumulating. Despite the pounding in his head, his curiosity had been awakened.

When the answer finally came to him, he stared in disbelief at a newspaper cutting he'd forgotten about years ago. He knew her, always had done. He'd just forgotten. He'd never believed she did what everyone said she did. She disappeared from circulation shortly after and fell from his – and everyone else's – memories.

Lillian. Fucking. Crosbie. The woman who ended two lives with one brutal and heartless action, and never paid for it.

THIRTEEN

'Malkie.' Thompson flapped a hand at him, indicated he should join her in her office.

She closed the door behind him and sat behind her desk.

He sat, smoothed his tie down his shirt-front, crossed his legs in a way he hoped came across as professional. He'd known himself to sulk for hours after her talking to him the way she had earlier.

'What the hell are you doing, you clown? I need you to break with normal routine and act like an adult for five minutes.' She glanced at her watch. 'Dammit. Get your coat.'

'Why? I'm nearly at my shift-end.'

'Not anymore; you and I are heading to Tulliallan. I'll drive. Try to tidy yourself up a bit before then, will you? At least tuck your bloody shirt tail in. How many times, Malkie?'

'Why, are we meeting someone important?'

'Megan Shaw. She worked in the old Livi Station back in the late seventies, early eighties. Louisa called a contact she'd developed at the National Archives in Edinburgh. Turns out a lot of the personnel records from that time were digitised and stored there, they're on a seventy-five-year retention period, I think. She found some records from around then and recognised Shaw's name. We now have a list of twenty or so officers who served there around the time Lillian Crosbie did. I called Shaw and she can spare us a half hour if we get over there quick.'

'She can spare us a half hour? Who the hell does she think she is?'

Thompson sighed, as she tidied papers and manila files into her desk drawer and locked it. 'She thinks she's Detective Chief Superintendent Megan Shaw, you idiot.'

'Should I know her?'

'She's about to become area commander for the whole of the North East Division. Do you pay any attention to the weekly briefing emails? Don't answer that. Meet me in the car park in' – she glanced at her watch, again – 'shit. Ten minutes. Not a bloody second longer, OK?'

She left without waiting for an answer.

Malkie spent five minutes hunting for some basic background on Shaw on the internet, found a recent press conference about her imminent promotion that apparently went sour, ugly questions asked about her past. He couldn't take time to watch to the end and made a mental note to get back to it.

After a further minute in the bathroom wrangling his shirt back into his trouser belt, re-knotting his tie, and wiping his shoes with wet paper towels, he found Steph waiting at his desk with a gleam in her eye. She glanced at her watch. 'Probably best not to piss off your DI and a DCS in the same day, I'd suggest.'

She irritated him when she nagged him, but she irritated him even more when he had to admit she nagged him and was right.

'I know. I'll be on my best behaviour. Promise.'

She stared at him in mock disbelief. 'I'd do better than that if I were you, old man.' She shook her head and didn't bother to hide a rueful smile from him.

The journey to Police Scotland headquarters at Tulliallan proved less uncomfortable than Malkie might have feared. He'd expected repeated dire warnings about the career-limiting damage possible from speaking out of turn to a DCS, but after a brief bio of Shaw – mid-sixties, private education, wealthy parents, married late in life then divorced soon after, forty-eight years in the job, well-respected and liked, expected to make area commander soon – Thompson seemed content to put some easy listening on the radio and concentrate on the road. Malkie took the opportunity to close his eyes for the half-hour drive. He'd get no sleep, but wanted to try. Though he tried to empty his mind, it took only minutes for the music to trigger him. Sunday mornings, teenage Malkie still in bed, Mum and Dad at breakfast reading the newspapers, Classic FM on the wireless, and the smell of toast wafting into his bedroom. Days long gone, now.

Fragments of images hammered into him, memories of sounds and smells and pain. His dad screaming at him, flames overhead. Choking, black smoke billowing down from the ceiling as he ran along the hallway to her bedroom door. He never made it into the room. His dad had said he got blown back, slammed against the wall by a backdraught when he opened the door.

Why did that bother him? He felt the menacing itch of an elusive revelation, something about that night, something he should be seeing but couldn't.

'Malkie. You OK?'

He opened his eyes.

Dark outside, headlights passing, car journey. Tulliallan. Back to school.

'Malkie?' Thompson, worry etched on her face. 'You were frowning and moving your head from side to side, like you were saying no to someone? Were you asleep?'

After a few more seconds, he reconnected with his surroundings. He rubbed a hand down his forehead, ground his fingertips into his eyes, shook himself, sat up straight.

'I must have nodded off. I'm fine.'

She glanced at him again. She couldn't give him a demanding stare because she was driving, so he smiled at her and gazed out the window.

What am I missing? Why does the backdraught through Mum's bedroom door bother me so much?

They arrived at Tulliallan. Thompson parked, and Malkie glanced at her. 'The college building?'

'Don't ask me. She said to meet her here.'

A receptionist directed them to an empty conference room as she reached for her phone. In the room, Thompson studied Malkie, seemed satisfied; not happy but satisfied.

'Please, for me, just this once, keep it shut, would you? You always mean well, but...'

Malkie stared at her for long seconds before putting her out of her discomfort. 'Already figured you'd want to do the talking, ma'am.'

She sighed and opened her mouth, but a short, compact woman in uniform but without her jacket walked through the door. Malkie and Thompson stood, but she flapped her hand at them to sit.

The woman sat opposite Thompson. She held a perfectly manicured hand out across the table to her. 'DI Thompson?'

Thompson nodded and smiled.

'And you must be DI McCulloch?' She held her hand out again.

He took it, found it cold but strong. 'Yes, ma'am. But I'm just a DS now.'

Thompson squeezed her fingers into her eyes and sighed.

DCS Shaw studied him, not unkindly. 'Your record shows you passed your DI exams?'

Malkie struggled for a response that wouldn't put Thompson into a complete tailspin, and – as always – fucked up.

'I didn't enjoy sitting at a desk ten hours a day, ma'am, so I didn't really work out as a DI. I can do less damage as a DS, anyway.' He grinned, but only for a second.

Shaw smiled with what looked like genuine humour. Thompson stared at her hands, her fingers interlaced and turning white.

'So, DI Thompson, you said you wanted to talk to me about Lillian Crosbie?'

Malkie pulled his notebook from his pocket, happy to relegate himself to minute-taker if it might keep his mouth shut for the rest of the session.

Thompson sat forward, probably happy to take over the talking and enter damage limitation mode. 'Lillian Crosbie served in the old Livingston Station at around the same time you did, and—'

Shaw raised a hand, smiled. 'Forgive me interrupting already, I really don't mean to be rude, but can I save us all some time? I'm only too aware of who she is, and why you're here.' She sat back, and her expression took on a more serious demeanour, as if remembering unpleasant memories.

'Lillian Crosbie was a constable when I did my probation in Livingston. She was one of those officers who seemed content to languish at a lower rank, never seemed to exhibit any ambition, you know the type?' She kept her eyes on Thompson, but they all knew she was drawing a comparison with ex-DI Malkie.

'I was already being fast-tracked. You probably don't know

that the eighties saw a big push to get more women into the job. I was singled out even earlier than that, in the late seventies, as a potential poster girl, as it were. So, I overtook her quite quickly, made sergeant only a year after joining up. I'm sure it pissed off some officers but I was too headstrong and cocky to care.' She smiled at them both, a gleam in her eyes. Despite himself, Malkie found himself warming to the woman.

'Crosbie was a good constable. She joined the force at a relatively late age, in her mid-twenties, under the women in policing initiative. She seemed more mature and had more life experience than her peers.' She hesitated again, and Malkie had to wonder if it was genuine or for effect.

'But in 1978, she was suspected of being responsible – but only indirectly and accidentally – for the death of a young girl she released from custody overnight on Hogmanay, although it was off the books, never recorded. I'm sure you both know how things used to be.'

Malkie knew the stories, the most popular being about the presence of a staff bar in the basement. It was said that if you needed a drink after your working day, you had a drink problem, because you should have been getting enough during your shift. He could imagine Hogmanay on night duty, the whole shift half-pissed and glued to *Scotch & Wry* on the TV.

'I decided the young girl didn't deserve a detainment recorded against her for minor misbehaviour, so I wanted to let her cool off in a cell then drive her home. However, Lillian – Constable Crosbie – released the girl during the night as some kind of misguided act of Hogmanay goodwill. It was a bad winter that year, worst since 1963...'

Malkie picked up where Shaw clearly didn't want to go into too much detail. 'She never made it home?'

Shaw's shoulders slumped. 'The poor girl was found dead from hypothermia on a bench in Almond Park the next morning, halfway home. Crosbie said she'd ordered her a taxi, but...'

Malkie had to wonder what uglier facts could cause the woman even further pause.

Thompson sat forward. 'So there's no record, anywhere, of this person's detainment? Do you remember her name? We should find something about this in newspaper archives, shouldn't we?'

'Her name was Alice Garten.' She had to stop, closed her eyes for a second, and if Malkie was any judge of character at all, the woman's struggle was genuine, painful and personal, but for what reason? 'No, there will be no record of the event. As I said, we thought it charitable at the time not to lock the poor girl up and record a detainment against her for mere disruptive behaviour. She was drunk and shouting at people in the street, but she didn't get physical. Just loud and threatening.'

Malkie chewed this over. No Police Scotland officer would want past indiscretions to stain her patch's reputation at a time when other forces were struggling to weather accusations of institutional sexism and racism and who knew how many more isms.

'You said "we".'

Thompson's head snapped around to look at him. 'Detective Sergeant McCulloch...'

Shaw frowned. 'Did I?'

Malkie battled with his inner idiot for a few seconds and as usual the idiot won.

'Yes, ma'am. A few times.'

Shaw stared at him: what looked like a warning or perhaps a request not to dig too deep, but he'd dragged them both too far in already.

'Best if we're appraised of all relevant facts if we're to do our utmost to avoid further besmirching of the Force's good reputation. Ma'am.'

Shaw arrived at a decision, but it looked like she'd rather have her perfect, polished fingernails pulled out.

'At the time of the incident, I was a Uniform sergeant, and PC Lillian Crosbie's immediate superior officer. I had no idea what Crosbie was doing, but I should have. As ranking officer that night, I should have known. Lillian was a good officer.' Her voice caught in her throat. 'And as I said, a good friend. But I allowed her to throw her career away.'

She lifted her gaze to Malkie's, her eyes bright with moisture. 'Lillian deserved none of what happened to her. She meant well. She always meant well. So, now I want to assist in any way I can to find her safe, if you'll accept my help. Subject to case-confidentiality and cross-jurisdictional considerations, of course. I'm staying in Edinburgh all of this week, so please let me be of assistance.

'I have another reason to hope you find her quickly.' She swallowed, as if reluctant to continue. Ashamed, even. 'Lillian famously barely said a word that wasn't necessary. We used to joke about her, saying she never used one word when none would do.' A fond smile lasted a second on her lips then faded.

'But after Alice Garten's death, Lillian was bitter. I was as close a friend to her as she ever had, and she told me in private, that my... betrayal of her, my punishing her and – as she thought – doing nothing to protect her, had hurt her terribly.' Shaw seemed to drift off for a second. 'I never before or since saw that much passion in her, but it was toxic. Furious. Vengeful, even. I actually feared her for a while.' She shook her head. 'Afraid of Little Lillian. Good grief.'

She sighed and closed her eyes for a second. 'I want to do all I can for Lillian, but please be discreet with what I've told you. And find her. Please.'

Thompson leaned forward. 'OK, ma'am. Can we start with who you remember being on duty, that night?'

'PC Claudette Crawford, PC Paul Gaddon, PC Sheila Ferguson, PC Mark Balfour, PC Lillian Crosbie.'

Malkie scribbled the names down, then glanced at Thompson. He wondered if she, as well as he, found it notable that Shaw could reel the names off as if it were yesterday.

'And, of course, me.' Shaw smiled at them both, and Malkie's hackles lifted.

FOURTEEN

[AF] [13:21]

Are any of you still in this chat? It's Fisher.

[13:22]

Answer me.

I'm going nowhere. Answer me.

[CC] [13:25]

Who are you?

[AF] [13:25]

Thank fuck for that. We need to talk, Claudette.

[CC] [13:25]

Who are you?

[AF] [13:25]

Don't piss about. We really fucking need to talk.

[13:26]

I mean it. What we were always afraid might happen? It's happening.

[CC] [13:30]

What was the name of our landlord in 1978?

[AF] [13:30]

Our what? You mean the barman in the basement pub in the old station? It was Docherty. Is this really necessary?

[CC] [13:30]

First name.

[AF] [13:31]

You mean the first Docherty or the second.

[CC] [13:31]

Explain.

[AF] [13:31]

You mean Sammy Docherty the ancient old sod with the handlebar moustache and the missing front tooth? Or his son, Duncan? Those Docherties?

[CC] [13:32]

What do you want? Is this about her?

[AF] [13:32]

Who else? She's gone off on one. Looks like even after all this time, she couldn't let things lie. She hired me to kill Crosbie, but she didn't fucking tell me who I was going up against.

[13:33]

Fuck's sake. This is bad.

Who else is in here? Who else is still alive and not already senile?

[CC] [13:34]

Delicate as ever. Tell me what's happened and I'll decide whether to drag them into this.

[AF] [13:35]

She contacted me out of nowhere. I hadn't
heard from her for forty-five years. Scared the
shit out of me. Offered me one job for a stupid
amount of money. Told me to do one old lady
and cover it up, said nothing about the old lady
being Crosbie. I was to make it look like a
burglary. I thought it was stupid to take risks
like this now, after all this time, so I tried to talk
her out of it. While I was doing that the kid I
sub-contracted the job to went in early.

[CC] [13:36]

Get to the point.

[AF] [13:36]

I don't know what happened. Yet. But my guy
fucked it up and ended up dead, himself, and
Crosbie has disappeared.

[CC] [13:37]

What the hell was the stupid woman thinking.
She actually sent you after Crosbie? Even I
haven't heard from Crosbie since then, and I
contacted every one of us specifically in case
something like this ever happened. Crosbie
never answered, then her phone got
disconnected, so I assumed she'd gone into
care. Or a hospice.

[AF] [13:37]

No, she wasn't in care, has her own home, and
I think it's safe to say she's not let herself
become some frail old biddy.

[CC] [13:37]

What do you mean?

[AF] [13:38]

She took out my man.

[CC] [13:39]

How? We're all in our sixties and Crosbie must
be in her seventies. How old was your man? As
old as us?

[AF] [13:39]

He was in his twenties, and fit. And from the
amount of blood I saw in her house when I
went in after her, she stabbed him and got
lucky. The place was sodden with it. And it
wasn't hers.

[CC] [13:39]

How do you know that?

[AF] [13:40]

Because when I first saw her, there wasn't a
mark on her. I think I cut her but I can't be sure.

[CC] [13:40]

So why is she missing if you went back to
finish her?

[AF] [13:40]

Because she's a lethal fucking weapon, OK?
Even at her age. She got the better of me.
When I came round, she'd fucked off and I
have no idea where she is now.

[13:41]

Or what she'll do next.

[CC] [13:41]

This is bad.

[AF] [13:41]

You think? We need to find her before she
comes after everyone she thinks might know
what happened, that night.

[13:42]

Who was the woman on the phone back then? I
never met her. Why did she start all this?

[CC] [13:42]

I don't know. I never knew. Only Mark Balfour
knew. She only ever called him. That's the truth.
This is too bloody serious to lie to each other.
Not now. What the hell was she thinking? Forty-
five years. More. Why?

[AF] [13:43]

I don't know. If I'd known who she was telling
me to kill I'd have told her to shove it.

[CC] [13:43]

Give me until tomorrow. I'll see who else is still
alive and kicking. Are you still fit?

[AF] [13:43]

Yes. She surprised me, that was all.

[CC] [13:43]

Not filling me with confidence.

[AF] [13:44]

I might never have been one of you lot but you
had no issues with me in the seventies when I
took your garbage out for you. Don't start any
shite with me now. We need to deal with this
together.

[CC] [13:44]

Anything else I should know? Any witnesses?
Were you seen? I'm guessing the police will be
involved – are you on their radar? At all?

[13:45]

Were you?

[AF] [13:45]

Who is she? I need to know. I can't work in the
dark now. Not now.

Who is she?

[CC] [13:45]

I told you. Only Mark Balfour ever knew who
she was. He dealt with her and farmed out the
jobs to us, remember?

[AF] [13:46]

And he disappeared not long after that night.
Which would explain why I never heard from
her again. Until last week. I'm tempted to
believe you. I'll need to find out more directly.

[CC] [13:46]

Do you think she'll come after all of us? Even Shaw?

[AF] [13:46]

You kidding? Especially her.

[CC] [13:46]

Aye, I suppose so. I don't think we should stir this up any more than she has already. If we let it lie, she might, too.

[AF] [13:47]

When did you get so naïve?

[CC] [13:47]

Were there any witnesses to your cock-up?

[AF] [13:47]

Mind your tone. No, nobody saw me.

[CC] [13:47]

That had better be true.

FIFTEEN

Back in Thompson's office, Malkie was first to voice what he knew Thompson must be thinking, too.

'Something's not right, there, boss. Gucci's looking for a duty roster for that night but it was forty-plus years ago. She's already fact-checked what she could of Shaw's version of events and found nothing odd. But I'd bet my pension something's not right.'

Thompson sighed, her expression telling both Malkie and Steph she thought so, too. She glanced out her office window at a few stragglers in the CID room, too swamped to fit all their paperwork into regulation working hours.

Malkie pushed on. 'I'll admit most of what she told us rings true. Yes, she should have had better control over things that night. But even if Crosbie had a momentary lapse of judgment and pushed poor Alice Garten out the door in the middle of winter, it sounds out of character given her clean service record. And Shaw's credible opinion of the woman. Also, in my experience, management only ever worry about their own backsides. Present company excluded, of course, ma'am. But I believe Shaw's grief, or regret, or guilt, or whatever else brought those tears to her eyes, had some basis in reality, too. But there's something else there. Something more personal, more than just forty-five-year-old guilt for letting an old mate down.

'I think she does feel bad about letting her old friend down, and I suspect she's carried some guilt around for far too long and punishes herself far too hard. Very unhealthy, that.'

Thompson and Steph shared a look, which Malkie also ignored.

'But we also need to bear in mind that she's a ladder-climber who really wouldn't want something like this coming to light. Even if we get Crosbie back safe, the media will have a field day with this. "Senior Police Scotland detective linked to death of innocent girl during the bad winter of 1978. Cover-up suspected." That sort of thing.'

Thompson and Steph both stared at him. Thompson voiced what they were probably both thinking.

'You're not often right, Malkie, but when you are we all wish you were bloody wrong.'

'You mean you think the same? Both of you?'

Neither confirmed or denied, but that, in itself, told him all he needed to know.

'Fuck me – sorry, Susan – so not just me, then. We agree she sounded genuine... ish, but we also agree she didn't tell us the whole story?'

Steph looked to Thompson for her reaction. Malkie would have preferred to have Steph with him during the interview but even he'd realised they couldn't go in mob-handed to interview a DCS.

Thompson waved Malkie's thorny question aside. 'OK. We'll struggle to find a copy of Garten's autopsy report or death certificate now, but put Rab on it. I think St John's didn't even open until long after all this happened.'

Steph flipped back a page in her notebook. '1989.'

'What else did you find?'

Steph set her notebook down on the desk and folded her arms in front of it. 'Not much at all, really just what I could find in newspaper archives. She was seventeen. Learning difficulties. Absent father, mother pregnant at seventeen years old and still drinking right up to full term, so the newspapers made a big thing out of that. No mention of Alice being in any trouble until that night. After allegedly being a sweet wee lassie her whole life, she was arrested in the town centre for squaring up to three lads twice her size. She was screaming at them and took a swing at one but didn't manage to land a single blow. By the time officers attended, she was sat at a bus stop in the central boulevard, sobbing and screaming at anyone who came near her. A witness said the three lads were long gone and he hadn't recognised any of them. Garten was taken into custody, and the rest we know. Well, we know what DCS Shaw has told us.'

She turned a page. 'Only her mother, Polly, attended her funeral. She complained to the newspapers for a week that the *bloody polis* had killed her daughter but no one took her seriously. A month after the funeral she stopped talking about it but went right off the rails. She died in 1993, hepatitis from dirty needles and fifteen years of drowning her grief. Bloody tragic.'

Malkie groaned. 'Fuck's sake. Always someone, right?'

Thompson queried him with her eyes.

'Worse off. Always someone worse off. What a shitty end to a short life. Poor bloody mare.'

Thompson sighed. 'If there was anything dodgy about that night, we can at least find out the truth on her behalf, right?'

Malkie and Steph glanced at each other and answered together. 'Aye.'

'OK, anything else on Lillian Crosbie?'

Malkie sighed. 'Nothing, boss. Absolutely bloody nothing. The old dear's house—'

Thompson cut in. 'Ms Lillian Crosbie's house.'

Malkie held his hands up to acknowledge the verbal spanking. 'Ms Crosbie's house was as bare of any identifying documentation or personal effects as any I've ever examined. No bills, no utility company letters, no council tax bills, no bank statements, nothing. We found a single photo of her and some bloke with a message scrawled on the back. It was being used as a bookmark in an old paperback. The photo has to be decades old but we had to use it for the MisPers web page. Anyway, only photo we have. It's like she was always just living there temporarily. SOCO initial report is in – blood type of the mess on the floor matched Billy Irvine's. No other blood types found, although I'm sure I saw blood on her hands. She was holding her side as if that big, ugly bloke got a hit in.'

'And we have no bloody clue where she is now?'

'No, boss.'

'So much for our Golden Hours, then, if we're exactly nowhere.'

Malkie glanced at Steph, bracing himself for a kicking, but Steph's attention was on something outside the window. Thompson caught his look. 'Oh stop that. We all know there's never a good excuse for lack of progress. I'll get it in the neck from management so you're getting it in the neck from me. That's the way it works. Steph, you with us?'

Steph didn't react. Odd for her to drift off during any meeting.

'Hello?' Thompson frowned at her. 'Planet earth to Steph?'

Steph tore her eyes from the view outside the window to look at Thompson, took a few seconds to come back from wherever she'd gone, folded her arms but still said nothing.

'What did you say was written on the back of the photo, Steph?'

'It said "Time and Silence". Rab said he'd try to identify what it means, see if it's a quote from somewhere.'

'Rab Lundy? Our DC Rab Lundy? What does he read that doesn't involve crayons?'

Malkie smiled, but only briefly. Steph's face remained stony.

'OK, so what about the neighbours?'

Steph took a second, frowned, looked like she couldn't be bothered, but then seemed to have a word with herself and straightened in her chair. 'Door-to-doors gave us very little. We got her name from her neighbour at number 37, but even she couldn't tell us anything else. Said Crosbie came and went, never said a word to a soul, never had any visitors except for repairs and stuff like that, and they never heard a peep from her house except for Saturday nights when she watched musicals and she cranked the volume up. Weird old bird, for sure.'

Thompson frowned. 'Old and lonely. Poor thing.' She stood. 'Well, if we really do have nothing, I'm going home to a takeaway pasta and wine then bed. This is going to get political, so I'm ignoring it until morning.' She grabbed her coat and her bag and headed for the stairs. She turned in the doorway. 'You two get some sleep as well. I've got a feeling this just got messy, so I need you both on form, OK?' She didn't wait for their confirmation, just turned and stomped away.

Steph sighed, slumped in her chair, looked bruised by this one, already. Her gaze returned to the window, almost as if she meant to shut Malkie out, to deny any attempt at conversation.

Malkie couldn't let this go; she was somewhere less than happy and he needed to bring her back any way he could. He drummed his fingers on his lips, his brow knotted. 'Why political?'

'What?' Again, a scowl.

What the hell's wrong with you, Steph?

'She said this was all going to turn political. Why?'

Steph sighed, cast him a look of disappointment that never seemed far from her expression where he was concerned. 'DCS Shaw is tipped to climb further up the greasy pole, and soon. She's being touted to take the next step up, any time now.'

'And that would be make her a ... What will that make her?'

'Good grief, Malkie, really? She's about to become North East Divisional Commander.'

Malkie had the decency to look embarrassed. He rarely gave a shit about anything that happened above DCI level, but maybe he needed to start. At least Steph was back in the room now. Better to see her irritated with him rather than languishing in some private misery.

'Any idea what people think of her? Is she well-liked? Any ugly rumours or history?'

'No. I've not heard anything specific, but I can ask a mate I know works at Marischal College.'

Malkie returned yet another in a long line of blank stares.

'Aberdeen. Police Station. Building with lots of coppers in it, although much less than there used to be.'

'Fewer.'

'What?' Genuine irritation edged her voice, now, but he couldn't help himself.

'Fewer coppers. Not less. You can't have less of something that can be counted.' He shrank inside as her expression turned dark.

Steph stared at him for long, cold seconds, then also stood. 'I have something I'm already late for. I'll look at all this again with a fresh head in the morning. I suggest you do, too.'

'You got a date, Steph? Try not to break him, OK?' He grinned, hoped to recover some old pal points.

'You know, sometimes you're not as funny as you think you are, Malkie.' Then she was gone, leaving Malkie replaying his final comment for what he'd said that triggered such uncharacteristic venom in her parting comment.

What the hell? Steph, troubled? Time to grow up and step up, old man.

SIXTEEN

'Joey? Fisher.'

'Fisher? Christ, it's been years. Hang on – what the fuck do you want? I'm skint, so don't ask.'

'I'm not on the scrounge, Joey. Look, mate, I'm in a bit of a bind, and I do need a favour. Urgent, like.'

'I'm fine, mate. Thanks for askin'. The girls are good, too, just started at uni. Haven't seen Iris since '95.'

'Yeah, sorry, Joey. My head's a bit up my arse just now.'

Joey seemed to catch something in Fisher's voice, and his tone changed.

'What do you need?'

'Sapphire Blue BMW 5. JNM18Y.'

'You know I'm retired now, right? Fishing rod and camping chair, all that shite.'

'I know, Joey, but you still own that MOT garage, don't you. I really need help bad, this time.'

'You're not going to pull a you-owe-me, are you? I know you had something to do with the bookie they found upside down in that Seafield sewage tank, but I didn't need any help. I had him in hand.'

'I know you did, Joey, and for the record, if I had escorted that wee shite to Seafield, I would have done it because he was a wee shite and had it coming, OK? You owe me nothing. I'm asking a favour, one mate to another.'

'Is that what we are, Fisher. Mates?'

'We always were, Joey. You know that.'

'The fuck we were. You wouldn't know a mate if he bit you on the arse.'

'Yeah, fair comment. Can you help, though?'

There was silence on the line for a few seconds, and Fisher knew Joey was weighing up the risk of getting involved with him again, weighing potential returns against risks he'd thought himself long shot of.

'Really up to your neck in it this time, yeah?' In other words, how far could he push his luck. Fisher decided that time was scarce, and expediency demanded he agree to whatever the little weasel was about to ask for.

'Two grand. No arguments.'

'Cheque or credit card?'

'Very fucking funny, Fisher. What number are you on?'

'Yeah, you're a comedian too. Call you back in ten minutes?'

'Should be enough. Listen, if one of my girls answers, you tell them you've got a wrong number and you hang up, OK?'

Fisher felt like telling Joey that if he ever spoke to him like that again, he'd be seeing the inside of a sewage tank himself, but he needed the man's help.

'Fine. By the way, what happened to Iris? You divorced?'

'You're kidding, aren't you? You never heard? She was playing away. Two guys on the go at once. I sent her packing. Never did get my hands on the bastard she was podging, though.'

'Ach, that's a shame. You didn't deserve that. Ten minutes, then.'

Fisher hung up, then he laughed. If he'd known Iris was that easy with her favours, he would never have fucked her in the first place.

He was still chuckling to himself when he called Joey back. He scribbled down an address.

'You're sure?'

'Of course I'm sure. I'm unpleasant, not bloody incompetent.'

'Alright. Thanks, Joey. Actually, Joey?'

'What?' Irritated now.

'What's her name?'

Joey paused. 'You don't know, already? And what do you mean *her*? It's a bloke owns that car. What's going on, Fisher? What are you dragging me into?'

'Nothing, Joey. Nothing. I only caught a number plate, complete stranger. Maybe his wife was driving or something like that.'

'The owner's name is Jonathan Norman Montrose. Thirty-four years old. Edinburgh address. I'll text it to you.'

Fisher trawled his memory but came up with no Montroses. Around thirty years younger than she was; had to be her son.

'Fisher, you bloody listening? I said two grand in my account tonight, right? I don't usually work on credit, but I made an exception for you.'

'Yeah, you're a saint, Joey. What's your account number?'

He listened as Joey read off the number but didn't bother writing it down.

'Got it. Cheers, mate.' He hung up. Joey would be exceedingly pissed off when the cash failed to appear, but the last thing Fisher was afraid of was an amateur like Joey, and the loss of the little shit's good faith wouldn't exactly be a great handicap.

He looked again at the name he'd scribbled on the notepad. Jonathan, thirty-four years old.

Fisher grinned. Even a cow like her must love her own flesh and blood.

. . .

He waited until dark then drove to the address. The Manse was one of Edinburgh's richest neighbourhoods, every house walled off and perched at the end of long gravel driveways. He could almost smell the cash. Whoever she was, she'd done well for herself.

He waited an hour in his car. Nobody came or went, and the drive remained empty of vehicles. He sneaked up the side of the house behind a row of sculpted bushes. No lights at the front of the house, but he knew that the front-facing rooms in these places were always kept immaculate, while the residents scruffed around in more lived-in lounges at the back. He reached the back garden and saw no lights on there, either.

He walked to the back of the huge, immaculate lawn until he could see every window right to the roofline. No lights.

He ran his eyes over the windows, and quickly spotted one above ground-floor level which looked accessible. He climbed a drainpipe but his arms and legs complained, and he registered the unhappy realisation that time was marching on. He peered through the glass. A bedroom, single bed, dresser, wardrobe. No clothes or other effects about the room. He'd got lucky first time and found a guest room. Any damage he did to the window while opening it wouldn't be noticed before the household retired and he went about his business.

He pulled his multitool from his back pocket, unfolded the large blade, and worked it between the upper and lower frames. He found the catch, and a few seconds of vigorous pushing saw it pop up. He closed the knife and pocketed it again, then lifted the lower frame and climbed through. He eased the window back down quietly, crept to the door and listened. Nothing.

He pushed the handle down and eased the door open. An empty hallway.

He checked the rooms on the first floor: all empty. He

searched the second and ground floors more confidently: nobody at home. On a console table in the massive, parquet-floored entrance hallway, he found mail addressed only to Jonathan Montrose.

Only two upstairs bedrooms looked used, one obviously that of a young man, so the other had to belong to Jonathan's mother. The woman he'd known for decades as only a voice on the phone.

Montrose. The ex-employer and cold-blooded monster he'd never met.

Her bedroom told a story. No recent photos, no clutter, no keepsakes, just books and a desk and a chair with clothing draped over it. The desk drawer looked easy to force, but he didn't want to tip her off he'd been there. Not yet.

He considered leaving a less visceral message for her so he could get out now, but he also wanted to make sure he left her in no doubt. What he had in mind, she'd never forget, and that would make it worth waiting for.

He chose an adjacent room that looked like a guest room, closed the door and settled himself behind a dresser, hidden from the doorway. As long as no one actually came inside, he'd be fine. It took him some time to get comfortable, his joints not as flexible as he'd like. He realised he hadn't slept soundly for two nights, needed to find some way to keep himself awake. On stakeouts years ago, he'd learned to ease himself into a state of meditation, his mind idling but his ears trained for the smallest sound. She or her son might be home, so he closed his eyes and started to count backwards from a thousand, breathing deeply and regularly to the rhythm of his count.

He got as far as eight hundred and fifty, then got bored. He pulled his multitool out again and started carving chips out of the beautifully varnished side of the antique – and very expen-sive-looking – mahogany dresser.

SEVENTEEN

When Malkie finally gave up trawling the case file for a blinding flash of insight that never came, he logged off, and grabbed his jacket. He made the mistake of taking a few minutes to enjoy the peace and quiet of a near-empty CID room.

DC Louisa Gooch appeared by his desk, a slip of paper in her hand and looking sheepish.

'Sorry, sir. I know you were on your way out the door, but—'

'Dammit, Gucci. How many times. It's Malkie, OK?'

'Sorry, boss. We just had a call from a concerned citizen in Edinburgh. Believes she might have seen our missing old lady.' She checked the clock on the wall. 'Just thirty minutes ago. I can attend if you want?'

Ah, Gucci, if only we had more like you...

'Thanks, Lou, but I'll take it. Our Fearless Leader is already pissed off at me, so I could do with scoring a few brownie points. What's the concerned citizen's name and address?'

. . .

The Waverley Church Mission was a dilapidated and crumbling old pile at the foot of Old Tolbooth Wynd. Malkie parked where he spotted a makeshift sign indicating the location of the place. It hung by two grubby nylon straps from a railing festooned with ivy, set back in the high, ancient-stone wall that led along the Calton Road towards more modern, and swanky, student accommodation.

Handwritten in black marker on a sheet of card taped carelessly into a plastic document holder, it didn't augur well for a reliable witness statement.

He pushed the gate open, stiff on rusted and noisy hinges, and ventured into a shadowed tunnel through the dense branches of untended and rampant bushes of some kind. The heavy oak doors at the front of the building, once high and wide and probably very impressive, now hung on rusted hinges, defaced with multiple layers of graffiti – much of it stuff you couldn't repeat to your granny. Windows set high up in the wood were reinforced with wire cages, as were the windows in the walls either side of the doors.

He did note, though, that the ground around the door and ten yards out into the dark alleyway had been swept clean and three plastic wheelie bins stood neatly to one side.

He found a video doorbell to the left of the doors and pressed the button. Seconds later he heard footsteps, then three different bolts pulled aside and two heavy locks turned. The door opened a few inches, and a wrinkled face peered out past a security chain.

The woman looked ancient, her face made-up but overpowdered, her silver hair tightly curled. A hint of lavender wafted out.

'Can I help you, young man?'

He held his warrant card up for her to see through the gap. 'Good morning, madam. Are you Elizabeth? I'm Detective

Sergeant Malcolm McCulloch, Police Scotland. You called about a sighting of a missing person?'

The woman's face relaxed. The door closed, the security chain was removed, and the door opened wide.

She wore a pair of faded jeans and a sweatshirt with the words 'God Will Provide' in faded print. She smiled warmly, stood aside and gestured Malkie inside.

'Please. Please come in.'

Malkie smiled and entered.

As the woman locked and bolted the door behind them, Malkie studied the interior.

Worn floorboards stretched the length of a long hallway running straight back from the front door. The walls were panelled in oak, the light fittings obviously original. An old rotary phone sat on a side table, beside a battered and ancient-looking phone book. Malkie fingered the phone dial, remembered a succession of phones like it throughout his childhood. Like the one his mum used to spend ages on to her reading-group pals.

'Oh, that doesn't work,' said the woman. 'I keep it there because it makes me feel like I'm still in the seventies.' Malkie saw a twinkle in her eye and decided he liked her.

'I'm Elizabeth Taylor. Not that one. Call me Lizzie. I run this little scrap of paradise.'

Malkie couldn't help but smile and she wrinkled her eyes back at him.

'You called the Police Scotland call centre about a lady we're concerned about and would like to find as quickly as possible?'

'Yes.' She hesitated, glanced to the side, seemed to hold an internal conversation with herself. 'I saw her. Yesterday. Here. I think she was hurt. I saw blood on her wrist and she kept one hand pressed to her side and walked tilted to one side.'

Dammit. That fucker did get a blow in.

Malkie stared at her. He was used to 'I can't be sure, but...' or 'She's much older than in the photo...' but he heard only conviction in Lizzie's voice. This was no flaky old bird; this woman was as sharp as Steph's tongue. She pulled her phone from a pocket in her skirt and opened an app. After a few swipes and presses, she showed him a shot from the video doorbell. The quality was outstanding, and Malkie had no trouble seeing the young woman in Crosbie's photograph grown older.

'That's her. Can I get a copy of all the video and photos you got of her, please?'

Lizzie pulled a memory stick from her pocket and handed it to him. 'I'm not quite as old and crusty as this place, Mr McCulloch. Not quite.'

She stepped past Malkie and carried on talking as he followed her down the hallway, smiling.

'Before I tell you about our visitor, I need to explain a few things, Mr McCulloch.'

Malkie followed, his curiosity piqued. She led him to a small office off the hallway and indicated he should sit at one of two chairs in front of a desk on which sat a keyboard and mouse and computer monitor. She pressed the space bar, then clicked on a desktop icon. A video window opened, showing a man in a bed. The video was low-res and grainy, not top-quality equipment, but it showed enough detail to reveal the man was not well. The bed looked like a full-function hospital bed, with raised bars at the sides and various knobs and buttons on a control panel built into the headboard.

'This, Mr McCulloch, is my longest-staying guest, Mr Ben Hutchison.'

Malkie recalled the photo found in Crosbie's house: 'Love, Ben'.

Lizzie had drifted off, her mind somewhere else.

'Lizzie?' He made his voice gentle.

She roused herself from some reverie. 'Ben has been with us

here for more than forty years, Mr McCulloch.'

Malkie gaped. 'Forty?'

'Forty-five. He came to us one evening back in '78. A taxi driver said he got the impression Ben had discharged himself from hospital against nurses' advice; he asked to be taken here. He gave the driver twenty pounds to swear he'd never tell a soul where he'd brought him. That was a lot of money in 1978, Mr McCulloch. The next day, some solicitors arrived with a lot of legal documents and a very long-term care agreement, very generous, too.'

Malkie nodded, smiled, gave her room to continue in her own time.

'Ben settled in, seemed at first only moody and sullen, showed no interest in forming any kind of relationship. He never went out, never had any visitors or phone calls. Apart from a brisk walk he took religiously around the grounds out the back for an hour every day, he sat and watched TV all day, every day. He didn't even seem to care what he watched. Whatever other residents put on, he sat and watched it. He'd eat at mealtimes, looked after himself well enough, just never made any attempt to open up to anyone. In all those years, not even to me. Eventually, he stopped his walks round the grounds. As time passed, he seemed to withdraw, close up, like he was shrinking in front of me, until he was like those poor people in that film, the people who were asleep and awake at the same time. If you lift them they stand. If you put food in their mouths they eat and swallow, sit them on a toilet and, well, you know...'

She slumped, seemed to exhaust some reserve of steel she'd summoned in preparation for this tale.

'Mr McCulloch. All that would be strange enough...' She swallowed, clearly struggling to continue. Malkie gave her time.

'At some point in the past, before he came to me, Ben had been...'

She stared at her lap, fiddled with a handkerchief Malkie

hadn't seen her produce from any pocket, then lifted her gaze to him, the steel back in her eyes.

'He's been hurt. Really very badly. And repeatedly, Mr McCulloch.'

Malkie stared at her, looked for the telltale signs of a needy witness embellishing their statement to more fully bask in their moment of importance. He saw nothing. She believed what she said.

What the fuck do I say to that?

'So, the old lady?'

Lizzie relaxed, as if the hard part was over.

'She appeared at the door late yesterday evening. It was raining so I let her in right away. She was soaked, and looked confused, almost haunted. She kept looking at the inside of the front door as if she was checking I'd pushed all the bolts home.'

Lizzie stood, indicated Malkie should, too. She ushered him out into the hallway then led him further into the building.

'She asked to see Ben, as if it was common knowledge he was here. She's been the first person, other than the solicitors who checked on him once every year, to ever visit him. I was in two minds, obviously, but she seemed so fragile, so desperate. I let her see him.'

She opened a door at the end of the hall and led Malkie into a kitchen. She crossed to what had to be the very back of the building and opened another door, a small door, set deep into ancient-looking three-foot-thick walls. She stood in the doorway, her hands on the handle of the open door, and waited for Malkie to look her in the eye.

'You know, she didn't even have an umbrella? Her hair was plastered to her head and rainwater was running down inside her coat as if she had no clue it was raining.

She was here on her own. She wasn't kidnapped. What the hell?

Lizzie pushed the small door fully open to reveal a utility

and wet room. In an alcove at the back, the foot of a flight of stairs turned sharp right and appeared to run up the inside of the back wall of the building. Lizzie crossed to them and waited for Malkie to join her.

'I have no idea what she said to him or if she managed to get any kind of response from him. Lord knows I rarely have. When she came back down those stairs, she walked past me, waited at the front door for me to unlock it, then disappeared into the night without a single further word.' She stood to one side and indicated Malkie should continue alone.

As he climbed the stairs, he heard her speak.

'Mr McCulloch, I have signed affidavits from a prestigious Edinburgh law firm that Ben was like he is now when he arrived, and that nothing illegal was involved in accepting him into my care. I need you to know that.'

Malkie peered up the stairs.

What the fuck am I going to find up there?

EIGHTEEN

Fisher started when he heard voices downstairs. His mind had wandered. Some arsehole little town in Bosnia. At work on some terrified sod they'd hauled in. Interviewing, they called it. Some poor kid who took a ten-year-old Kalashnikov from a psycho warlord and set out to change the world one atrocity at a time. He'd suffered beyond imagination at Fisher's hands but they got nothing from him; the boy had pissed and shit himself in minutes then passed out from blood loss and never regained consciousness.

Fisher had been wondering whether he could be that cold and empty and vicious again if he had to be, and he'd completely failed to hear tyres on the gravel drive, or the front door opening.

He heard two voices, one male and one female.

'You want a nightcap, Mum?' *Bingo.*

'No thanks. Been a hard day, so I'm heading for bed. I won't need the car tomorrow. My driver will pick me up. Goodnight, Jonathan.'

He heard keys drop onto the side table, then footsteps on

the stairs and the first-floor hallway. A light came on in what had to be her bedroom. He found his multitool in his hand without realising he'd even unfolded it.

He waited, heard drawers opening and closing, then a shower running. He eased the bedroom door open an inch to listen. He heard the shower door open and close and the sound of the water change, and he waited. He listened to the shower stop running, then he listened to her hair dryer, and he waited. He heard her move about her bedroom, sighing a few times, then she went quiet. Still, he waited.

When her bedroom light went out, he gave it another thirty minutes then crept through. Waiting time was over.

She lay in bed, her breathing slow and regular, her mouth open and slack. He tried to get a clear look at her face, thought he felt a tickle of recognition, but she slept with her face half-buried in her pillow and he couldn't risk disturbing her. He glanced around the room for a handbag or purse, anything that might provide a better ID than just Montrose, but he saw nothing. Must be downstairs, on the console table with her keys. He debated whether to risk sneaking down for it, but he could hear a TV somewhere and couldn't risk running into her precious offspring.

He crossed her room on the balls of his feet and hid a motion-triggered camera between two books on a top shelf, then pulled his mobile out and stood over her bed; she was vulnerable and almost innocent-looking in her sleep, one leg hanging out over the edge of the mattress. He was disappointed to find she slept in a shapeless T-shirt and leggings, had expected something upmarket and classy, for some reason. He took one photo on his mobile, dark and grainy because he couldn't risk the flash, then back towards the unused bedroom and the window he'd entered through.

He slept in his car, a burner phone plugged in with a

message ready to send and set to chime when the bookshelf camera detected movement.

After a few false alarms when she shifted in what he hoped were haunted dreams, he finally saw her wake and sit up. He only realised now the images were softer and grainier than he'd have liked, but they'd do the job. He pressed send on his phone and watched, an eager grin on his face. She sat up as if shocked, reached for a drawer in her bedside table, and took out a phone, held it as if it might bite her. Not the one lying in plain view on her bedside table: had to be her burner, the one she used to contact him. The screen lit up. She dropped it and jumped out of bed as if it had bitten her.

She sat on a chair beside the bed. Then stood, sat, stood again and stepped to the window.

The phone lay on her pillow, untouched, hopefully because the thing terrified her. A picture of her, asleep, Fisher's fingers teasing a lock of hair from her forehead. He doubted the message could be any clearer.

I can get to you.

Her response would dictate the length of her remaining life expectancy. If necessary, he'd escalate. It would be messy and ugly, but if she raised the stakes that high, she'd leave him no choice.

She ran from the room and returned, closing the door with her back and slumping against it. He assumed she'd checked every room in the house.

When she returned to her bedroom, looking flustered, he saw her notice his muddy footprints on the carpet. He'd made a point of not cleaning garden muck from his boots. At the bathroom doorway, she reeled when she saw where he'd stood, and aimed a furious kick at a laundry basket.

She screamed her rage, her hands bunched into fists, her face contorted. Then, deflated, sat heavily on the floor, pulled at her lower lip as she rocked backwards and forwards. Her son appeared at the bedroom door and spoke to her, the audio too muffled to make out his words. She said something, then shouted at him, and he retreated, looking shocked.

Mission accomplished. She would be nowhere near as cocky after this.

NINETEEN

Malkie breathed deep before pushing open the door to Ben Hutchison's bedroom.

He managed to avoid gagging at most crime scenes and post-mortems, but his rage never lessened.

The room inside was clean and tidy. Tellingly so. Reminded him of Lillian Crosbie's home. No personal effects adorned a battered old dresser. Framed prints hanging on one wall all looked like cheap mass-produced stuff you could buy in any homeware store. Not one item of furniture looked less than forty years old, and Malkie got an immediate feeling he was disturbing a place of sanctuary that had protected the man for half a lifetime. Malkie watched Hutchison's chest rise and fall, slow and steady. He looked at peace, showed no evidence to explain Lizzie's comment – 'Hurt. Badly. Repeatedly.'

He stepped up to the bed. Fully clothed, the man lay on his side, his heavy-lidded eyes fixed on a TV set running rolling twenty-four-hour news coverage. He looked to be in his late sixties, his eyes rheumy and glassy, thin veins in his hands covered by no more than a thin, dry, papery coating of fragile-looking skin. Older than his years, by a long way.

He gave no indication he was aware Malkie was there.

'Mr Hutchison? I'm Detective Sergeant Malcolm McCulloch from Police Scotland.'

Nothing.

'May I sit? Talk to you for a wee while, Mr Hutchison?'

Again, nothing. Malkie pulled over a heavy and ornately carved, but battered and chipped, dining chair and placed it by Hutchison's bed, careful not to obstruct the man's view of the TV. He saw no glimmer of anything that suggested Ben Hutchison was even aware of his presence.

Malkie sat for a few minutes, watched dust motes dance in a sunbeam that shone through old, heavy sash windows. The frames had seen better days and needed repainting, but he noticed that the glass was pristine. As was, he now noted, the carpets and skirting boards and the bedclothes Hutchison lay on. Malkie was happy to label Lizzie Taylor as Good People.

He leaned forward until he guessed he impinged on Hutchison's field of view, but the man's eyes didn't move from the TV screen. He blinked, slow and lazy, but his gaze didn't shift from a tanned and shiny newsreader with thick, perfect hair and blinding teeth, currently describing some awful event in practised, sombre tones.

'I'd like to talk to you about a visitor you had yesterday, Mr Hutchison. A lady who was here late yesterday evening? Do you remember what you talked about?'

Nothing.

Malkie leaned into Hutchison's field of view. The man's eyes refocused onto Malkie but no other reaction followed.

'Mr Hutchison? I'm concerned for the lady's safety, sir.'

Nothing. No interest, no recognition, no reaction.

Malkie sat back, and the man's eyes returned to their thousand-yard stare at the TV.

Malkie sighed; he'd wanted to hear Hutchison confirm the

old lady's name, rather than feed it to him, but that clearly wasn't about to happen.

'Mr Hutchison? May I call you Ben?'

Nothing.

'Ben, I really do have serious concerns about Lillian Crosbie's safety, given the violent events of last night.' He chose his words with care; perhaps curiosity or concern might rouse the man from wherever he was hiding.

Nothing.

Malkie rubbed his hands down his face, suppressed an urge to whisper a quiet *for fuck's sake* to himself.

He cast his eyes around the room again, as his mind fumbled for another approach.

He noticed the man's wrist was exposed under his shirt cuff, where his head rested on his palm. His wrist was scarred. Two clean, separate cuts. Down the wrist. Hutchison had tried to check out permanently, but only once, and had made no repeat attempts.

Malkie pushed Hutchison's cuff further down, saw the scars ran for several inches and further under his sleeves, straight down the inside of the arm, where too many previous, ugly cases had taught him ran the best veins for doing the job right first time.

'That's the least of it.'

Malkie jumped at Lizzie's voice from the doorway, quiet and gentle, sorrowful, but a shock in the silence that hung in the room, heavy with Malkie's shame at being caught invading Hutchison's personal space so intimately.

'Those scars were fresh when he came to stay with us. With me. He was brought straight from hospital, jabbering away that he didn't do that to himself, and that he wasn't the one they needed to protect.'

She crossed to the other side of Hutchison's bed, stood with her hands clasped in front of her like a stern but protective matron.

Malkie sat back in his chair. 'He sees me, but he won't react to me.' He suddenly felt like the insensitive clod most thought him to be. 'I mean, you see me, don't you, Mr Hutchison? Do you hear me, too? Ben? Can you talk to me, Ben? It's important.'

Nothing.

Lizzie took a breath. 'Come round here, please, Mr McCulloch.'

Malkie, confused, obeyed. After a moment's hesitation, she whispered to Hutchison, 'Please forgive me if this is not what you'd want, Ben. Please.'

Malkie's mind stumbled along, trying to guess what was coming before it hit him unprepared.

Lizzie lifted Hutchison's shirt and pulled it up to reveal his back from shoulder blades to waist.

Cigarette burns. Razor slashes. Scald burns. Gouges and holes. Scars upon scars.

A tear dropped from Lizzie's eye onto Ben's vandalised skin and still he failed to react. Malkie stared. Bile threatened to burn its way up his throat. No wonder the poor bastard's mind hid behind walls of his own making.

Despite long years of witnessing the worst atrocities human beings can inflict on their own kind, he could never harden himself to the soul-battering impact of the kind of brutality he saw now. He hoped he never would, or he'd retire.

Lizzie replaced Hutchison's shirt, smoothed it down, stroked his hair once, then left her hand resting on his shoulder. Her tears dried, burned away by a fury in her eyes Malkie found shocking but understandable.

'He never said a word about who did this to him or why. Not even in those first few weeks before he closed himself off completely. I've tried, Mr McCulloch. I've sat with him many an evening, talked to him, pretended he was answering. I've read that book to him about a hundred times, because he seems so attached to it, even though I'm the furthest thing from a reader you could ever meet. The only time I ever see any kind of reaction from him is if I change the TV from the news channel. Then he rocks gently in his bed and mumbles words I can't make out until I put the news back on. Always the news.'

Malkie returned to the TV side of the bed and switched it off. Hutchison's eyes fastened onto him but still no words or sound came. He held his gaze longer than Malkie could bear and switched it back on. Hutchison's gaze turned back to the screen.

Malkie stood. 'Lizzie. You need to tell me everything, and I mean absolutely everything, you remember about Ben's visitor yesterday. I'm going to find her, and – if I can after so long – whoever did this to him.'

TWENTY

Why the hell is she doing this?

Why does she want to hurt me after all these years? Or is it not just me? There were six of us. Five, not counting her. Is she going after the others, too?

And why? What does she hope to achieve?

Stupid, stupid woman.

I've stayed quiet all this time, so what's made her rake it all up again? Doesn't she realise I want the past to remain the past as much as any of us do? Does she think I don't punish myself every day for what was done that night?

I need to finish what I should have finished back in 1978. What was I thinking? Time could never heal wounds like those. I caused her so much trouble, led so much grief to her door, but I suffered much more. And she went on, survived it, so why drag it all out into daylight again, now.

Didn't I hurt her enough with my first stupid mistake. And it was a mistake, they must all have seen that?

Oh, God. Oh, dear God, no. Is she looking for—

Stop this. Get a grip. She's one woman. You can survive this.

Where did I put the damned thing? If she gets her hands on it... Oh, God. Where is it?

Stop it. She's one woman. Just one woman.

TWENTY-ONE

Malkie headed for the canteen immediately after the morning briefing, wanted to give both Thompson and Steph as much cooling-off time as possible. Thompson looked up as he returned, but he walked past to his desk, refused to make eye contact.

Steph sat at her desk, glaring at Rab Lundy, a DC for eight years and the only man other than Malkie in Livingston CID known for actively resisting any prospect of promotion. Rab's rough-edged personality guaranteed any promotion beyond DS would elude him forever, but he never displayed any inclination to rise above DC.

Rab turned to Malkie and crossed his feet at the ankles on his desk, the grin on his kisser as smug as fuck. Steph lowered her eyes to the papers on her desk and sighed.

'What?' Malkie asked, preparing himself to be less than impressed.

Steph spoke without lifting her eyes from her screen. 'Ask anyone, sir. I don't think there's a soul in the building hasn't heard about it.'

Malkie sighed, the 'sir' sounded all wrong coming from

Steph. It might indicate residual anger from the previous night, but he'd never expect grudges or petulance from her.

What the hell is eating at you, Steph? This is not like you.

He hoped she'd look at him, see his concern, his worry, but her eyes remained on her screen. Malkie removed his jacket, placed it on the back of his chair, sat, waited several more seconds, and only then turned to Rab. Rab's grin hadn't shifted an inch.

'Well, after I'd exhausted all the usual sources, you know – electoral roll, credit agencies, DWP...'

'I know the routine, Rab – get to the point, if you would.'

Rab ruffled a little at this interruption to his no-doubt well-rehearsed build up but continued. 'Well, on the off-chance, I ran a check against the paper files in the archives, what with her being a pensioner and all.'

Malkie waited, eventually bid him continue with an impatient lift of his eyebrows.

'So, I turned up two missing person reports from March 1978, under her name. Lillian Crosbie.'

Malkie was intrigued, despite his best efforts not to let Rab see it. 'Who made the enquiries?'

'Some bloke called Ben Hutchison.'

Malkie gaped at him.

Fuck. Me.

Rab looked surprised that this small nugget of police work seemed to hold some significance. 'You know him?'

'Was there an address?'

'Aye, hang on.' He consulted his notes. '44 Old Smithy Road, North Berwick. But that was forty-something years ago.'

'As much as it pains me to say this, Rab, well done, mate.' He pulled Lizzie Taylor's memory stick from his pocket and handed it to him. 'I just met Mr Hutchison. He's a...' Was he a guest or a patient? 'He's staying at a shelter in Edinburgh, but he's really not well. Crosbie's been there. Photos and videos on that, see what you can get from it, aye?'

Rab turned back to his PC, happy to have something to do that didn't involve physical effort.

Outside, Steph caught up with Malkie halfway to his car. He veered away from his car and headed for hers. 'You mind driving? I'm a bit knackered, didn't sleep well.'

'Fine.'

Oh, shit. Fine meaning anything but fine.

He needed to re-establish communications, couldn't bear to think he'd upset her so much as to even lose her friendship, even temporarily. 'Shitty dreams.'

'About the fire again? Talk to me.'

He felt a pang of shame; even when so obviously pissed off at him, she wouldn't leave him to deal with his own troubles alone. He didn't come close to deserving her.

'Ach, just the usual, Steph. Until I find out, or remember, or someone else tells me, what I missed that night, why she died, I'll continue to assume I'm to blame. No point trying to change my mind until then.' His voice broke. 'My mum, Steph. My own fucking mum.'

'OK. Easy, partner. Close your eyes, sleep if you can, or enjoy the drive.'

'I'm sorry for upsetting you last night, Steph. Didn't mean to. I hope you know that?'

'It's fine. I'm fine. I mean, I will be. You know what? I'll put some cheesy, middle-aged guff on the radio, help you nod off.' She turned the radio on before he could say any more.

Malkie tried to sleep, but peace wouldn't come to him. 'Lillian Crosbie. She's not young, is she? She can't go on the lam, not at her age. Where's she going to go?'

'Maybe she has friends?'

'I don't think so. Even from the little we saw inside her

house before the SOCOs arrived, that woman was a loner, a recluse.'

Steph said nothing, concentrated on negotiating a sharp turn into one of Livingston's many roundabouts.

'It's as if she had no life, Steph. There were no family photographs, no holiday postcards, not even any numbers in her telephone speed-dial. Just one crappy old paperback and a photo with some cryptic message scribbled on it. It's as if she knew no one.'

'Some old people get like that. Maybe she just didn't have any kids?'

'Possibly, but most people have at least a couple of acquaintances. You know – chums from the bingo, that sort of thing?'

'And she had none?'

'Not a trace, that I can see. That house felt as if she was getting ready to move out.'

He stared out the window, found himself looking for pensioners to compare. He'd always thought of old people as one homogeneous demographic group. His grandparents had died when he was still at school, so he'd had very little first-hand experience of the blue-rinse and twin-set brigade. Now, he noticed how so many of them stood chatting to each other, passing the time, and their warmth towards each other seemed genuine – no facades, no social politics. It occurred to him that the older they got, the more they must value the acquaintances they formed, unlike Crosbie, who had seemed to make efforts to avoid all social ties.

He also noticed how none of them looked capable of fighting their way out of a wet paper bag, let alone take down a healthy six-foot lad in his twenties and an older but even bigger bloke.

The more he thought about old Lillian Crosbie, the more he wondered if young Billy Irvine had the slightest clue what he was up against.

'Rab had better get that info to me before we get there,' he grumbled.

'Ben Hutchison's sister, Rebecca. Ran her own riding school, built with family money, now she's a stay-at-home. Does a lot for the community, apparently.'

Malkie stared at her.

'Couldn't help myself. Rab stopped looking after he'd turned up his little bombshell. He seemed to think he'd achieved enough for one day. Probably gave himself a headache getting that far by himself.'

She smiled, then wiped it again; possibly too soon to go easy on Malkie.

'So, I picked up where he'd left off. Only I didn't see the need to brag about a bit of basic police work.'

I wonder if Rab will get as far as tracking down the investigating officers? Malkie wondered, idly.

Steph reached into her inside pocket and handed her notebook to him.

'Last page.'

Malkie took the notebook, flipped to the last page. 'Your handwriting's rotten, you know that?'

TWENTY-TWO

Fisher woke with a start, the shriek of a mobile deafening in the early morning silence.

Montrose?

His head felt about to crack open and it took him long seconds to remember the previous evening. A dash to his flat to stuff whatever he could grab in two minutes into his old army kit bag, then a hunt for a shitty hotel that would take cash and pretend not to notice his obvious nerves. He'd have preferred somewhere outside of the city but knew it would look suspicious if he checked into a motorway hotel with no credit card and no car registration. The hotel bar – all chipped Formica tables and sticky vinyl chairs – had been open late and stayed empty. He'd decided even she wouldn't find him in a dive like this and proceeded to get hammered. He knew he'd stop himself before crossing the line into being dangerously vocal, but he was no stranger to rum, and could go a long way before reaching that particular line.

He grabbed his mobile from the bedside table, checked the display, saw nothing; had to be her burner.

He noticed the time, after eleven. How the hell could he

oversleep with all this shite going on? He needed to smarten up his act or he'd end up banged up in Saughton or at the bottom of Harlaw Reservoir.

She wanted to talk. Good sign or very bad sign? He needed a clearer head before finding out.

He lay back, fingers squeezing his eyelids, trying to blot out the sun blasting through the curtains he'd forgotten to close in his rush to merciful sleep. He could have got up to close them, but he knew he'd suffer if he asked too much of himself too soon.

Unable to get back to sleep, he couldn't help but chew over his current situation.

He'd watched his own front door for an hour before he'd risked entering. After a quick recce to make sure there wasn't already someone inside, he'd double-locked the door, left the lights off, and packed only enough clothing for a few nights, plus the file he'd started on Crosbie.

He had to hope the message he'd sent Montrose would penetrate her stubborn skull. He wanted out and was capable of bringing all kinds of pain to her door if she insisted on dragging him further into her idiotic plans.

He grinned to himself. He'd watched her on the camera he'd hidden in her room, and she'd freaked more than he could have hoped when she'd discovered the photo. Things could now go one of two ways. Either she'd decide against taking on a newly emboldened Fisher and cut him out of her efforts to find Crosbie. Or she would go overboard, take them both on. Trouble was, he was the very resource she used to hire to do her dirty work. She would have to be a little more self-sufficient and creative if she wanted to start that particular fight.

He laid back down and was about to open the file when his mobile shrieked at him again. Once more, the number was withheld.

This time, he took the call.

'What?' he barked, less than enthusiastic about conversation in his present state.

'Hello, Fisher.'

He froze. A familiar voice, but he prayed he was wrong.

'Who is this?' He failed to keep a tremor from his voice.

'An old friend. How are you?'

The voice was soft and musical, almost camp. But slurred, as if drunk.

Fisher swallowed, his mouth suddenly dry. It was him. It couldn't be, but it was him.

'Cut the shite, pal. Who is this?'

'My name's Michael. We need to talk, you and me.'

'Who are you?'

'I'm the bogey-man, Fisher. Her other attack dog you all knew existed in the seventies. We need to talk. I'll be in touch.' The line went dead.

He wished he could believe it was only the drink that had him bent over the toilet two seconds later.

He was real, always had been.

They'd all heard rumours about her – Montrose's – other operative. A psychopath. Too violent and unstable for most jobs, he was thought to be used only for the dirtiest of work, the kinds of jobs even Fisher baulked at.

He was real, and the thought of going up against an unknown like this Michael character carried a whole level of risk he hadn't had to consider for decades. This man could be the end of him unless he was very, fucking careful.

After rinsing the bitter burn of stomach acid from his throat with water from the minibar, he repacked his kit bag. He left it sitting on the chair by the door, handles together, ready to be grabbed on the way out if he had to.

Next, he checked the window. It opened but a lever locked the gap at four inches. He made short work of that with his multitool. It would still lock when closed, but he could push it wide open now, if needed.

He sat on the edge of the bed and ran through it all again. It calmed him, focused his mind, eased him into the professional mindset, and he regained some of his self-composure, with a concrete and specific problem to get his teeth into.

His biggest problem was that he hadn't gone tooled up for years. He hadn't the faintest idea who to talk to about arming himself. He could try Joey again, but he didn't want that wee shite holding any more on him than was necessary.

That said, he knew Michael's reputation. Mad Mike. The maniac never did anything at a distance when he could get in close, really enjoy himself, so even a shooter might be useless.

Rumours varied, but most agreed that Michael served in the Northern Ireland border patrols, until he was court-marshalled and discharged extremely dishonourably after a spectacular cluster fuck deep in County Armagh. The target was so sensitive, even the RUC had no idea they were there. The squad leader had requested Michael's removal from what was supposed to be a discreet mission, but HQ failed to respond before kick-off and the ensuing bloodbath went down in British Army folklore.

He'd always thought Michael a myth. He'd guessed that Montrose used other men occasionally, but he'd never imagined even she would use someone as lethal as Michael was reputed to be.

He snapped back to the present, realised he'd lain back on the bed, arms crossed behind his head, far too relaxed.

He opened a window and breathed deep. The February air was cold and sharp, the sky a bright blue. A day to make hiding just too big a price to pay for a long life. He could wait here for Michael, tell him just where to come, try to take him on his own terms, but an alternative plan occurred to him.

Montrose had set a rabid animal on him, so she could call

him off. The photograph he'd left on her pillow had rattled her. He doubted she'd respond to a reasoned request to call it quits. He genuinely would be prepared to disappear, never show his face again, and keep her dirty little activities to himself, but her pride could never accept that, even if her sick, paranoid mind could bring itself to believe him.

He'd hoped the photo had sent a clear enough message – *I can get to you* – but even knowing he had stood above her while she slept, knowing he could have done her there and then, it seemed she had called on one of the most unstable and dangerous men he'd ever feared going up against.

The woman was incapable of backing down, even when common sense dictated she cut her losses and leave well alone.

He was also aware that his temptation to sit tight betrayed weak and irrational hope resorted to by most people in danger: *if I ignore it, it'll all go away.*

As much as he wished otherwise, Fisher knew his best bet was to take the fight right back to her, get in her face, scare the fucking shit out of her, appeal to the one instinct he could be sure drove her. Her desire to save her own filthy skin, above all else.

It would be unpleasant. He would have to get his message across in such a way that even she would baulk at coming after him again. He was going to have to hurt her. Nothing short of complete and utter degradation would get through to her.

He needed darkness for his next move, so he had no choice but to lie low, stay in his room, watch crap TV, and wait.

As soon as dusk fell, he and his multitool had a long overdue appointment with Mrs Montrose.

TWENTY-THREE

Malkie had pictured the address as a mass-built box, detached at best, and so was greatly surprised to find that Old Smithy Road was a long, tree-lined avenue, with no two properties less than forty feet from each other. All had old drystone walls and gates behind which gravelled drives led to double garages and impressive sandstone and granite homes which wouldn't have looked out of place up the moneyed end of The Grange, back in Edinburgh.

As Steph parked on a gravel drive between immaculate and lush lawns, he sat up and groaned. He'd wakened with a muscle tight and aching in his neck and was now less than looking forward to a face-to-face with anyone with an attitude typical of this level of obvious wealth, but he'd give it his best because he was already on warnings. It occurred to him that he couldn't remember the last time he wasn't on some kind of warning.

The door was answered promptly by a young lad in jeans and a sweatshirt, fresh-faced and pink, a sheaf of papers tucked under one arm and a pen behind his ear.

Malkie smiled. 'Rebecca Hutchison, please?'

The boy looked from him to Steph and back, seemed perturbed.

'Can I ask who's calling, please?'

Malkie loved this bit. 'Police Scotland CID. Please tell her we'd like a wee chat.'

Malkie's smile broadened. He did so enjoy the typical reaction to those words.

'Just... just a second, please. I'll see if...'

He tailed off, glanced nervously between them both again as he closed the door.

'*See if?*' said Steph. 'How can he not know if she's at home?'

'These kinds of people probably dread scruffs like me appearing on their doorstep.'

Steph stared at him, disapproving. 'These kinds of people?' She raised one very judgmental eyebrow but Malkie simply smiled back.

'Steph, you really must stop repeating everything you hear.'

She was about to retort when the door opened again, and the lad ushered them inside. He avoided eye contact, looked everywhere but at them.

'Please take a seat in the day room. Miss Hutchison will be down in a minute.'

'Lovely. Thank you,' said Malkie, pleasantly.

Once they were alone, Steph repeated, 'These kinds of people? Maybe I should ask the questions today?'

Malkie feigned disappointment. 'Steph. Please. Have some faith.'

At that moment, the day room door opened, and Rebecca Hutchison glided in.

She was dressed exactly as Malkie would have expected – heavy tweed skirt, sensible shoes, blouse and cardigan, her silver hair in a tight bun. He and Steph stood.

'Good morning, Miss Hutchison. Sorry to disturb you. I'm Detective Sergeant Malcolm McCulloch and this is Detective

Constable Stephanie Lang. We'd like to talk to you about your brother Ben, if we may?'

Steph smiled but, as ever, it didn't suit her.

'Please, sit.'

She sat opposite them, ankles crossed, and smoothed her skirt across her lap, a picture of elegance. But for all her calm appearance, Malkie detected a tension in her posture.

'So, what do the police want with my brother? I have to admit to being intrigued.'

Malkie noticed Steph staring very pointedly at him and decided to draw on his limited reserves of tact and diplomacy.

'We're looking into an attack on an elderly lady a few nights ago, and our investigations have led us to two historic missing persons reports concerning that same lady.'

Miss Hutchison nodded, patient and indulgent. 'And how can I be of assistance?'

'Well, the reports were filed by your brother. I visited him but... I got no information from him.'

Hutchison's eyelids flickered for only a second, then she cleared her throat. She found some invisible piece of lint on her skirt and picked at it as she spoke. She took long seconds to begin.

'You visited him?' Her voice failed her on the last word. 'Mr McCulloch, I haven't seen my brother for more than forty years.'

She paused, seemed to need to gather herself before continuing. Malkie waited.

'I last spoke to Ben a few days after he was attacked in Edinburgh one night in 1978. He was hospitalised, nearly died.'

She inhaled deeply, obviously still troubled even after so long, had to push her next question out. 'How is he?'

'He was physically well, but... uncommunicative. Miss Hutchison, do you think you'd be OK to answer a few questions? It would assist us greatly.'

Tears welled in her eyes. She pulled a cotton handkerchief from her sleeve and dabbed at them, then replaced the handkerchief, as if making a point of putting away her momentary lapse. 'I'm fine. I reacted badly because of the aftermath of Ben's attack. I was never happy with the way certain things went.'

Malkie glanced at Steph. She too now looked intrigued. Malkie sat back, crossed his legs, attempted to appear relaxed and non-threatening.

Miss Hutchison licked her lips, gazed out of the front window at her immaculately landscaped garden for a few seconds.

'Ben was found at the seafront at Granton in Edinburgh by a taxi driver who took him to the Western General Hospital but didn't wait for the police. I was notified by our family solicitor and made plans to go to see him. They tried to find the taxi driver but back then there wasn't a camera on every street corner. Ben was interviewed but claimed to have no idea who had attacked him or why.'

She paused, obviously more affected by her recollections than she'd expected. She took a few seconds before continuing, and Malkie waited silently.

'Back then, we were expanding our stables and I was extremely busy, so I called him first. He told me not to hurry, that he was fine and the end of the week would do. The day I was supposed to go down, I received a call from the hospital to tell me that Ben had discharged himself. He called a few days later, said he was OK, but needed some time to rest. Said he'd call me when he felt better.

'Over the years, Ben called less and less. He wouldn't discuss that night, and he wouldn't give me an address or telephone number. He wrote occasionally, but his letters were always very vague and disorganised. Over about a year or so, he became more and more distant and withdrawn, and eventually he cut me off completely, stopped calling. His last letter to me was the most upsetting. He claimed he wanted a complete break from the past, to start a new life. He promised he'd be OK, and asked me not to worry about him.'

She looked back at Malkie, as if she'd just remembered he was there.

'I never heard from him again. I asked our solicitor for his address, but he cited client confidentiality and said Ben didn't want to be found. I've had no reason to believe he's even still alive, but I preferred to believe he instructed his solicitor to share at least news of his passing should it transpire.'

She smiled, took hold of her composure again.

'And that's about all I can tell you, I'm afraid. I haven't thought about it for a while, I have to admit. It's been such a long time.'

Malkie smiled as warmly as he could. He was genuinely sorry to have raked it all up again for the poor woman.

'Please don't apologise, Miss Hutchison. You've been a great help. Can I just ask, what's your family solicitor's name?'

'Oh, I'm afraid he died some years ago. His firm still handles my business, though. Thomas Fairfield & Co. In Edinburgh.'

'One last question, Miss Hutchison. Did Ben ever talk to you about the missing persons reports he filed?'

'I don't think so, but as I said, we talked less and less after his attack. What were the names of the missing people?'

'A Miss Lillian Crosbie?'

Hutchison's head snapped up. She stared straight at him.

'Yes. Certainly. Ben never stopped talking about her before his attack.'

Malkie's heart skipped. He had nothing else. He needed something to set his investigation in some kind of clear direction.

'Ben went through cadet school with Lillian Crosbie then he got posted in the Borders and she got posted somewhere else, I'm not sure where. Ben carried a torch for her for all the years between starting work and his attack, but I think she never reciprocated. According to what Ben told me back then, they were close friends, but she said that was all they'd ever be and that hurt him deeply.

'Everyone thought Ben was a tough guy. He was an exceptional constable, extremely fit and had an aptitude for martial arts, such as they were in the seventies. The day he said he wanted to apply for a detective rank he was the most excited I'd ever heard him. But I worried because he wasn't tough enough inside. He could take care of himself, and he was so strong and fit I even found him a little intimidating sometimes, but emotionally and psychologically Ben was very fragile, and he wore his heart on his sleeve every time he fell for someone. He didn't meet many girls he took a shine to, but he jumped in with both feet every time, and ended up getting hurt a great deal. He always said Lillian Crosbie's rejection was the kindest and most gentle he'd ever received. Even though it broke his heart, he never said a bad word about her.'

Malkie suddenly realised he'd taken none of this down. He glanced at Steph, who was scribbling away. He looked away again before she saw him.

'Miss Hutchison, can you recall any other names from around that time? Anyone else Ben spoke to you about?'

She frowned. 'He never said much about his colleagues, but he complained a lot about problems Miss Crosbie had with one of her colleagues, her boss, actually. A real bitch, apparently, if you'll excuse my language.' She actually blushed. Rebecca Hutchison obviously led a very sheltered little existence. He envied her that, hoped he and his dad might yet get to enjoy the same kind of seclusion and peace he imagined this woman enjoyed.

'Do you remember that boss's name, Miss Hutchison?'

Hutchison studied him, as if assessing him, and seemed to come to a decision.

'Where did you find Ben, Mr McCulloch?'

Malkie sighed. *Why did she have to ask me that? But then, how could she not?*

'I'm honestly sorry, Miss Hutchison, but I can't tell you that. The person who called us did so under extreme duress, but I'm still bound by your brother's stated desire for client confidentiality. I wish I could tell you. I do.'

Hutchison relaxed, closed her eyes. Malkie frowned at Steph, who shrugged back in equal confusion.

'That's OK. I suppose I'm happy to hear you respect his wishes, and his safety, as much as that hurts me. Is my brother in any danger, Mr McCulloch?'

Is he? I have no idea. 'It's possible. But we know very little at the moment, which is why we need your help.'

'Ben's boss was a woman called Megan Shaw, and Ben hated her. I believe Crosbie did something terrible and Ben thought Shaw should have protected Crosbie better. But Shaw let Crosbie down in the worst possible way, ruined Crosbie's career, her whole life.'

I'm starting to believe she did, Miss Hutchison.

TWENTY-FOUR

Another doorstep, another doorbell, this one next to a massive, glossy black slab set into the ground floor entrance of a Georgian pile on Ainslie Place, in Edinburgh city centre. This was the kind of doorbell that promised Malkie would leave disappointed and no further forward.

Ainslie Place was home to many prestigious law firms, solicitors and architects. Some occupied one or more floors of a towering, stately pile, but a few – like Thomas Fairfield & Co. – filled the whole building, which meant a distinct possibility he was about to get one of those looks. The one that said 'Oh dear' in appalled and pitying tones. The one that never failed to get his back up and set him on a path to confrontation borne of his uncontrollable need to slap down entitlement and superiority wherever he could. The joys of a warrant card and the power of his legal authority over even the lofty heights of privilege that could afford an entire Georgian tenement on Ainslie Place.

He was shaken from his pre-confrontation attitude when a scratchy but unmistakably plummy voice blared from the intercom.

'Thomas Fairfield & Co.? Can I help you?'

He noticed, only now, the small lens above the speaker grill. He held his warrant card up to the lens. 'Detective Sergeant Malcolm McCulloch and Detective Constable Stephanie Lang. We'd like a word, please.'

'Please pull your warrant card back from the lens a few inches.' The intonation suggested a polite request, but one which expected full compliance without question. He did so, with a heavy sigh he didn't bother to hide.

The door buzzed, and Steph pushed it. She held one finger up in the air between them and arched an eyebrow but felt no need to articulate her warning. He hated it when she did that.

Inside, a long, wide hallway extended from the inner glass doors to several other doors at the rear of the building. Everything was mahogany, polished and buffed but no attempt had been made to repair various scratches and scrapes that testified to the authenticity and antiquity of the decor. Everything here was worth a fortune, and Thomas Fairfield & Co. wanted everyone to know it.

A small, wiry lady appeared from a side door, all smart trouser suit and pixie-cut white hair; a woman growing old about as gracefully and fashionably as Malkie could remember encountering. No way her trouser suit came from any Princes Street chain store. Harvey Nicks, maybe.

'May I see your warrant cards again, please?' Her smile carried professional warmth alongside a touch of 'Do you know who you're talking to?'

Malkie and Steph showed her their cards again. She studied each for a few seconds, before seeming to settle her mind. 'Thank you. Now, what can I help two officers of the law with today?'

Malkie found himself warming to the old bird. She was, after all, a product of a profession steeped in tradition and privilege and might be completely different in a social situation.

Maybe this would go OK, after all. Then he smacked himself mentally for such naïve optimism.

'We'd like to talk to whoever handles the affairs of a Ben Hutchison, brother of Rebecca Hutchison, a family I'm given to understand your firm has represented for decades.' He realised he'd unconsciously stuck a couple of plums in his mouth, and the realisation this old woman made him feel so inadequate stung.

The woman turned on her heel and walked back into an office. Malkie and Steph shrugged at each other and followed her.

She sat behind a huge desk, almost certainly also ancient mahogany, and tapped away on the keyboard of a computer so sleek and modern it looked out of place in the surroundings.

'We do have accounts with the Hutchison family, yes. I'll need to see if our Mr Truscott is available to talk to you. I have to say, though: Mr Truscott is a senior partner so his time is very valuable. Please take a seat in the waiting room, down the hall-way, on the right. Thank you.' She reached for her phone but waited for them to leave before dialling.

Malkie and Steph seated themselves in the waiting room, as plush and New Town Georgian as everything else. A huge bay window looked out onto an immaculate garden, at the bottom of which a high hedgerow obscured what Malkie knew would be a spectacular view over the Dean Bridge and the terraced and tree-covered slopes of the gorge through which the Water of Leith wended through the west of the city to the Firth of Forth. Its source lay up in the Pentlands, near Harperrig Reservoir, where the cabin waited for him and his dad to finish work and move in. Not for the first time in recent days, he wished he could be sitting on the porch with his dad and hot coffees.

A man appeared in the doorway. Middle-aged but fit-look-ing, his suit trousers and waistcoat dark navy blue, and even Malkie's less-than-sophisticated eye could tell his attire was custom-fitted. His shoes probably cost more than Malkie's whole wardrobe. This had to be senior partner Mr Truscott.

The man closed the door behind him and took a seat opposite them. He crossed his legs, and Malkie got a close-up look at his shoes, which did, indeed, look more expensive than his car. 'I'm Phillip Truscott, senior partner. How can I help you, officers?'

Malkie led but reminded himself of Steph's warning: she knew him better than he knew himself, most of the time.

'We're investigating a missing person who has disappeared under rather violent circumstances. We found a link from our missing person to Mr Hutchison. We spoke to his sister, Rebecca, who told us he's been incommunicado, for want of a better word, for more than forty years. I had cause to meet Mr Hutchison, and...'

Malkie considered how to describe what he'd seen. 'He had been tortured, Mr Truscott.'

Truscott studied Malkie, made him feel like some job applicant who'd just admitted to having form for embezzlement.

'I don't recall anything sinister in Mr Hutchison's files, but I'm afraid that without the appropriate authorisation to override his client confidentiality, that's about all I can share with you. You do understand, I trust?'

Malkie sighed and didn't bother to hide it.

Truscott seemed to deflate a little. He removed his glasses and pulled a lens cloth from his pocket. Malkie was amazed at how much less a pain in the arse the man looked without them shrinking his eyes to what Malkie thought of as weaselly.

Maybe give the guy a break, old man?

Truscott finished cleaning his glasses but didn't replace them on his face; perhaps he knew too well the effect they had on his appearance.

'You know, I get really very tired of that look, Mr McCulloch. No, please don't bother denying it. It's the look we always get when we tell you we can't share information or we'll lose our jobs and possibly our liberty, and you look at us as if you're just itching to charge us with obstruction of justice.'

Malkie waited, his discomfort building.

'If a journalist asks you to share inside information on a case, you wouldn't dream of complying. Well, most of you wouldn't, I like to believe.'

Malkie nodded and lifted his eyebrows to acknowledge this unfortunate fact.

'Tell me. Is it all the mahogany and brass, or our crusty old reputation, that puts officers like yourself on the defensive before we even open our mouths? Can you imagine how tiresome that can be, how much it puts *us* on the defensive, and so round and round it goes? So unfortunate.'

Malkie sighed, slumped himself, a little.

'All fair points, Mr Truscott. All fair points. We are, after all, supposed to be on the same side, looking after the rights of the innocent and catching bad guys, right?'

Truscott smiled and shrugged as if to say 'indeed'.

Malkie glanced at Steph, who shrugged too, as if to say 'no argument from me'.

'Mr Truscott, if you could tell us what little you can, professionally, about Mr Ben Hutchison, we really would appreciate it. Ms Taylor at the shelter told us he was an ex-policeman who was attacked and taken to the Western General Hospital by an anonymous taxi driver in 1978, and that he moved into the Waverley Church Shelter and was given an open-ended contract to care for him, with regular checks on his well-being and newly fitted security measures, arranged by yourselves. That's what I know, and if you can add anything to that, it might aid our investigation and help us find our missing person before she comes to harm.'

'She?' Truscott's attention suddenly caught.

'Lillian Crosbie. A close friend, possibly more, until Mr

Hutchison chose to cut himself off so completely. He served in Uniform in the Borders; she was West Lothian.'

Truscott considered his next comment for long seconds.

'Mr Fairfield, the founder of our firm, told me he once asked Mr Hutchison why he wanted to cut himself off legally from his family, from everyone and everything. Mr Hutchison said something about him being a danger to Ms Crosbie if '*she*' found him again. Who '*she*' was we didn't ask, but Mr Fairfield was certain he was not referring to Ms Crosbie.'

Truscott paused for what seemed like an age, stared out the window at the gardens. Malkie gave him all the time he needed, realised the man had just bent the rules more than he was comfortable with.

'Cutting off all contact with Ms Crosbie hurt Mr Hutchison deeply, so he had to have had the best of reasons.'

Truscott stared at him. Malkie nodded. Truscott nodded back, a bare tip of his head, then stood.

'Until then, Mr McCulloch, Ms Lang.' He extended his hand; Malkie shook it, as did Steph.

Malkie turned in the doorway. 'I apologise, Mr Truscott.'

'For what?' The man's surprise looked genuine.

'For pre-judging.'

'As do I, Mr McCulloch.'

TWENTY-FIVE

Malkie paused before pushing yet another doorbell. So much of his working life seemed to consist of pushing doorbells. At least this one carried no real risk, despite being in a part of the New Town that reeked of such conspicuous wealth and entitlement that pressing any doorbell could prove hit and miss for a scruff like him.

Malkie had asked to be assigned to a private therapist after it became apparent that the department-assigned shrink and he were never going to be anything other than mortal enemies. He'd never before been made to feel like a specimen being examined, poked and prodded. Questions he considered none of her bloody business asked in a tone of voice that suggested somewhere close to zero real interest beyond ticking her boxes and getting him out the door again. The fact that someone had grassed him up to her for calling her 'the therapist from hell' hadn't helped and had almost resulted in yet another disciplinary on his already shocking career record. He had volunteered to find himself his own therapist, at his own expense, and she'd agreed on condition that he showed her all his homework signed off by a registered mental health professional.

Malkie had taken a recommendation from Rab Lundy, which should have been a warning sign, but by that time Malkie was due another session and desperation made him reckless.

Malkie had to pay for his sessions with Timothy Crichton himself, since the man wasn't on, and never would get anywhere near, the department preferred-supplier list. This stretched Malkie's failing financial situation even more, but Timothy had turned out to be the mother of all blessings. While technically qualified, Timothy's adherence to accepted psychiatric and psychological principles and consulting practices tended to be of the lip-service kind, at best. Much like Malkie's approach to standards and procedure. Malkie found him a breath of the freshest of air; a medical professional not so far up their own arse they'd forgotten what daylight looked like.

During their first session, Malkie had mentioned his struggles to pay his dad's mortgage on top of his own rental property. Timothy had dug deeper, gently, and learned all about the house fire that had left his dad homeless and killed his mum, and about Malkie's stubborn but unjustifiable certainty of his culpability. Timothy had told Malkie just how loaded his family was and offered to treat Malkie for less than a third what other practitioners asked. Timothy often made Malkie feel like a specimen under glass but he couldn't turn down a discount like that.

Malkie pushed the doorbell and waited for the usual performance to begin.

'Timothy Crichton, how may I be of service?'

Malkie's mood had been foul until he heard Timothy's over-the-top greeting. Gucci's wee info-bomb about Lillian Crosbie being ex-Uniform had energised the whole CID room, the prospect of something a bit tasty, but Thompson had insisted he keep his appointment and promised to update him afterwards.

But Malkie smiled now; Timothy had that effect on him. 'Camp' didn't come close to describing Timothy's self-affected persona. One which – Malkie had learned – masked a lifetime of bitter shame and guilt from his teen years in the fifties when admitting to homosexuality guaranteed you a good booting from the Pigs.

'Troll up here you bona sharpy, you. Been too long since I vardered your dolly old eek.'

'In English, Timothy? No one's spoken Polari since paisley cravats went out of fashion.'

'Paisley cravats will never go out of fashion, Malkie. Now be a good lad and troll up here, you old dish.' After a click from the intercom and a buzz from the door lock, Malkie grinned, shook his head, and entered the tenement stair.

Timothy, as always, waited in his open doorway. Malkie endured the traditional squeezing past between the doorframe and Timothy's ample girth, and tried to ignore the satisfied sigh Timothy made no effort to hide.

'You're a perv, Timothy.'

'I have to be me, Malkie. I have to be me. What do you have for me this time, sweet man?'

Malkie fished a bottle out of his coat pocket and read the label. 'A cheap blend today, I'm afraid, bit short on ready cash this month. Sorry.'

Timothy took the bottle, turned his nose up at it. 'I'm sure you'll make up for this massive faux pas next time, dear boy. Why don't you stretch out in your usual scruffy but lovable recumbency, and I'll sit at my desk with my bumper book of *Times* crosswords and pretend I'm listening, OK?'

'You moved on from sudokus?'

'Had to. I've been detecting ever so slight tendencies in myself to lapses in memory, mild confusion when operating that damned air fryer, you know the sort of thing. So, in the spirit of exercising my mind as thoroughly as I used to exercise this now-travesty of a body, I've stepped up a gear. Cryptic crosswords.'

'You seeing a doctor, Timothy? I need you sane and able to mollify my boss for another few years, mate.'

Timothy's eyes twinkled; he and Malkie had learned to read each other so they never embarrassed themselves with sentimentality. Or rather, Timothy had learned not to try to tease Malkie into any kind of emotional bond, much as he always professed that he'd like to.

'I'm fine, Malkie. Just taking all possible precautions, considering my age and my delicate sensibilities.' He flashed Malkie a grin that was more pout than smile.

Malkie stretched out on the chaise longue by the massive bay window that looked out onto private gardens the likes of which riffraff like him would never own a key to. He realised he'd forgotten to bring something to read as he usually spent these sessions doing, and he was far too wound up to sleep. He closed his eyes, listened to the slow, gentle thuds from inside Timothy's huge and ancient grandfather clock, and to the sound of Timothy's pen on paper, and his occasional tuts.

His mind wouldn't rest. A new fear sprang into vicious and confidence-rattling form. Hutchison had spent decades – not just years, decades – hiding from something appalling; by visiting him, might Crosbie or Malkie have led that same trouble right back to him? Did he need to request protection for Hutchison, even if he could justify that to Thompson? The man he'd seen in Crosbie's home looked dangerous. He'd seen for himself – against all credibility – the old woman getting the better of the brute because he'd seen her put him down, but he'd also seen the man land a solid blow to her abdomen, then blood on her side and her hand. Was she OK? Would she survive? Lizzie Taylor's sighting of her earlier today at the hostel proved Lillian Crosbie had given the guy the slip but where was she now? And where was the brute? Did Hutchison have anything to do with it all, or was he nothing more than Crosbie's oldest friend, and his torture nothing more than some kind of collateral damage? But then what about Phillip Truscott's comments about Hutchison locking himself away to protect Crosbie? She'd known where to find him after the attack in her home, so how long had it been since she'd found him and yet never visited him? Lizzie Taylor said she'd never seen Crosbie before.

'What a fucking mess.'

'What was that, Malkie, my sweet?'

Malkie opened his eyes. 'Shit, did I say that out loud?'

'You certainly did, lover. Want to talk about it?'

Malkie realised that unlike every other previous visit to Timothy, this time he did feel a need. He sat up, turned to face him.

'I have a stabbing and a MisPer and a man who's spent forty-five years hiding in a Church Mission Shelter from someone who tortured him. I haven't a bloody clue what the hell's going on, Tim, old boy.'

Timothy tutted at Malkie's use of this most hated forms of his name but waited in silence.

He hesitated. Despite their relaxed professional relationship, Malkie knew Timothy to be as discreet as they come. He'd rather have his favourite velvet smoking jacket torn to shreds than betray a confidence.

'The man I saw had been...' Memories of the carnage inflicted on Ben Hutchison stopped Malkie's words in his throat, until he swallowed and pushed himself to continue. 'Aw Christ, Tim. The things they did to the poor bastard.'

He sighed, braced himself to stop his usual self-flogging tendencies colouring his description of events; he needed to hear Timothy's honest and unalloyed opinion.

'Our MisPer, a seventy-three-year-old woman, was attacked in her home by what we thought was a volume crime mouth-breather, an opportunist looking for easy cash. But – and believe me I'm struggling with this evidence – what I saw suggests she stabbed the mouth-breather in the neck. He died a hundred yards away, bled out. Then I saw her – and again, I can only repeat what I saw – she took this bloke down. Six foot tall and built like a brick shithouse. Makes no sense. Then she turns up at a homeless shelter in Edinburgh, injured and distressed, to visit a gentleman of similar age who's been closed off and unresponsive for decades. Then she scarpers again in a terrible state when he seems not to recognise her. As if the poor old bird's last support got kicked out from under her because he just wasn't really there.'

Malkie rubbed his eyes then bent forward and hung his head as low between his knees as his paunch would let him, as if extra blood flow to his head might kick his brain up a gear.

When he straightened again, Timothy was studying him, his crossword book discarded on the desk.

'Malkie, my dear boy. Correct me if I'm wrong, but I imagine you attended this refuge for society's unfortunates following a lead of some kind?'

'Aye, the woman who runs it called it in when she found our old lady's photo on the Police Scotland MisPer page.'

'So, did you have any choice? Was ignoring the lady's call an option?'

Malkie scowled at him. 'Of course not.'

'So, you had no choice but to attend and interview this lady?'

'No.' Malkie's temper started to fray because he'd realised where Timothy was taking this.

'Then even if you did enable someone to locate the gentleman, or perhaps it was your frail old lady who did so, you would have been remiss in your responsibilities had you failed to attend, correct?'

Malkie surrendered. Held his hands up. Timothy smiled at him; no smugness, no told-you-so, just a fervent desire for Malkie to stop flogging himself for self-manufactured sins. The man knew him almost as well as Steph did, which was a major pain in the arse.

'Thing is, Tim, she's the second old lady I've let down in ten months, mate, and I don't think I can handle losing another one.'

Timothy thought for a few moments. 'Malkie. Love. Would you hate yourself more if you put everything you have into finding her even if you don't get her back safe and sound, than if you just didn't bother trying at all? And yes, that's about as loaded a question as you'll ever hear from me.'

Malkie smiled at him. When it came to making him see the bloody obvious that was already right in front of him, Timothy was an artist.

Mind made up, the only way he could have decided, Malkie settled back to try to doze for the remaining twenty minutes of the hour he was struggling to pay for.

TWENTY-SIX

After a long, frustrating day hiding like some pathetic coward, Fisher was bored to hell and impatient to act.

He'd found extra security at Montrose's house. He'd watched her lose it big time when she'd discovered the photograph he'd left her, knew he had got to her.

He'd been surprised she'd continued with her idiotic plans after that, but knowing her as he did, he had to admit that letting the whole thing drop would have been out of character.

He'd found a house with a garden which backed onto hers, and with nobody home. A shed against the adjoining wall stood under a large oak tree, whose branches dropped down to the roof, giving him an ideal place from which to observe without being seen from any of the surrounding properties.

He spent a half hour watching the new muscle, scanning the exterior by eye, and the interior through compact binocs, his elbows braced on the roof felt of the shed.

They looked good enough that he didn't want to have to go up against them. He could probably take one, but both would be beyond him.

Fortunately, these guys were lazy. Either they didn't expect anyone to be stupid enough to attempt entry during broad daylight, or they weren't paid enough to take the job seriously. In either case, Fisher could see their minds weren't completely on the job.

It didn't take him long to spot a third man. Two patrolled the perimeter of the building. They should have stationed themselves front and back with regular perimeter checks, but they both stood, fags in hand, at one rear corner of the building, looking bored.

The third sat in the kitchen, with a mug of something and a newspaper. He didn't even face the window, angled instead across and slightly away from the glass. Fisher watched every other room in the house and saw no one else.

He only had to wait five minutes. Smokes finished, the two on the back wandered around the side of the house. Fisher waited, and when they reappeared at the opposite side, he could tell from the time-gap that they didn't believe in hurrying.

He allowed them to complete a couple of circuits to check for random variations in their routine, as any half-trained idiot would know to do. They didn't.

Satisfied, he waited for them to disappear one more time, then confirmed that the man in the kitchen still sat engrossed in his paper, and dropped to the ground.

He sprinted across the lawn. He didn't bother to keep low – he was as exposed as he could be – and his boots made no sound on the perfectly mowed lawn. He reached the back wall of the house, and immediately sprang up the same drainpipe he'd used last time.

His ageing muscles complained, but he scaled the wall quickly and reached the window to the same spare room as before.

He paused, flattened himself against the wall. The two goons appeared, ambled across the back of the house, and disappeared again. Too busy talking about some footie match last weekend, they didn't look up, or even around the garden. He would have a long, boring wait until she came home and fell asleep again, but waiting was easy.

He turned, examined the window. He spotted the new security measures immediately. Magnetic sensors mounted where the two halves of the sash windows met. The presence of the man in the kitchen didn't necessarily mean that the entire system was disabled. If it was sophisticated enough, it would be zoned, and the windows might still be alarmed even if the internal motion detectors were switched off.

He perched on the left corner of the window ledge, stretched over to the adjacent ledge, and neatly stepped to the next window. Another spare room. It also was alarmed, but he noticed that the sensor wires hadn't yet been boxed in, meaning the installation was still in progress. He pressed his face to the glass, peered as far around the inside wall as he could, scanned the side wall of the room.

His eyes traced the wires along the skirting board, followed them to the doorway, and there he spotted the bare ends. A toolbox sat on the hallway floor, just outside the door.

As he watched, a man in overalls stepped into the room.

Fisher ducked but could find nothing other than the window frame to hold on to. He had to hope the man didn't spot his fingertips on the wood.

After a few seconds, he heard the man's boots on the wooden floorboards. He risked peeking over the bottom of the window frame.

The electrician stood examining a small plastic connector block, a frown on his face. He poked it with a screwdriver, peered inside it, then tossed it to the floor and turned away. Fisher spotted his head bob down the staircase.

He couldn't stay long where he was: the crack security operatives were bound to glance upwards sometime, if only out of boredom. He gave the sparky a few seconds to get downstairs, then took a deep breath, took out his multitool, and inserted the blade between the window frames. He flipped the catch and lifted the lower frame. It slid up easily.

He stepped inside, lowered the window again, and slipped behind a single bed. The sparky should have no reason to look on that side of the room, and he seemed to be finishing up anyway.

He froze when he heard the sparky return. The man pottered about for a few more minutes, then left again. He heard his footsteps descend the stairs, and breathed a sigh of relief.

He was settling in for the long wait when the sparky returned again, entered the room, and crossed straight to the window.

Fisher rolled quickly against the side of the bed, managed to get some of himself under the bedspread, but if the man looked his way, he'd be fucked.

The sparky released the catch, gripped the handles at the bottom of the frame, then shouted over his shoulder, 'Testing.'

He waited for an answering call from downstairs, then lifted the frame.

A piercing siren sounded from the hallway. The sparky lowered the frame again and latched it, then hurried back to the hallway.

'Right, turn it off now.'

The siren died.

Fisher heard the door close, and eased himself onto his back again.

His heart pounded and his head swam. He was way too old for this shit.

The remainder of the afternoon passed mostly without event. Every couple of hours or so, the door would open and close again, so he assumed the security detail were going through the motions, but none of them ever bothered to actually look round the inside of the room.

When he heard the front door open and close, then silence, he risked creeping to a window at the front of the house and saw both the electricians and the security detail get into their vehicles and drive off. He returned to the same room, stretched out on the bed, and settled in to wait.

The tedium of the passing hours gave him far too much time to contemplate what he was about to do. He tried his relaxation exercises but couldn't stop his mind chewing on the night's coming events.

As much as he believed she had it coming to her, years – decades of remembering her as one of the scariest people he'd ever known – made him wary of taking her down so brutally. He suspected she wouldn't buckle easily. He'd have to be at his most brutal and creative.

He'd tried to intimidate her with the photo, had hoped she'd finally realise it was all getting a bit real and back off. She'd have her hands full if Crosbie decided to come for her now, so he hoped she might see the sense at least in getting Fisher off her back.

But he'd received a stark reminder of who she was. It wasn't in her to back down from anything, regardless of the consequences.

So now he had to hurt her.

The hours passed, and Fisher worked his way through the extensive list of ways he'd learned over the years to break, humiliate and – call it what it is – torture a human body. Some he disregarded as beyond even these desperate times, and some he grudgingly admitted were acceptable given his present constraints. She needed to agree quickly, and sincerely, to leave well alone, and never come after him again.

He decided his old favourite would do fine: simple, brutal, and excruciatingly painful for the minor damage it did.

· · ·

When he heard footsteps on the wooden floorboards between the hall carpet and the bedroom he realised he'd drifted off. Never fully asleep – his training was too deeply ingrained for that – but certainly not completely conscious. Not nearly good enough.

He felt adrenaline course through him. He'd long ago learned that you couldn't suppress the electrifying rush, you just had to handle it, allow it to sharpen your senses, work for you.

He rose silently, stretched his arms, legs and back, eased knots and kinks from muscles aching from long inactivity on a hard floor.

He pulled his multitool from his pocket and eased out the miniature pliers. He could only hope he didn't need to find more imaginative uses for the various other tools lurking in its steel casing.

He crossed to her bedroom door, ajar a few inches, and heard the shower starting.

It was time.

He eased the door open and slipped through, keeping close to the wall so she couldn't see him from inside the bathroom.

The lights were on, the bathroom door open. He could see steam floating into the bedroom. He found his hands were shaking. He wasn't on a job, out to hurt some lowlife who might well have deserved it. This was personal.

He breathed slow and deep, steadied himself, then stepped towards the bathroom.

He heard the bedroom door click shut behind him. A languid and slurred voice spoke.

'Hello, Fisher. Lovely to meet you at last.'

TWENTY-SEVEN

Fisher felt a sting at his neck. He froze but refused to drop his weapon.

'Now that we've got the "*who's still got it*" out of the way and you lost, I'm going to sit down and we're going to talk, Fisher.'

When Michael's steel withdrew, Fisher spun round, backed up, put his back against a wall, found himself on the balls of his feet, arms loose but ready. Coiled.

Michael chuckled. 'Not lost it, then, old man?' He turned his back on Fisher as if he couldn't be less afraid of him and returned to his chair behind the door. He lowered himself into it with a grunt.

Fisher's mouth turned as dry as a budgie's floor mat, and a knot of fear lodged itself in his throat. 'What do you want, you fucking psycho?'

The man's face darkened. 'Not anymore, Fisher. Not got the heart for it these days. World's changed, left our kind behind, hasn't it?' The man's disappointment looked genuine.

Fisher relaxed. Not completely, but enough to ease the aches burning in his leg and arm muscles. He let his hand holding the multitool drop to his side, but kept it held, light but ready, in his fingers. Michael's gaze followed it down, and he smiled again.

Michael opened his jacket, some manky garment that looked like he'd slept in it. He stood and Fisher flinched. He laid the kitchen knife in his hand on a sideboard, turned a full circle, gave Fisher every chance to pick up on any other weapons. 'I'm clean, Fisher. I haven't carried for years.'

He sat again, let his jacket fall closed.

Only now did Fisher notice – just as Michael had struggled to stand, he'd had to ease himself back into his chair, too. The years hadn't been kind to him. He noted, too, a slight slur in his words, a clumsiness in pronunciation. Parkinson's? Alzheimer's? Was that why he claimed to have mellowed? Because he had only a limited time left? Men like them often topped themselves before letting someone wipe their arse for years.

Fisher crossed to the bed, sat on the edge, kept his legs tensed under him so he could rise quickly if he had to. 'Time's not been kind to you, has it, Michael? I've got a few creaky bits and I grunt when I get out of my armchair, but what the hell happened to you?'

Michael made a show of examining himself, cast a hurt look at Fisher. 'Cruel, Fisher. True, but hurtful, mate.'

The 'mate' set Fisher's alarms blaring. Men like Michael never had mates; the concept of one human being caring a damn about another was an alien concept to his type. In their eyes people were either lumps of meat they were allowed to kill, or everyone else.

'So, are you here to do me?'

Michael considered Fisher for a while, then leaned forward. 'She did ask me to do you, Fisher, but – and this will come as a shocker to you – I want *us* to do *her* before she drags us down with her.'

Fisher reeled. Her mythical psycho attack dog asking for help? This was wrong, beyond any measure of common sense, and trusting a man like him could only end one, very final, way.

'Don't look at me like that, Fisher. Think it through. You want to retire. I want to enjoy whatever time I have left without worrying about her nonsense. She's obviously as loopy as a bag of frogs to drag all this up again after so many years. Who are you more afraid of? Me or her?'

'And just how long do you think you have left, Michael?'

Michael shrugged, his expression resigned. 'Do any of us know how long we have left to us, Fisher? Do we want to know?'

An ageing, decrepit, philosophical psychopath. *The world's turned upside down.*

'The way I see it, old chum, is as follows. For whatever reason, she's raking up a past we all thought was done with. She asked me to deal with you and Crosbie, but I propose a two-stage alternative plan. First, we find out why she's raking it all up again. Then, we end her. It's a complex plan but I feel two experienced veterans like us can pull it off. What do you say?' He tried to beam, but one side of his face failed to rise as high as the other.

Has he had a stroke?

Fisher chewed this over, until an uncomfortable thought intruded. 'Where is she, anyway? She can't come home and find us in the same room but not tearing lumps out of each other.'

'Relax, she's at some fancy dinner, schmoozing with a lot of twats in suits she loathes but needs to impress.'

'You're sure?'

Michael pulled a mobile phone from his jacket and tapped the screen a few times. He turned the display towards him and Fisher recognised some kind of Follow My Phone app. He leaned forward to focus, made out a flashing yellow dot on the other side of the River Forth, forty miles west of Edinburgh.

Michael grinned. 'You're not the only one who's been poking around her bedroom while she slept the sleep of the sinful. Nice bit of kit, that camera, by the way. Don't worry, it's still there, she looked but didn't find it, but it was too easy to hack so I connected my phone to its IP address too. Hope you don't mind. She's got some temper, doesn't she?'

Fisher saw no way out other than to humour him. He could never trust him, and Michael would never believe it if he tried to pretend he did, but if he really did want *her* dealt with more than he did Fisher, then mutually beneficial assurances could be agreed on. Until she was an ex-problem, then he had no doubt they would return to business as usual.

'Fine. Who does what?'

Michael smiled. 'Before we get to that, you know why the silly cow is going after Crosbie after so many years, don't you? You know what happened? Or what they said happened?'

'I didn't, but I do now. Crosbie released some girl, turned her out of the old Livi Station and left her to find her own way home on Hogmanay in the middle of that bastard of a winter in '78. Girl was found on a park bench, next morning, frozen to death. That's as much as my newspaper clippings said.'

Michael sighed, disappointed. 'Is that it? That's all you have?' He leaned forward and grunted, smacked a hand to his back. 'I bloody hate getting old, Fisher. It's no fun.'

He straightened, took a few seconds for some ache or twinge to pass. 'I'm going to dig. I'm good at digging.' He held a thin, white and gnarled hand out to Fisher.

Fisher kept his by his sides. 'Funny man. Don't push your luck.'

TWENTY-EIGHT

After returning to the station from his session with Timothy, Malkie kept his head down until shift-end. Steph had got herself bogged down in rereading door-to-door interviews for anything they might have missed, which tended to put her in a foul mood. He'd managed to avoid her attention all afternoon, but it had only been a matter of time. Before risking departure for the evening, he tried to head off a lecture he suspected had been brewing for hours.

'OK, I admit it. I pre-judged Truscott, OK? I expected everyone in that building to be toffee-nosed, plummy-accented snobs, so I never gave them a chance, OK? I went in there looking for a face-off with some entitled jobsworth with an axe to grind with us *polis* and far too much self-importance to see our point of view, and who looked forward to nothing more than sending us scurrying back to management for a warrant meanwhile they can have great fun telling us to take a hike because some of their rules lay our rules over a barrel and fuck them royally. OK? I don't need you to tell me I was a clown in there.'

He took a breath. 'OK, off you go, let rip, give it to me.'

She hadn't broken her gaze all through his ranting monologue. Now she shook her head as if in disbelief. Possibly amusement, too.

'You finished?'

He nodded, indicated she should commence laying into him.

'I went in there with the same attitude, you idiot.'

He opened his mouth but shut it again; her expression said she wasn't nearly finished.

'You think you're the only one who hates some of the twats we meet in our line of work? You think I don't get pissed off at jobsworths? Of course I bloody do. But I keep it to myself, try not to let my prejudice colour my approach to people who might not be such twats.'

Malkie's phone buzzed in his pocket, but he dared not reach for it while she was in full flow.

'As soon as Truscott walked in, I thought the same: that we were in for the usual nonsense and we'd be sent packing empty-handed.'

Malkie's phone continued buzzing.

'Well, you know what I mean. That man wants to tell us something. He was bursting to tell us. Trouble is, Ben Hutchison is not the MisPer, Crosbie is, so how do we get a warrant to look at Hutchison's legal affairs based only on a forty-five-year-old crush on Crosbie? And answer your phone, for Pete's sake.'

She turned to stare out the window. She chewed the inside of her cheek, pursed her lips, which he knew meant she was concentrating. He pulled his phone from his pocket.

'DS McCulloch, Police Scotland.'

'Who did you tell where Ben was, Mr McCulloch? Who did you tell?' Her voice rose to stridency as she asked the second time; the woman sounded furious.

Malkie, taken aback, stammered an answer. 'Only my

colleague DC Lang, Ms Taylor. It's not even in the case notes yet.'

A lump of dread landed in Malkie's guts. 'Why are you asking, Ms Taylor? What's happened?'

'He's gone, damn you. After all these years, someone's taken him. You get here now and look at what you've done, Mr McCulloch.'

She hung up. Steph turned, opened her mouth, saw Malkie's expression. 'Oh God, what now?'

When Lizzie Taylor opened the Waverley Shelter door, Malkie could swear the temperature around him dropped ten degrees. She stood aside, nodded a hello to Steph but made no eye contact with Malkie. Inside, she closed and bolted the door, all five bolts, and walked past them in the direction of the rear of the building and Ben's room. She led them to the top of the stairs, pushed the door open with her foot, then folded her arms and stood aside.

'I haven't touched anything. I didn't want to interfere in you fixing your mess.' She stared ahead, her lips clamped tight, her eyes blazing.

Malkie and Steph stepped past her, and Malkie's day turned even worse than he thought it could.

Shards of glass covered the carpet under a broken pane in an opened sash window.

The bedclothes had been dragged half onto the floor.

Malkie rubbed the bridge of his nose, pushed his fingertips into his eyes, hard, as if punishing himself for his imminent newest fuck-up. He held his hand out and Steph slapped a sealed bag of shoe covers into his hand without needing to be asked.

They surveyed the room, one half each, then returned to the doorway as close as they could remember in their own footsteps.

Malkie sighed, a long, desolate venting of his culpability in whatever had happened here. Ben Hutchison had, Ms Taylor had told him, done nothing and said nothing of his own volition for decades – literally decades – until Detective Sergeant McFuckup led someone to him and destroyed what bleak and lonely peace the man still clung to.

Well done, arsehole. Well done.

'Stop that, Malkie. Don't even start your nonsense.'

He looked at her but didn't bother to ask what she meant. She, as ever, was merciless and continued anyway.

'Whatever happened here, you had no choice but to follow the lead.' She pushed the door closed on the waiting Lizzie Taylor, then whispered, 'She called you, identified Crosbie as Mr Hutchison's mystery visitor, what the hell else could you do?'

'I know, Steph, but—'

'No. No buts. You're not laying this on you. Not happening, mate. Don't make me get really stroppy on your arse. I mean it.'

His mouth wouldn't be stopped. 'The man was fine – relatively-speaking – for fuck knows how many years. I came here yesterday. Whatever happened, he's not very fine now, is he?'

She placed a hand on his arm, waited for him to meet her gaze. 'Let's find out what happened first, OK? If it turned out you did something stupid...You didn't, did you? Never mind, don't answer that. Let's get the SOCOs here, hopefully get some initial answers by morning? Deal?'

When she reopened the door, Lizzie Taylor looked twice as furious as before, if that were possible. 'Well? What are you going to do about this? How are you going to fix this? You stupid, stupid, man.' She broke down. Malkie reached for her without thinking, but Steph pulled him back and took the woman in her arms, waited for the sobs and the wails and the grief to peter out. Malkie stood, clueless as to what to say or do. He pulled his phone out again and called it in. Thompson couldn't mask a heavy sigh at the news. 'So, do we have two MisPers now?'

Malkie gazed around at the room: blood and signs of a struggle and a window smashed from the outside. 'Aye, I think it's safe to say we have two MisPers now. Sorry about that.'

'Don't be stupid. Not your fault. Probably not your fault. Stop loading yourself with other people's shite. That's an order.'

When the SOCOs arrived, Malkie and Steph waited. Lizzie Taylor made them both a coffee but said nothing. After an hour, Malkie's patience broke. He knocked on the door, eased it open.

'Give me something, guys? Please? You're killing me out here.'

One paper-suited figure, male from the build, straightened up from dusting the bedframe and sighed. 'I don't know how you do things in the sticks, DS McCulloch, but—'

'I know, I know. I'll wait for the report, but you know what they say about the first twenty-four hours, don't you? Can you give me anything? At all?'

The SOCO studied him for a few seconds, then his shoulders loosened. 'Window glass on the inside suggests forced entry but could have been faked. I know, I know, but it's a possibility. The earth around the outside of the window's been smoothed out with a rake we found lying out there, and the rest of the back yard is paved, so not much chance of shoe impressions but we might get lucky. Blood type we'll get tomorrow. Prints, too, if you're lucky.'

Malkie thanked the man, tried to keep the disappointment from souring the sentiment, but knew he failed.

Steph punched him on the arm. 'Back to Livi. See if Gucci has turned up anything new on Crosbie, or – wonders can happen – see if Rab took the initiative and followed up on any other contact between her and Hutchison. Tomorrow will be a brand-new day and with a bit of luck there'll be a shiny new SOCO initial report waiting for us.'

Malkie tried to thank Lizzie Taylor, but the look she turned on him shook him to his core, bore into him and shamed him. He could hope she'd reconsider his culpability later, but the fury in her eyes now would, he knew, keep him from sleep tonight.

TWENTY-NINE

Fisher waited in his car. He forced himself to close his eyes and breathe easy.

He couldn't trust the man who claimed to be called Michael, that much was beyond doubt. Why would the man suggest turning on Montrose and lose a healthy payment as well as an excuse to kill people?

He needed Michael to believe he was onside with his plan, and meanwhile find Crosbie first, as insurance.

He waited until Michael appeared at the opening to the driveway. He walked to a black Audi, and Fisher noticed a stiffness in his posture, a dragging of his feet. Aye, he'd had a stroke, at some point. None of them were getting any younger, and Fisher intended to get a lot older before his time came. Michael drove off. Fisher checked his headlights were off and followed him.

The Audi seemed to drive around at random, then circle back to the same street they'd started from. Fisher parked a block away and watched.

Neither the Audi nor Michael moved for an hour, then Fisher saw two BMWs enter Montrose's driveway – her son's and another. He watched Montrose enter the front door. Her security detail, two of them, followed her in then left again minutes later. They climbed into their BMW and drove away.

Michael climbed out of his Audi, stiff and slow, and walked towards the house. Fisher waited ten seconds, then sprinted after him. He saw Michael turn back into Montrose's driveway.

What the hell are you playing at?

Fisher approached the driveway and peered towards the house. Jonathan Montrose's BMW sat at the front door, and a light shone in a downstairs window. Michael was nowhere to be seen. Fisher crept closer, hunched over, his knee aching from his stooped posture.

He found no chink in the curtains to watch through and swore under his breath. What the hell was Michael doing back there right after proposing they murder her? His mind ran wild; nothing made sense. He forced himself to calm down and walked a circuit of the house. He saw no other security and found no doors or windows open. Montrose must have sent her security away at Michael's request. As he agonised over what to do, he heard the front door open and crept back to the front.

Her voice sounded, low and quiet. 'Are you absolutely positive he trusts you?'

'No, he doesn't, but he'll realise he has no choice.'

'And there's no chance he has it?'

'No. One of the others has it, if anyone.'

A pause.

'Get it back. Whatever else you need to do, get it back. You never used to be this incompetent, so bloody fix this mess. Has that penetrated that thick skull of yours?'

Michael stepped close, his nose nearly touching hers. He towered over her. 'If you ever talk to me like that again, I'll fucking end you, and to hell with your big fat fee. Now, has that penetrated *your* skull?'

She looked shaken. She also looked familiar. He'd not seen

her face at the shopping centre, and hadn't been able to make out any detail in the darkness of her bedroom as he stood over her, but he saw her clearly now. He knew her from somewhere but couldn't place her.

Michael walked away. Fisher waited until he heard her front door close, then crept after him, one eye on the lit window.

Fisher caught up to Michael and slammed him forward over the top of his car, one twisted arm up his back.

'What the fuck are you playing at, Michael, if that's your real name? Tell me now or I swear I'll break your arm in three places.'

The man's breath hissed from between his teeth. 'Fuck's sake. Let go and I'll explain. That bloody hurts.'

Fisher eased up enough to allow Michael to talk. 'Talk. First, how long until her security come back?'

'No idea. We'd better get in my car. Frisk me if it makes you feel safer.'

Fisher did so and found nothing.

'Keys.'

Michael rummaged in his pocket with his free hand, pulled a bunch of car keys out. Fisher unlocked the doors, then released Michael's arm and opened the driver's door, but held on to the keys. 'Get in.'

Michael did so, and Fisher got in the passenger side. He scanned the street in both directions but saw no sign of the security detail returning. He checked the glove compartment and under the passenger seat for weapons, then handed Michael the keys. Michael massaged his upper arm and grimaced. His pain looked to be genuine, even though Fisher had gone easy on him. Just how knackered was the man?

Michael started the car and drove off. Three blocks away, Fisher told him to park.

'What, the fuck, are you playing at?'

Michael sighed. 'I'm playing her, not you, Fisher.'

'Montrose? Explain.'

Michael seemed to appraise him. 'She approached you, aye? Asked you to kill Crosbie?'

'Aye.'

'Well, she asked me, too. Crosbie then you.'

Fisher swore. Why did he ever listen to her? He had a decent enough retirement lined up. Why did he have to be greedy?

Because a refusal can offend and result in early death. That's why.

'So why didn't you try, already? You had me cold. Why not do me right there?'

Michael cracked a rueful smile. 'You're kidding, right? Look at me, man. You were right about one thing: time hasn't been good to me.'

Fisher couldn't argue with that. He'd thought he was struggling with his age-creaky joints, prostate the size of a golf ball, eyesight and hearing failing – but the state of Michael gave him a sharp dose of perspective. The man was a wreck.

'What happened to you?'

Michael glanced at him, sharp and intense, then relaxed. 'Ach, to hell with it, I've got no self-respect left anyway, mate.'

Again, Michael bristled at this familiarity from a man with such a vicious reputation, but he could detect no artifice in his words, no false tone.

'I got old, Fisher. I'm about the same age as you and you're not looking too fresh, either. You name it, I've had it. A stroke, two heart attacks, diabetes, and old Parkinson's is in the process of moving into my knackered old head, too.'

He chuckled. 'I'm fucked, mate. And you wonder why I'm reluctant to try to take on both you and Crosbie? I only got the better of you in there because you had such a hard-on to get at her you forgot to check your corners. After that, the rest was all bluff. Have you always been so gullible?'

Fisher could find no words. He'd been terrified of this man. Of the idea of this man, the legend, the spook story. Many people had lived in fear of Montrose's secret bogeyman being sent after them. The man's cruelty and viciousness were legendary, which was why many thought him a myth.

'OK. I'll take a punt. What's your burner number?'

Michael told him. Fisher dialled it.

'You don't trust me?'

'No. Make me.'

'Fair enough. You ever heard of a guy called Ben Hutchison?'

'No.'

'Shame.'

'Don't fuck me about, Michael. Who is he?' Fisher pulled his multitool from his pocket and held it in his fingers.

'Steady, Fisher. We're on the same side now, remember? I know he and Crosbie were close, back in the day. No, I don't know how close. All I know is "close". You find him, you find her.'

Fisher studied him. Seeing him pull his multitool out had rattled him. And looking again at the state the man was in – thin and scrawny, hunched-over, lopsided and wobbly – not only would he be of bugger-all use to Fisher if things got hairy, he might be better off sent packing and no longer a distraction.

'Tell me your plan, again.'

Michael sighed, as if talking to a backward student. 'First, we dig, find out why she's stirring up all this shite after so long. Then, we kill her and put her out of all our misery.'

Fisher smacked a fist into his kisser. Michael's head snapped back, and Fisher heard a crunch as cartilage crumpled.

'I propose an amendment to your plan. Michael, are you listening to me? Pay attention, man, don't be rude.'

Michael managed to face Fisher again, his eyes streaming and his nose pouring blood.

'First, we dig around, find out why, etc., etc. Second, we kill her; I like that bit. Three, and this is the critical part, Michael. You listening? Three, you disappear and I never see your fucking ugly face again.' He leaned forward and Michael recoiled. 'Ever.'

He put a hand on Michael's and gently guided it to his nose. 'Pinch it and put your head back. I've heard your nose can recover completely even after damage like that. Better?'

Michael glared at him.

Fisher flexed his aching fingers. He couldn't tighten his fist as much as he used to. 'Are we clear, Michael? Is that even your real name?'

Michael groaned, long and miserable, but he nodded.

Fisher opened the car door and climbed out. 'After all I've heard about you, I have to say I'm disappointed, mate.'

THIRTY

'Oh, you fucking, shitting, bloody, fucking bastard.' Malkie sucked his thumb and wondered if the head of the hammer had chipped a bone. It hurt enough to have done real damage. He waved it in the air in a futile act of doing any irrational and pointless motion he could, rather than just sit still and let the pain swamp him. Flailing it about seemed to increase the blood flow and the pain doubled.

'Oh, you absolute bastard. Jeez, that bloody hurts.'

His dad poked his head out of the cabin door. 'Run it under some cold... Oh aye, there's no running water yet, is there? Go and dip it in the loch. That should be freezing this time of year.' He nodded and smiled as if to say, 'You're welcome,' then returned inside.

Malkie wandered down to the loch side. The water was, as expected, bloody freezing. After less than thirty seconds the pain from the cold eclipsed the pain from the hammer blow. He removed his thumb and dried it on his sweatshirt. He sat on his favourite rock, the one with a surface just flat and even enough to perch his arse on and level enough to be comfortable. Harperrig Reservoir stretched away in front of him. He closed his eyes, listened to the water lapping at the rocky shore, heard sheep complaining to each other in the fields north and south of the water. A vehicle drove along the A70 a half mile to the north of the loch, distant enough to be softened into background noise. He'd learned during his teen years to zone out the sound of traffic on the road to Edinburgh. He'd hidden out here from his car-crash of an adolescence more times than he could remember, even when his dad managed to secure a few summer bookings of the cabin, before the age of the place had overtaken his DIY abilities and he'd had to withdraw it from holiday letting sites. As it turned out, the fact they'd never got the place into good enough shape to sell had saved them from home-lessness.

The family home had burned down earlier that year, an event which killed his mum, his dad's wife of fifty years, and left a yawning gulf of words unspoken and grief unvented since his dad had been discharged from St John's. Both knew there were further conversations to be had, but Malkie had only barely surfaced from his comeback case after a period of enforced leave. It had quickly become a shit show, not because of himself, for a change, but because of the reckless ambition of his then DI, McLeish. Malkie couldn't know if his dad had tried to find the 'right time' to talk about the fire, as he had, but neither had ever been the best at reading each other. Dad had always been that stalwart of Scottish family life: the outwardly dour and grumpy but solid and dependable father figure with a hidden heart of gold and a devilish, if as dry as a desert, sense of humour. Malkie had endured an adolescence he managed to make a mess of all on his own. Never comfortable with social conventions, he'd kept his gob shut most of the time because being thought of as a loner and a weirdo attracted less pain than trying to 'fit in' and fucking it up.

He stood, took another long look at the view he hoped his dad would get to enjoy for a good few years. That was, if he didn't fuck up again and lose his job or – worse – his pension. So much rode on him now, and it scared the shite out of him if he stopped to think about it. He wandered back to the cabin porch. Dad appeared, two plates of breakfast in hand. 'How's the injury? Will you live, you think?'

Malkie studied his thumb. No swelling, no discolouration, nothing. 'I think I must have the lowest pain threshold of any living person in history, Dad.'

'Oh, I don't know. You've suffered worse and come through it, son. I mean, how many take the beatings you've had to take in the name of your job? And nobody ever got stabbed stacking shelves in Tesco, right? And remember that silly wee girl's brothers, the ones that...'

His dad's voice faded, and memories pushed forward in Malkie's mind. He pushed them back, but not before heaving a long and pain-filled sigh.

His dad put his plate down. 'Sorry. That was stupid of me.'

Malkie scolded himself for letting his dad feel responsible for pain he should have let go of years ago.

Grow up. Stop lumbering other people with your own neuroses.

Dad picked up his plate again, chased a lump of porridge around his plate with a flimsy plastic spoon. They had forgotten, again, to buy some proper kitchenware while shopping the previous weekend.

'What was her name, anyway. The one who got you in so much trouble?'

Malkie sighed. As much as he hated thinking about her, maybe some small effort to share some of his less pleasant memories might bring them both some measure of comfort with each other. A few baby steps towards rebuilding the comfort of family affection that had been burned out of both of them, along with everything else his dad ever cared for.

'Her name was Sandra Morton. She came from a rotten

family, one of the worst. I ignored warning signs right from the start about what bad news they were because I was so blinded by the fact that an actual girl of the female persuasion might actually fancy me, I ignored my own common sense and jumped in with both of my size elevens. By the time I learned just how dangerous the Mortons were, Sandra decided I was hers, and turned completely psycho when I said I wanted nothing more to do with her or her family's drug business. She never admitted it, but I know she encouraged her knuckle-dragging brothers to hurt me.'

He glanced at his dad, who sat with his mouth open, his eyes appalled. 'I never knew any of this, son. I thought you got mugged or something, because you always refused to tell us what happened or who did it.'

'Why would you know? You were my dad and I was a miserable wee shite who preferred to keep my screw-ups to myself and flog myself for them rather than tell anyone what an idiot I'd been.'

Malkie thought for a second. 'Nothing's changed there, then, eh?' He realised he'd spoken out loud and accepted his dad's stern look of reproach with a lift of his hand.

'Do you ever see her these days? Or her brothers?'

'No. One of them died and the other one was never really an instigator, just followed his brother's lead. I haven't seen her since we left school a few months after I left her. I thought they'd forgotten me until they... Well, you remember.'

'I just remember they nearly killed you. And your recovery was horrible: the surgery, the therapy, your nightmares. No wonder you've never been a man to trust people.'

Both sat in silence for long minutes, content to allow the soothing sounds of the wind in the dark of the surrounding trees and the flutter of the occasional bat flying past to chase away the worst kinds of memories.

From out of nowhere, Malkie felt an urge to discuss the

night his mother died. He'd never stop believing himself to be complicit in the fire, despite a fire investigation report having established beyond all doubt that it was accidental: a scented candle had fallen onto her bedclothes and she'd been too weak from chemotherapy – that Malkie knew nothing about – to escape. From what little he'd learned from his dad, he knew that by the time his dad reached her the flames were already too fierce for him to do anything. His father had been slammed back against a wall by a backdraught when he opened the bedroom door, and was broken so badly he'd endured six lonely months in St John's, needing multiple skin grafts and three operations, then months of physiotherapy. As ever, thoughts of that aspect of his dad's injuries triggered a scratching on his mind, a tickle of something he felt vital to his understanding of events but which never came fully into view. Instead, it lurked on the periphery of his mind as if taunting him with withheld knowledge of whatever weakness or stupidity on his part had contributed to her death.

The itch became too great, too insistent. 'Why didn't you hear her until it was too late, Dad?' He realised as he spoke how brutal and accusatory his question sounded. His dad cast him an appalled look, as if not believing his own son could ask him a question that led to somewhere so awful.

'Sorry, Dad. I don't mean anything by that. I promise. I'm just surprised you couldn't hear her until it was too late. Did you have the TV on? Was the rugby on and you'd tuned your hearing aids to the TV? What was it? Have you any idea?'

His dad stared at him for long seconds and Malkie felt himself wither inside. Dad opened his mouth, then closed it again and rubbed his eyes with his fingertips. When he looked up again, Malkie recoiled at the pain in the old man's eyes. No anger, no accusation, no indication he resented the question, only a deep and debilitating fear of whatever answer he'd receive to the question that waited to sound from him.

'What do you remember about that day, son?'

Malkie reeled. Was his dad trying to find a way to reveal what Malkie had always suspected? Did he know only too well and too painfully what Malkie did or didn't do that night that sealed his mum's horrific death? He'd fought for months to piece together scathing fragments of memories, to order them into some kind of narrative that mental momentum might carry him to remember his ultimate failing.

'I remember giving her that candle. I remember she insisted on my putting it by her bedside and lighting it. I refused, told her it was asking for trouble.' He stopped, guilt burned up from his stomach and scalded the back of his mouth. He swallowed down the bitter taste, forced himself to continue. 'I remember leaving in a furious temper and letting her know how stupid I thought it was, a lighted candle right beside her bed.'

He swallowed, his throat thick with guilt.

'That's all I remember. I think I left without even telling you, I was so pissed off at her. Fuck's sake. I can't even remember what my last words to her were, but I know they were awful, Dad.'

Dad's eyes had softened, and they glistened, too, but he held Malkie's gaze. Malkie couldn't bear the honesty in their shared grief and looked down at his hands in his lap.

'Did I kill her, Dad? Did she die because I wasn't strong enough to refuse her?'

He heard nothing until he could bear the lack of a response no longer. When he looked up, his dad's eyes had turned hard again, troubled.

'And you don't remember anything else, son, no?' The question was gentle but the possible implication devastating: was there something else his dad remembered that he didn't?

He could find no words, nothing that wouldn't sound weak and needy.

His dad stood, turned to walk back into the cabin, but he stopped in the doorway.

'You didn't kill your mum, Malkie. Neither did I. It happened, and whatever we both did or didn't do might have contributed to it, but we didn't kill her. A stupid accident did. And that's the truth of it, son.'

Malkie's tears poured out of him. He strode away to the loch side to let them fall into the icy, night-black waters of the reservoir. He stared at his shivering, broken reflection on the surface, and despised it.

THIRTY-ONE

Sheila Ferguson had known this might come to bite them all one day, and – if she were honest with herself – she welcomed it. Waiting for the inevitable had been so hard.

She'd ducked out of Claudette's stupid chat thing years ago, got tired of her repeated demands that they move to new and more secure apps as time and technology progressed, rather than just let it all fade into a past best left behind.

Ferguson had prepared for the day. She couldn't know if Crosbie would come for her today or tomorrow or next week or three months from now. But after seeing Fisher pop up in the chat, she'd known that the end of the story they'd all feared was finally happening, and she'd never get to die peacefully in her bed.

After what they did, none of them deserved to.

What they did? No, what they didn't do. What every damned one of them should have done but was too scared to. And now it was too late, had been too late the day after it happened.

She'd always suspected that not knowing anything was the worst of it. Not knowing if it would happen had changed to not knowing when. The question that still terrified her was *how*. Crosbie had scared the shit out of her. She knew how to hurt people despite her timid demeanour, her painful shyness, her infuriating habit of apologising too much all the time, for everything. Maybe a complete lack of any kind of self-confidence was what made her join those classes. She remembered now, Crosbie had been one of the first to sign up to that thing about more women in policing in the late seventies. They fast-tracked Megan Shaw to... what did she reach in '78? Was it DI already? No, not in only two years. She'd made DS and was well on her way to DI. She'd joined the Force and someone thought she would make a perfect poster girl for its new female-friendly image. Was that why she didn't try harder to cover for Crosbie? Did management tell her to let Crosbie take her punishment and not get tarred with the incident?

The same organisation that rushed Shaw up the greasy pole too quickly had also started Crosbie on her path to becoming one dangerous little mouse. A vicious little rat of a woman, more appropriately. Ferguson had seen Crosbie's skills only once when they tackled a drunk mountain of a man outside The Dog & Parrot pub, a builder who'd just been sacked from the Livingston expansion programme. The man had turned violent as only excessive drink can turn some people, and two hilarious male officers had told her and Crosbie they were welcome to take this one on themselves, to score a point for the girls.

Crosbie had given them a look that wiped the smiles off their faces, turned to Ferguson, nodded her head towards the man-mountain as if to say, 'We need to prove a point here,' and piled in. Ferguson was seconds behind her but missed the bulk of the fight. No one quite saw what Crosbie did to the man, but he screamed in agony and choked, then vomited and tried to crawl away from them on his knees and one hand, the other clutching his face.

Doctors managed to save the man's eye, and he was never

seen in The Dog & Parrot again. No one ever asked where she'd learned to hurt people like that, although a rumour had circulated that she'd grown up in a huge family in one of the worst sink estates in Glasgow.

Ferguson glanced between the curtains to her front garden. As she noticed the garden gate hanging open, a hand holding a handkerchief slipped over her face. She took one involuntary breath of suffocating, acrid fumes and tumbled into darkness.

When she regained consciousness, she found herself tied to a chair with what smelled like her hessian shopping bag over her head. She tried to raise her hands to yank the bag off and found her arms were strapped to the chair arms. She tried to stand and found her ankles strapped to the chair legs. She peered down out of the opening of the bag and saw her plastic dish basin at her feet. Her breathing went into overdrive, and she gulped at what air she could draw through the fabric of the bag.

A hand rested on her shoulder, light and delicate, and a voice whispered, 'Shhh.'

Fear silenced her. She was about to find out the *how*.

'Lillian? I'm sorry. We all were, but what could we do? You remember what it was like back then? We were nothing, Lillian. Even if we had tried to do something we would just have been...' Her voice died as cold fingers slipped inside the hessian bag and caressed the back of her neck. She felt thin, old skin. The fingers withdrew then lifted the front of the bag. Not enough for Ferguson to see anything, but enough to reach inside and stroke her cheek. She lost control of her bladder, something she'd always promised herself she would never do when this time came.

The voice said 'Shhh' again as the fingers – the joints swollen with what had to be arthritis – stroked her cheek. The hand withdrew. Ferguson remembered now: the bloody woman never spoke more than she needed to, used her facial expressions instead. Those cold, soulless, grey eyes of hers. How could anyone so quiet and mousey turn out to be so vicious? Ferguson waited, her stomach in her throat and her heart pounding, but she refused to add begging and pleading to the shame of having soiled herself. If Crosbie was going to finish her, nothing would stop her, so she saw no benefit to be gained from demeaning herself further.

'Crosbie. Whether you believe me or not, I'm sorry. More sorry than you'll ever know. I was weak, and I put myself before you, and I've always hated myself for that. Now,' – she swallowed, her mouth suddenly dry and her tongue thick – 'I'd appreciate it if you'd make this quick. Please.' Her voice broke on the last word, but she didn't care anymore.

She felt a sharp scratch, then felt her blood run down the side of her wrist. She heard it drop into the basin, and – finally – she knew the how. And she knew why: the stories about that poor wee girl's death had always been true. She hoped this would prove a painless way to die.

A calm settled on her. Crosbie stroked her hair through the fabric of the bag, slow and gentle. Ferguson waited until she felt her thoughts start to float away from her but said nothing. She waited longer. Crosbie said nothing. Ferguson felt drunk, or how she imagined being drunk felt, having never touched a drop in her life: another regret. Her head spun, but still, she said nothing. The dripping of her own blood continued, reduced in frequency as – she imagined – the basin filled. A fitting way to go, considering.

When Ferguson guessed she had seconds left, she pushed five words past her thick tongue and cold, numb lips.

'Please believe I'm sorry, Lillian.'

THIRTY-TWO

After about the worst night's sleep Malkie could remember, he dressed in record time, drove like a maniac, and stomped into the Livingston CID room at a minute past eight. Heads lifted, eyes widened. Malkie being less than twenty minutes late simply never happened.

Malkie ignored them, headed straight for Steph's desk. She'd already logged on. Before he even opened his mouth, she spoke.

'Yes.'

'Yes, what?'

'The initial SOCO report is in.'

He waited. And waited. 'And?'

He sat.

'Lillian Crosbie and Billy Irvine or Ben Hutchison first?'

'Start with Crosbie.'

Steph rolled her mouse wheel and pages of the report scrolled down her screen. She stopped at the top.

'Young Billy Irvine's post-mortem is later this morning. Lin Fraser's going to do it. Was going to be tomorrow but Ben Hutchison's abduction got it expedited on the basis of a probable connection. Irvine's blood type matches that found all over Lillian Crosbie's house, but I think we already suspected it would.'

She scrolled down a few paragraphs. 'Initial opinion is that Irvine was killed by a single stab wound to the neck, just nicked his carotid artery, but barely, which is the reason he made it as far he did before passing out.'

'The weapon?'

'Something young idiots like him buy off the internet, probably imported and very illegal. You know the kind of thing, one serrated edge, one sheer, anything from three to six inches, that sort of thing. Although...' She scrolled again until she found a paragraph she'd highlighted. 'Lin called me to give me one very interesting initial observation she says she might not record in the report, just a hunch she had. The wound was barely an inch deep. Possibly because it was a weak old woman using it, but Lin thinks even a seventy-something pensioner could put enough strength into a blow to penetrate deeper than that. It was a clean wound, no indication the blade slipped, so it's not like whoever did it lost their grip.'

Malkie's brain kicked into gear. 'Like the attacker knew he or she only needed a jab at that spot to do maximum damage?'

'That's what I'm wondering. Which leads me to think it was the bloke you saw in the kitchen and not Lillian Crosbie. What did he look like?'

'Big. Tall and wide across the shoulders. Fifties, maybe early sixties. Mostly bald and trimmed to a number two or three at the sides. I feel like I saw a bit of a paunch on him but I can't be sure. He had something like a multitool in his hand with the blade extended. I don't think I saw any blood on it, or on him, but can't be sure.'

He surprised himself, his memory jolting him. 'Damn it, how could I forget? She had blood on her sleeve, and more than just a few spots.' He stared at Steph, his mouth open, his eyes wide. 'I think it was Crosbie that killed Billy Irvine, Steph.'

She frowned, seemed not to want to believe it but failing. 'So, who was the guy in the kitchen, then?'

They both sat in silence. Pamela Ballantyne wandered over, DS under everyone's least favourite DI, Gavin McLeish, and the last person Malkie or Steph felt like sharing their latest case findings with.

'Sounds messy. Sorry, couldn't help overhearing. Anyway, morning briefing in two minutes.' Pamela grinned, and Malkie wanted to smack her in her perfect white teeth.

As all present gathered for the briefing, Malkie turned over in his mind how the hell he was going to pitch this without starting another 'how long until he fucks up this time' sweepstake.

Thompson hadn't arrived yet, but McLeish started bang on time. Rather than cover his own cases first, as professional etiquette would normally dictate, he started straight in on Malkie. McLeish always insisted that his minions stand for the briefing but after the outstanding shit show McLeish's behaviour caused during their previous case together, Malkie gambled that the arrogant prick wouldn't push his luck for a while.

'One deceased, one MisPer. When I arrived at the scene, the deceased was already being loaded for transport. One witness claimed to have seen a senior citizen wandering around the park where the locus was situated but then claimed she disappeared. I called for backup...' He refused to glance at Steph. It wasn't her fault he barged into his own shit show before she arrived. '...then followed an evidence trail, fresh blood, to a terraced house adjacent to the park. I found the door open a few inches. I saw an older woman at an upstairs bedroom window. I pushed the front door open to call to her but saw her appear in the downstairs hallway and a male appear behind her from the kitchen, armed with some kind of multi-tool. I shouted a warning at her. She seemed to panic and threw a vase at me, scored a lucky hit.'

McLeish cast a stern gaze at the back row to silence an isolated and hushed snigger.

Malkie continued. His self-respect had long become immune to all but the worst of humiliations.

'I can only have been unconscious for a minute or two, but I found them both gone. In parallel, we received a call from the manager of an Edinburgh homeless shelter who claimed to have seen the woman whose photo we found in an upstairs bedroom and posted on the Police Scotland Facebook page. I visited the man that the woman had been to see, found out he was attacked and tortured forty-five years ago and has been virtually house-bound and uncommunicative ever since. The day after my visit, it appears someone broke into his room in the shelter and abducted him. Here endeth the lesson. Please feel free to rip into me, now.'

A silence followed. His update had consisted of more words than most officers heard from him in a week. Pammy Ballan-tyne spoke first, ever up for a chance to make Malkie's life difficult.

'Am I right in thinking a part of the crime scene was conta-minated when you sustained your head injury?'

Malkie failed to suppress a sigh. 'Yes, Pam. Next question. Anyone?'

McLeish stood from where he'd been leaning back against a desk. 'Who was your backup when you entered the premises?'

Malkie took a breath. The bastard already knew the answer to his own question. 'I was alone. I followed an evidence trail while waiting for backup, saw the trail lead straight through a front door that was slightly ajar, and pushed it open only a few inches to look inside. When I saw a man about to attack an elderly lady, I had no choice but to take some kind of action. I would have preferred to apprehend the man, obviously, but I was incapacitated too quickly.'

Another snigger. Another warning glance from McLeish, but he wasn't finished with Malkie yet.

'But you entered the premises alone, yes?'

DI Thompson chose that moment to arrive. She crossed to the front of the room without taking her coat off, her eyes on McLeish.

'Thank you for covering for me, DI McLeish. I'll take my officers' caseloads from here, thanks. Malkie: Lillian Crosbie and Ben Hutchison are both recorded as MisPers for now, yes?'

Malkie held McLeish's gaze a second longer before turning to Thompson. 'Aye. No sign of either of them. We'll start on that today. And the initial scene report from Hutchison's apparent abduction.'

Thompson nodded at both of them. 'Fine. Let me know what you have before the end of the day, please.'

Malkie nodded. 'Ma'am.'

Following a comparatively uneventful rest of the briefing, Malkie and Steph reconvened at her desk.

She opened a new email, then the attached document. 'Right, scene report from the shelter.' She read, scrolled. Read some more. Malkie waited but felt his impatience rise. She turned back to him.

'Pretty much what they told us last night. Blood spots on the book and floor match Hutchison's. Ms Taylor had a full medical file on him. Looks like someone broke in and dragged him away into the night. You think maybe someone followed Crosbie to the shelter? Or followed you? Maybe the man you saw attack Crosbie? But if it was that bloke, why? We've got too much *might have happened* and not enough *we can be certain about*. Even Billy Irvine. I doubt he broke into her place just for her purse and her jewellery. He was sent there.'

'By the big guy in the kitchen?'

'They have to be connected, no? Crosbie's and Hutchison's disappearances can't be coincidental.'

Malkie had to agree. He felt pressure behind his eyes, anxiety building. 'I'll take Crosbie, you take Hutchison for now, aye?'

'Will do. Second of us to get a decent lead enters all the case notes for this one, agreed?'

Malkie nodded, and he already knew he had a lot of typing to do before this one was over. 'Fine. I'll review Gucci's list of the officers on duty the night Alice Garten died.'

Steph turned back to her own desk and the initial SOCO report from Ben Hutchison's assumed abduction. Malkie scanned the list. Gucci, ever the perfectionist, had also looked for current addresses of the six.

PC Claudette Crawford had left the Force a couple of years after that night. No longer resident at her last known address in Blackburn, dropped off the electoral roll and no other obvious trace of her.

PC Paul Gaddon had also left the Force in 1978. No longer resident at last known address in Torphicen, and also dropped off the electoral roll, also so far untraceable.

PC Sheila Ferguson had also left the Force, but only a few months after that night. Again, no longer resident at last known address in Bathgate.

PC Mark Balfour turned out to have disappeared only a couple of years after the night Alice Garten died, his MisPer case never solved and closed thirty years ago.

DS Megan Shaw, now a DCS and on her way to bigger things and pretty much untouchable.

And finally, PC Lillian Crosbie went missing three months after Alice Garten's death, address only too well known but – again – not recorded on the electoral roll and no indication of employment or any other connection to modern life. And now very much no longer resident.

Crawford, Gaddon, Ferguson, Balfour, Crosbie, Shaw, and Garten.

Five constables, one detective sergeant, one dead girl.

Malkie sent the list to the printer. In the absence of any other promising investigative avenues to explore, he could at least review whatever notes Gucci and Rab had added to the case file and hope he might spot something they'd missed.

THIRTY-THREE

[AF] [08:04]

We need to talk again. It's urgent. DO NOT
IGNORE ME.

[CC] [08:07]

No need to shout. What now?

[AF] [08:07]

Remember the bloke you always thought was a
myth. A story she told us to keep us in line?
Had Sheila Ferguson terrified, remember? Well,
he's real. He came after me.

[CC] [08:08]

Rubbish. He never existed. I heard she used
some guy who made such a bloodbath of one
job she never used him again, but he wasn't
any bogeyman, just a nutter.

[AF] [08:08]

Aye, that's what you all thought. But I've met
him. Says his name's Michael.

[CC] [08:09]

This man. Michael. Does he seem as
dangerous as the man we heard about, back
then?

[AF] [08:10]

Every fucking bit. The man's a bloody animal.
Putting him down would be doing him and us a
favour. He's got old and he's not in great shape,
but I still wouldn't take him on unless I had to. If
that stupid bitch has dragged him into this
we're all fucked. I think it was him that killed
Mark Balfour. Come to think about it, why is
Balfour even still in this chat? No one's heard
from him since '78. He was on duty that night,
too, wasn't he?

[CC] [08:10]

I always hoped he was just hiding and might
speak up again one day, so I copied him over
every time we changed messaging app.

[AF] [08:10]

When did you get so naïve? Maybe Michael
killed him back in '78, and if Crosbie doesn't
get us first, he's going to come for us all now?
Crosbie included?

[CC] [08:11]

Do you think?

[AF] [08:11]

It's possible.

[CC] [08:11]

Christ, this is bad.

You never met Mark's mysterious contact,
did you?

[AF] [08:12]

No. I had even less chance of meeting her than
any of you lot did. I was useful to her because I
had skills you lot were too delicate to use, too
delicate to get your hands that dirty. Me and
him, there were only two of us, I think.

[CC] [08:12]

For a while I had a stupid idea about who she
might be but I couldn't risk talking about it even
amongst us.

[AF] [08:12]

Who? Who do you think she is?

[08:13]

Claudette?

THIRTY-FOUR

'DS McCulloch, visitor for you at the front desk.' Sergeant Bernadette Stevens managed to sound as frosty to Malkie down a telephone as she was face to face.

'Thanks, Bernie. Who is it?' He took another bite out of his cheese roll and continued reading a web page on the right way to repair cracked drainage downpipes. His dad had broken two already, trying to fix the cabin roof so they could sleep in separate rooms without waking up soaked.

'Hang on, I'll just ask your secretary to get her details. Just a second. OK. She says come down and find out for yourself.'

Malkie started to apologise but found himself talking to an empty line. He closed his browser down in case McLeish passed his desk, washed his mouthful of food down with a gulp of tea long gone cold, and stood. He pulled his jacket on, tightened his tie knot, and tucked his shirt tail back in. One day he'd find somewhere that sold shirts that didn't pull themselves out of his waistband every five minutes.

In the foyer, Bernie sat with her head down over some paperwork. Malkie waited a second before clearing his throat. Bernie looked up at him, her gaze cool and disapproving, as ever. He'd never worked out exactly what stupid comment he'd made to her in the five years he'd known her that had upset her so much. Pissing people off came so easy to him he'd become almost immune to their disdain. Almost. For some reason Bernie's obvious disapproval upset him. He liked Bernie. Everyone liked Bernie and she liked most people, even less pleasant members of the public. But not Malkie, and he'd resigned himself to never finding out why. She indicated behind him, over his shoulder with her pen and returned to her paperwork.

'Thanks, Bernie.'

'Sergeant Stevens.'

'Sorry.' He started to turn away but stopped himself.

He waited until she sighed and looked up at him again.

'I mean it. I apologise.'

She looked confused. 'For what?'

'For whatever I've done or said that's obviously pissed you off. I'm sorry. Really.'

He thought her about to say something, but she seemed to have second thoughts, frowned, and lowered her eyes to her paperwork, again.

He'd tried. Rome wasn't built etc. He turned to the visitor seating area, desperate for any relief from his current ignominy, and his heart stopped.

Sandra Morton. Sitting bolt upright, her back straight and her chin up, her eyes seeming to plead with him not to just turn his back on her and walk away.

He turned his back on her and started to walk away.

'Please, Malkie. Five minutes. Please?' She sounded broken. Crushed. Desperate. Sounded like she couldn't care less about how she was laying herself bare to him in front of complete strangers.

His first and only schooldays girlfriend, a troubled and troublesome soul who'd had her brothers try to kill him just for breaking off a relationship with her. Once as violent and hard as they come, now she sounded timid, even frightened. His stubborn compassionate streak overrode the alarm bells sounding in his head. He turned back to her.

Hope flared in her eyes, and Malkie found himself unable to believe it was fake. He sighed; despite every scrap of better judgment, he walked back across the foyer to her. She stood, clutched her handbag in front of her. He noticed that her feet pointed slightly inward. Pigeon-toed, he believed they called it.

He stared for long seconds, locked his gaze with hers. He'd spent so many years remembering her as the most spiteful person he'd ever known that to see her drop her eyes as if shamed, shook him.

She's not faking this. Fuck's sake, where have I heard that before?

He'd been taken in by a woman's tears before, but he thought tears from Sandra Morton might just be too much for even him to fall for. He nodded towards the front doors. She stepped past him.

Outside, the air was bright and sharp with mid-February frost that sparkled on the landscaped lawns that surrounded the Livingston Civic Centre, home to Police Scotland and courtrooms and the West Lothian Procurator Fiscal. He led her to a bench. Not the one he liked to escape to on the rare occasion he got to spend lunchtime at the station; he wouldn't spoil that spot with memories of her.

They sat. She adopted the same pose as when he'd first seen her in reception. Bolt upright, perched on the edge of the seat, she clutched her handbag in her lap. She stared straight ahead. He said nothing, watched her swallow several times, refused to make this easy for her. Whatever this would turn out to be.

Eventually, she turned to him. 'I suppose a "sorry" wouldn't go down well? Even if I really, really meant it?'

He realised she was trying to be cute, to cut through the

tension that hung between them, thick with history and pain. He said nothing and she cast her eyes down again.

Malkie waited. She'd destroyed his faith in intimacy and relationships, and her brothers had nearly killed him for putting his own safety before her. Unless she said something to change his entire world view, he meant to walk away again in minutes. For his own emotional health, if nothing else.

She stared down at her lap. He could feel she had something to say but was struggling to find the words. As much as he loathed her presence, as much as he itched to tell her to fuck off and never talk to him again, the part of him, the soft, stupid, naïve part of him inside, needed to be as fair as he could be. If she'd made the effort to seek him out and found the guts to face him after what she and her brothers did to him, she might have something to say that even he needed to hear. So, he waited.

'How have you been, Malkie?'

'You mean for the past thirty years? Just peachy, Sandra. You?' He regretted his words, instantly. Thirty years. Can someone change in such a long time? Was he now the one inflicting his own bile on her without giving her a chance? But then, could she ever change so much he could even think about forgiving her for damage already done? Was he hoping she'd say something to confirm his loathing of her, give him an excuse to hurt her, to throw hate at her with a clear conscience? Could he ever be that cruel to another human being? He hoped not, so he gave her a chance. Gave himself a chance to be bigger than the hurt she'd caused him, so long ago.

'I apologise. I've been fine. Had a rough year, but Dad and I are getting through it.'

She stared at him, her eyes appalled, her mouth clamped tight on what he assumed to be more tears. She couldn't hold his gaze, looked down again.

He turned towards her. This pain he was seeing was real. Whoever she had been in the past, however brutally she'd set her brothers on him in their youth, she now looked as broken and grief-ridden a person as he could ever remember meeting. Apart from his dad when they both lost Malkie's mum, but that was pain he still laid claim to, until someone proved otherwise.

'What's wrong, Sandra? I hate to see anyone in this state. Even you.'

She swallowed, took a long, shuddering breath, dabbed at her eyes then wiped her nose on a handkerchief she pulled from the sleeve of her cardigan. Only now did he notice how she was dressed. Gone was the designer gear and conspicuous wealth of her adolescent wardrobe. Now, she wore flats on her feet, a woollen skirt and tights, and – of all things – a twee knitted cardigan. It had flowers along the shoulder line, and flower-shaped buttons.

What are you up to, Sandra? You wouldn't have been seen dead dressed like that when we... We were young then; now we're both knocking on fifty.

'What's going on? What can we possibly have to say to each other? This just hurts, Sandra.' A bitter lump of long-buried anger thickened in his throat and his voice broke. She glanced at him, her eyes wet and betraying a guilt-ridden *mea culpa* that told him whatever else she'd done, the last thing she wanted now was to inflict more pain on him. This confused him. How could she turn from wishing him dead, albeit thirty years ago, to seeming to care deeply that she wouldn't cause him any more pain? Can people change that much?

She half turned towards him. He edged away from her; his resolve had failed before because of the slightest physical connection to a woman.

She opened her mouth. 'I...' She broke down, gripped the edge of the seat with her hands, sobbed quietly.

I can't handle this. I owe her nothing. Nothing. But she seems so different, more than I could have expected. Can she have changed enough to deserve a second chance? Even from me?

His phone rang. For once, he thanked it for its timing. He stood.

'Sandra, I have to go. I'm not someone you can rely on for comfort, and I never will be. You did too much damage for that ever to happen again.'

She folded forward, hunched over her handbag, clutched her hands to her chest as if to hold her heart together. People turned to stare. Malkie stood. As much as he painted himself as the cold and hurtful bastard – and wasn't he so used to people thinking that? – he felt pressure greater than ever before to run, to flee, to put her behind him once more, and hope she stayed there.

He turned to walk away.

She called after him.

'I was pregnant, Malkie.'

He stopped, couldn't help himself. As much as he wanted to turn and look at her, to gauge her honesty, to ask her *with whose baby?*, he couldn't. This was too much, if it was even true. He felt his grip on himself, already fragile, slip at precisely the time when he couldn't afford any distractions. Lillian Crosbie needed him.

He carried on walking, sick to his stomach and shaking but unable to turn around. He'd felt shame at his own weakness many times before, but nothing on this scale.

He veered away from the station entrance. He couldn't face Steph or Thompson or Ballantyne or McLeish. He felt unworthy and worthless. Despite the lack of progress on Crosbie's case, he decided today he had a perfect reason for a rare lunch break. He wanted to talk to a man who could never talk back. A man Malkie had fought for but let down, one of life's collateral victims. A man Malkie would always feel a kinship for.

A man who had known how shit it felt to buckle under pressure.

THIRTY-FIVE

Malkie parked outside the Lothians Ex-Services Outreach Centre on the north side of Airngath Hill. He forced himself to stop, to make the effort to enjoy the simple pleasure of the stunning view, clear and bright across the Forth Estuary to the low hills of Fife. He watched the shadows of clouds roll across their mottled and muted green and brown slopes. For a few seconds, he lost himself, let his eyes wander across the vista. He considered getting away with his dad, across the bridges and northwest, maybe a cabin on the coast, spend the days walking and the evenings doing jigsaws with pieces missing eating rubbish and watching the sun set on the other side of the massive grey Atlantic. It had been too long. The last time, it had been the three of them, but he and Dad had to start facing up to the future at some point.

Investigations during his previous case had led him here to the Outreach Centre in a search for Walter Callahan, a troubled ex-squaddie with PTSD who ended up on the run and getting shot for something he didn't do. The cruelty and injustice of that case, still raw and painful from only three months ago, haunted Malkie, and always would. The wrong man dead and in the ground and the man who should be there walking around free. Malkie had interrogated himself many times since that case was closed, and rated his performance during the investigation somewhere worse than woeful.

He promised himself he'd take some leave and get him and his dad away for some peace and quiet and restorative boredom. Just as soon as he found little old Lillian Crosbie. When he'd broken his jinx and finished at least this job with the right result.

He turned to face the main building. Set into a high drystone wall was an iron gate, its glossy black paint glinting in the lunchtime sunshine. The impressive lady who ran the place, Dame Helen Reid, had told him he was welcome to visit the private cemetery that lay beyond that gate as often as he wished. Malkie couldn't bring himself to believe she thought he'd done all he could to save Callahan, but she'd made the effort to let him know at least that she didn't blame him.

He climbed out of his car and stood for a while, one elbow resting on the top of the open door. He watched the zinc and glass front of the modern annexe built onto the side of the original Edwardian pile which he knew from two previous visits housed the admin and medical departments and the residents' rooms. The new annexe held the dining room and physiotherapy suite and a hydrotherapy pool.

He took a long, deep breath that did nothing to calm his nerves. As much as he wished he could, he allowed himself no illusions; he wasn't here to make abject apologies to the man he'd failed to save from an armed police officer's bullets. At least, not only for that reason.

He scanned the storey-high windows of what he knew to be the dining room, despite the hour being nowhere near any mealtime, for the face of the person whose lopsided smile he'd thought of every day since his first visit.

Deborah. Flight Lieuy Mad Bitch Deborah, she claimed her

ex-RAF colleagues called her. A victim of MOD spending cuts to maintenance budgets, she'd died three times under surgery after a helicopter she was testing had fallen from the sky and nearly destroyed her. He'd met her the day he came to interview Dame Helen Reid about Callahan, and again on the day of Callahan's funeral. Malkie, Dame Helen and three others said goodbye to a brave but broken man who deserved none of the hell he was put through. Deborah had held Malkie's hand throughout the eulogy, and he could still remember being surprised at the soft, velvety feel of her scarred skin as she laced her fingers into his.

A short lunch afterwards in the LESOC bar had ended with him and Deborah promising to keep in touch as tradition demanded, but Malkie then did his usual and over-analysed everything. As he'd done so many times before, to so many other people, Malkie punished both Deborah and himself with his own stubborn refusal to allow himself any chance of comfort for his failure to save Callahan.

He pushed the gate open and stepped through. A lawn surrounded by some kind of flowering bushes, the grass dotted with modest grave markers, all the same style. Polished granite memorials no bigger than shoe boxes with simple brass plates detailing the names, ranks, and birth and death dates of all interred there. He found Callahan's grave and crouched down on one heel. A worn and battered brass flick-lighter sat atop the stone, engraved with a regimental insignia, and Malkie had to choke back a surge of fury at the man whose fault it was that Callahan suffered and died as he did.

'I have no fucking idea what I'm doing here, Callahan. Walter. I don't believe in any kind of afterlife, so I must just need to hang on to my memory of you, mate. That's the only reason I can think I've been wanting to come here for the last two months. Well, that and – you know – her, maybe.

'Are you happier now, Walter? Or at least less unhappy?

What those fuckers did to you...' He cut off his own next words; this wasn't about him and how he'd failed the man.

'I'm back at work. Struggling but still turning up every day. What else can we do, right?'

He paused, wished to a god he didn't believe in that Callahan could answer him back. He dropped his head, felt the warmth of tears build in his eyes. He let them fall to the grass; Callahan at least deserved the honesty of his grief.

'Hello, Mr Dirty Old Man.'

He jumped, turned, found Deborah watching him from her wheelchair. He wiped his eyes on his coat sleeve and cleared the taste of ashes from his throat.

'I beg your pardon?'

She grinned her lopsided smile. As before, Malkie couldn't help noticing that despite the damage inflicted on her hands and legs and face, despite the striated and leathery texture of her skin and the milky film across one of her eyes, her teeth remained perfect. Her smile warmed him every bit as much now as it did the first day he'd met her.

She wheeled herself forward. Malkie noticed toned muscles tighten across her shoulders and down her forearms as she pushed.

She followed his gaze. 'I've been working out, only way I'll get out of this chair for good.'

If anyone can achieve that, Deborah...

She grinned at him. 'Remember the day we met? You told me you were operating undercover. As a dirty old man. And I said you were the nicest dirty old man I'd ever met. Remember?'

He did, and he smiled. 'I remember. You were feeding the ducks. That nurse looked like she wanted to call the polis, until she saw my warrant card.' He made a show of examining himself from chest to toe. 'She probably had every right to be worried.'

She laughed, and her eyes shone, with more life and vitality than Malkie could ever remember feeling in himself.

'You feel like pushing me back to the duck pond, Mr Dirty Old Man?' She grinned and reminded him of Steph at her best.

After a silent goodbye to Callahan and a promise to return, he pushed Deborah's wheelchair back through the gate and across a lawn to the duck pond where they'd first met.

She set her brakes and adjusted her position, wincing in pain as she did so.

'You OK, Deborah?' He stepped forward, desperate to help but clueless as to how he might do so.

'I'm fine. Really. Felt worse.' She grinned again and Malkie felt unworthy of her company.

'Stop that, Malkie. Please. Don't come here without telling me you're visiting then go on a downer with me.'

'Hang on. How did you know I was here?' The fact that he'd not asked Helen Reid to pass on the info was either down to his being afraid of seeing Deborah, or wanting too much to see her. He couldn't work out which.

'Helen told me. She called my room, told me you were here.'

Malkie scanned the window in the front of the building where he knew her office was, but saw no sign of her. This didn't surprise him; Dame Helen Reid was the kind of person to set things in motion then let them run their course without feeling a need to hand-hold.

'How have you been? Are you back at work?'

He sat on the nearby bench. 'Aye, and hating every second of it.'

'Pretty crap is it, your job?'

'Mostly, aye, but it brings occasional pleasant surprises.' He smiled at her, and realised he felt no embarrassment at his not so cryptic admission.

'You silver-tongued devil. What are you after?' She laughed.

What am I after, Deborah? What am I doing here?

'I didn't mean anything by it, Malkie.' The worry in her eyes cut into him.

'No, you're fine, really. Sorry.'

Her face turned serious, as if she wanted to turn the conversation to a different tack. 'I've missed you, dirty old man. I'm glad you came back for a visit, even if not for me.'

Her eyes told him she was teasing again, and he pushed his fear and his guilt down.

He had to push the words out, but they felt right and true when they did come.

'I've missed you too, Deborah. I didn't ask Dame Helen to tell you I was coming but I hoped I'd bump into you.'

She smiled again, never seemed to stop smiling, and Malkie wondered how someone with so little to be happy about managed to shine like she did.

'I'll take that. Do better next time, OK, old man?'

He laughed, an odd feeling he wasn't used to. 'Yes, young lady. I will.'

Deborah tilted her head back to let the sun soothe her face. Malkie watched her, thought that just sitting with her and believing she could be happy to have him there might be all he'd ever need.

Then his phone rang, and he knew without looking at it that his day was about to be ruined. He glanced at the display – Thompson – and frowned an apology at Deborah.

'My DI. Sorry.'

Deborah nodded at him to take the call.

'Boss?'

'Get back here, Malkie.'

'Can it wait? I'm—'

'Megan Shaw's in Intensive Care. She's been stabbed. Someone tried to kill her.'

THIRTY-SIX

In Steph's car, rolling along the M8 towards Glasgow, Malkie considered trying to get Steph to talk about whatever was upsetting her, but he worried that doing so might rattle her when she needed to stay sharp. He considered sharing his own troubles with her. His ongoing certainty of his culpability in his mum's death that he just could not shake. Sandra Morton's claim that Malkie was a father. He couldn't help but wonder what kind of woman his child – and how those words hurt his soul – had grown into; she'd be in her early thirties now, with a life of her own but possibly no dad. But none of those conversations could go anywhere worthwhile, and the last thing he wanted was Steph going in there pissed off at him. DCS Megan Shaw struck him as far too perceptive a person to miss trouble in the ranks.

So, he watched the world slide by: the flat, green expanse of West Lothian giving way to the grey, urban sprawl of West Glasgow.

When they reached the hospital and entered her private room, DCS Shaw was already sitting up in bed, and dabbed repeatedly at her face and neck, dripping with sweat.

'Doctors don't me want sitting up yet, but I want out of

here, and I already know she didn't cut me too deep. She meant to kill me, I'm sure of that, but she's as old as I am and much less fit, so she didn't manage much more than a shallow flesh wound.

'Take a seat, both of you.' She swung her legs round to hang out the side of the bed, but grimaced and grunted with pain as she did so.

Malkie asked the question that had to be burning on Steph's lips too. 'She?'

Shaw stared at him as if not believing anyone could be so stupid. 'Crosbie. Who else do you think tried to kill me?'

Malkie gave himself a warning to watch his mouth, but he refused to compromise on basic police work. 'You saw her, ma'am? You saw Lillian Crosbie and she stabbed you?'

Shaw seemed to run out of patience. 'Detective Sergeant McCulloch. Lillian Crosbie stabbed me in my own back garden. By the time I'd fallen to the grass and recovered from the shock, I saw her disappear around the house towards the street. I'm sure the crime scene report will corroborate that, if you can't take my word for it.'

A nurse charged through the door from the nurses' station outside. 'Ms Shaw, you're not ready to be out of bed yet. Please. The doctors—'

Shaw closed her eyes and took a breath, then waved a hand at her. 'Nonsense. I only have a few stitches, and I believe it wasn't a deep wound, so I'm discharging myself as soon as I can walk and dress myself, young lady.'

The nurse sighed, exasperated, but walked off. Shaw opened her eyes again.

'There's a secondary reason I sent for you, DS McCulloch.'

Sent for me?

She leaned forward, braced her hands on the side of the bed, and pushed herself to her feet. She grunted again, but held a hand out to stop Malkie from taking her arm for support.

When she could breathe again, she continued. 'You know

I'm following this case closely. I have "skin in the game" I believe the popular phrase goes. I've been contacted by someone I'd rather never have heard from again. An ex-army man turned to private security. We used him on occasion as an informant and occasionally asked him to do some digging where rules and regulations rather hamstrung us, if you catch my drift. As I said previously, we worked in a different world back then, with different norms and standards.'

You mean you were cutting corners all over the place, ma'am? Using known criminals to do your dirty work?

'He's threatened to blackmail me. This was before Crosbie tried to kill me. The bloody man knows nothing about what happened the night Alice Garten died, but he says he has proof that I knew about Crosbie letting that poor girl out in that terrible weather and he claims I tried to cover it up for her sake. That's just not true. Poor Lillian was subjected to the full weight of the rule book, and all I could do was stop it being escalated to criminal charges.

'I explained all this to the man and he seemed to lose his bluster somewhat, but I fear if I refuse to indulge whatever demands he may yet make, he'll interfere with your investigation in some idiotic attempt to muddy the waters and harm my reputation just as I'm about to be elevated to a very senior rank in the Police Scotland executive.'

Are you reminding us of that for a reason, Shaw? Was that a warning to back off?

'The man's name is Anton Fisher. I have a photo of him in my bag. I got it from his army personnel file, but please don't ask me how I got that back in the seventies.' She took a step. Pain hissed through her teeth, but she reached inside her gown and her fingers came out dry. 'Told you my stitches would hold.' She crossed the room one slow, painful step after another, to her handbag. She rummaged and produced a notebook, from which she pulled a photograph, folded in two. She turned to walk back to her bed.

Malkie saw her black out before she even went down. She crashed to the floor, took a bedpan and jug of water with her as her reflexes threw an arm out for support even as she collapsed. Malkie and Steph barely got to Shaw before a nurse pushed them aside and tended to her. 'Outside, please. Now.' Her voice left no room for argument.

Malkie and Steph took seats in the waiting area. Malkie produced the photograph and unfolded it.

Steph gaped. 'You stopped to grab the bloody—' She stopped when she saw Malkie's face darken. 'What?'

Malkie couldn't answer for a few seconds. Steph reached for the photo, saw a head and shoulders shot of a man in his twenties. Big and broad, he looked muscular under his army uniform, and his face suggested violence given any excuse.

She looked back at Malkie. 'You know him?'

'It's an old photo, but aye, I know him. That's the ugly bastard I saw attack Lillian Crosbie in her house.'

Steph looked again. 'I need to get this to Thompson, right away. And I'll get Rab or Gucci onto tracing an address. If we're lucky he's local and there can't be many Antons in West Lothian.' She pulled her phone from her pocket and tutted. 'No bloody signal. I'm going back to that cafe at the hospital foyer. I'll grab us some coffees and send this to Thompson from outside. Might be a while: this ward's at the other end of the hospital from the entrance.' She walked away, her eyes on her phone at arm's length in the air.

Malkie saw a nurse open the curtains around Shaw's bed. She examined the readouts on the various displays around the bed, seemed satisfied. Shaw lay asleep, looking peaceful.

A nurse approached him. 'That is one very stubborn woman. She was told to stay in bed until her wound had at least granulated under those stitches. What was she thinking?'

Malkie stood. 'How bad is the wound? We got minimal information over the telephone.'

The nurse studied him. 'Are you family?'

'No, I'm a police officer, but...'

The nurse opened her mouth and held an arm out to usher him away, but Malkie spoke over her.

'But Ms Shaw specifically asked for me to come to see her. So can I at least see for myself that she's OK?'

The nurse pointed at the floor as if to tell him to wait and went to confer with a colleague at the nurses' station. She returned looking more relaxed. 'Sorry, I had to check. Yes, seems you were asked for. Her stitches held so there's no apparent further damage. She's had a mild sedative to settle her, but you can sit with her for a while, if you like.'

The nurse gave him a professional sympathetic smile and walked away.

Malkie entered Shaw's room and took a seat beside her bed. Asleep, she looked like anyone's favourite auntie, not the fierce and prickly DCS Megan Shaw. Malkie's brain chewed over her producing a photo of the man who he'd seen attack Lillian Crosbie. Shaw's revelation that Crosbie had stabbed her supported the possibility that the old woman was capable of escaping the man he now knew to be Anton Fisher. And if she was capable of that, might she also have been up to killing Billy Irvine in the first place? But who the hell was Anton Fisher? Shaw had said nothing about him other than his intention to blackmail her, and had offered no motive – simple greed? – for the man to go public with a story about her trying to cover up Crosbie's negligence. Negligence that led to the death of young Alice Garten, cold and alone and wretched, lost halfway home and frozen to death while pretty much everyone else in West Lothian was getting pissed and celebrating the start of a fantastic new year.

The ugliness of the whole story turned Malkie's stomach.

'What's going on, Detective Chief Superintendent soon-to-be Area Commander Megan Shaw? There's something else, something you're not telling us.'

He whispered the words, didn't mean her to hear them, didn't expect a reaction.

She muttered something.

Malkie checked that none of the nurses were watching him and leaned down to Shaw's ear. Without thinking, he pulled his phone from his pocket and double-pressed the power button to start it recording. Less for what other people might say to him, more so he could play back what he'd said on occasions when he feared his gob might land him in the shit.

'What was that? What did you say, Megan?'

She muttered more, unintelligible, barely formed words, but then a slurred string of words came out he did manage to pick up.

'I'm sorry, Lillian. They made me...' Even in her sedated state, Malkie heard anguish in her words, a miserable and penitent whine.

She went silent again.

Malkie's heart hammered in his chest. He replayed the audio. Did he hope he'd misheard her? The recording was ambiguous but damning. 'I'm sorry, Lillian. They made me...'

Did he dare tell Steph? The recording would be inadmissible but even she would have to take this seriously, wouldn't she? Could she deal with this, the state she was in? But then, keeping information from her on their last major case had nearly burned away the last of their friendship.

He wandered back to the waiting area to wait for Steph, didn't want her even finding him in Shaw's room. Not until he'd decided whether to play it to her. He leaned forward, rested his elbows on his knees and hung his head.

The shit just keeps coming, doesn't it?

THIRTY-SEVEN

Am I even sure what happened that night? It was so long ago, and I forget so much these days.

That stupid girl. I didn't mean to hurt her. I thought I was doing her a favour, letting her go home by herself. How could I know she'd get herself lost and... I meant well. Didn't I? Yes, I meant well.

Why is she stirring up so much grief from so long ago? It was done and it couldn't be undone. I regretted it. It wasn't my fault how the fallout went, where the blame was laid. What good would have come from punishing me any more than I punished myself.

Why? Why now? What did she hope to achieve? Or was it just that she finally, after so long, couldn't handle it any longer, the pain I caused her? She's exposed wounds we all thought long healed, if not forgotten.

Is it going to end with one of us in the ground?

Not me. I don't deserve that, even after what I did. I paid my price. I did all I could to make amends, and it was never enough. I couldn't give any more, I couldn't lay myself open to any more hatred. There were circumstances. It wouldn't have hurt only me. I had others to think about. Other lives to save from being ruined.

And the other thing... Oh God, I didn't know. None of us did. How could we have known?

But she wants us to remember now, doesn't she? How broken and toxic can she be, to want to remind us of that? We couldn't have known...

THIRTY-EIGHT

Malkie and Steph returned to the station. Neither spoke a word the whole way.

When they reached the CID room activity levels had heightened, focused around DS Pamela Ballantyne's desk. Malkie wandered over.

Pam and three others stared at a newly arrived incident report. All looked grim. Malkie peered at the screen, scanned the fields at the top of the form that held the headline information, then wished he hadn't.

Pam noticed Malkie's attention. 'Nice of you to join us, DS McCulloch.' Malkie bit his tongue; wrong time to try to take Pam on.

'Suspected homicide. Victim's name Sheila Ferguson.'

Malkie's guts sank.

Ferguson was one of the names on the list Gucci had got from the National Archives in Edinburgh. The six officers on duty in Livi Police Station the night Alice Garten died.

Crawford, Gaddon, Ferguson, Balfour, Crosbie, Shaw. Five constables, one detective sergeant. One dead girl.

'Fuck. She's on the list,' he said.

'I know,' said Pam. She sat back in her chair, thought for a second. 'You'll be taking this one, Malkie?' Even she held off on her usual scorn for Malkie in the face of what was going to bring at the very least heightened pressure on them all to get a result, and at worst a shitload of overtime.

'Aye, I'll take it, haven't even got my jacket off yet.' He glanced at the form on the screen for the address, fished in his pocket for his notebook but found Steph already at his side and scribbling it in hers. 'I'll come back here if I finish up at the locus in time, otherwise morning briefing.'

'Aye.' Pam reached for her mouse and switched to another window. They were dismissed.

Malkie and Steph returned to their desks. He rolled his chair over beside hers, leaned close. 'You OK, Steph? I could do with you at a locus, always prefer you to assist, but...'

She smiled, squeezed his arm. Malkie thought he saw her eyes glisten, but she gave him no time to confirm. 'I'm fine, old man. Let's go see if this might help us find your little old lady, shall we?'

Normally on turning up at a locus, at the ones they got to fresh, Steph would produce sealed packs of nitrile gloves and shoe covers from some secret compartment in her jacket, but this time they arrived to find a whole circus already in full flow. A terraced cottage, one of nine or ten. Arc lights bathing the place in blinding white light. A SOCO van parked up on the pavement, the back doors open. They stepped over to the van. A figure already clad in a paper onesie turned from logging something on a clipboard, pulled her face mask down, and grinned.

Malkie beamed at her. 'Sally. How lovely to see you. Has been ages, hasn't it?'

Sally chuckled. 'No, Malkie. I was in that shelter the old boy got abducted from. You looked right at me but as usual you were too focused on the job. Good job I'm fond enough of you not to take it personally.'

Malkie grinned, sheepish. 'Sorry, Sally. You all look the same to me in those stylish onesies you all wear.'

Steph stepped forward. 'Any chance we can get inside sometime tonight, Sally?'

'Aye. Sorry. Hang on. I expect miss will be a size eight so...' She rummaged in the van and handed Steph a sealed package. 'Small for you, Steph?' She appraised Malkie. 'And sir will be needing something for the more generously proportioned gentleman.' She rummaged again. 'XXL, very roomy.'

'XL will be fine, you cheeky sod.'

Malkie and Steph suited up, added foot covers and gloves and face masks to their stylish ensembles, pulled their hoods up and headed along the raised footplates already laid down the garden path and into the hallway. Malkie stopped for a second on the threshold. The humour at the SOCO van was a necessary thing, but when officers – decent officers – turned to the reason for their attendance, respect and solemnity took over. Not the fake solemnity worn by newsreaders to signify to less-perceptive viewers a switch from something light-hearted to the day's next awful tragedy. Those attending a heavy-duty scene like this treated the locus, the victim, with respect and moderated their comments accordingly. Certainly when Steph was in attendance, if they knew what was good for them.

Inside, the victim, Sheila Ferguson, strapped to a chair, her arms and legs secured. A basin on the floor, full of blood, drained from long deep cuts down the length of one forearm. The woman white beyond any pale skin Malkie had ever seen.

He swallowed bile. The sight and smell of any murder scene could cause a few upset stomachs or a rush to vomit outside of the scene integrity tape. But this...

This was no crime of passion, no release of pent-up frustration or lashing out at an abusive partner or a robbery gone wrong. This was premeditated, a useful word that masked a multitude of horrific implications – planning: cold-hearted and methodical actions taken by one person to end the life of another. The conscious and calculated ripping away of all that made some poor sod who they were. An entire life ended. Every achievement and celebration and golden moment that made the victim a person, a being that lived and loved and laughed and wept, a person that gave life to other people, who would also have the hearts ripped out of them. Doubly so when the news of their death was followed by details of how they died.

No. Any person who suffered death at someone else's hands, they didn't die: they were killed. Robbed. Our lives, the fundamental thing that belongs to each of us, to the exclusion of all others, was stolen from them. Malkie had always struggled with the finality of death, no more so than when dealing with his own mother's recent passing. But when death crossed over to this depth of cruelty...

Malkie left the house. The SOCOs would examine and record and collate and compile the scene into a safe and anodyne mass of words and numbers and diagrams on sheets of paper and computer screens, and Sheila Ferguson would spend the night cold and alone, in a steel drawer surrounded by other poor bastards who deserved just as little to be there.

Outside, he ripped his mask off and heaved in a great lungful of air. Steph joined him.

'You OK, old man?'

'No.'

'No. Me neither. This one is...'

'I know.'

THIRTY-NINE

[AF] [16:38]

are you there Claudette?

[PG] [16:39]

i don't think she is are you online claudette?

[AF] [16:39]

Apparently not. Why did you take so long to
respond, Paul? We're all in deep shit, right now.
Don't you care? Are you not worried?

[PG] [16:39]

of course i am shes got to have lost the fucking
plot completely to be digging this shite up
again its been more than forty years

[AF] [16:40]

Forty-five. Do you know who she was? Who
she is?

[PG] [16:40]

no only mark spoke to her and only ever on the
phone you know that

but Claudette warned me shes a vicious cow
and obviously stupid enough to send you after
crosbie and its blown up in her face and itll
probably blow up in all our fucking faces what
the fuck was she thinking

[AF] [16:40]

Poetic as ever, Paul. I've missed your lyrical
turns of phrase. And your charming phobia of
punctuation. How the hell have you got your
phone not auto-correcting all the tripe you
write?

[PG] [16:41]

ever the fucking joker fisher so youve heard
from claudette

[AF] [16:41]

Aye.

[PG] [16:41]

is she ok

[AF] [16:41]

No idea. She came on here a couple of times
but she's not responding now. I hope she's OK.

[PG] [16:42]

not like you to worry about someone else fisher
you got a thing for her

[AF] [16:41]

None of your business.

[PG] [16:41]

ha ha who would have thought you and
claudette you dirty dog

does claudette know why the stupid cow went
after crosbie after all this time

[AF] [16:42]

I don't think so. I just want it cleaned up. I
heard about an old acquaintance of Crosbie's.
He disappeared too, apparently, a month or so
after Crosbie went quiet.

[PG] [16:42]

ben

[AF] [16:42]

Aye. Did you know him?

[PG] [16:43]

no she just mentioned him once or twice i think
he was a uniform based in the borders

[AF] [16:43]

You got an address?

[PG] [16:43]

no

ill keep trying claudette she wouldn't just drop
out of contact I hope crosbie hasn't got to her
that woman was a fucking animal when she got
goaded out of her little miss shy act

[AF] [16:44]

What about you? Did you have a soft spot for
her, Paul?

[PG] [16:44]

for crosbie are you fucking kidding me the quiet
ones are the ones that eat you alive

[AF] [16:45]

No, for Claudette, you prune. You sound like
you miss her.

[PG] [16:45]

i suppose i do she was alright nice arse too

[AF] [16:45]

You haven't changed, Paul. Did you ever hear
from Mark Balfour? He was never one for
holding back his comments, either.

[PG] [16:46]

none of us have heard from that prick since
1978 thats why the work dried up because he
disappeared selfish prick

[AF] [16:46]

Who was she, Paul? Not Crosbie. Her. The
voice on the phone, the one that Balfour got us
the jobs from?

[PG] [16:46]

who

you mean claudette what the fuck are you
talking about

[AF] [16:46]

No, not Claudette.

[PG] [16:47]

oh christ you mean her i told you i never found
out and i mean to keep it that way she was a
voice on the phone that only ever called mark
and i didnt want to know any more than that

she was a bad one fisher whoever she was

[AF] [16:47]

Aye, but we all took her money didn't we?

[PG] [16:47]

you kidding it was too much not to take

[AF] [16:48]

But we're paying for it, now, aren't we? And
Crosbie's collecting. I suppose after what
happened she deserves some payback.

[PG] [16:48]

crosbie was a mouse and a fucking timid one
until you got her back up if she comes for me ill
have her fisher ill fuckin gut her so i will

[AF] [16:48]

I'm glad I never got on your bad side, Paul.

[PG] [16:48]

who says you didnt

FORTY

When the SOCOs finally left Sheila Ferguson's home and released the crime scene to them, Malkie and Steph braced themselves to re-enter.

Steph, as always, produced gloves and shoe covers from nowhere.

'Where the hell do you stash this stuff? I mean, that jacket looks thin and there's nothing of you—'

She slapped his hand away from lifting one side of her jacket.

'Hands off, or I'll report you to HR. Again. Dirty old sod.'

She smiled, but her comment reminded him of the only other person who called him that, or close enough. Deborah. He glanced at his watch, wondered if he could fit a detour into his drive home to the cabin and dinner. Two visits in a week would send her a message, but he realised he didn't give a toss if it did.

'Malkie? I was kidding, mate.'

He returned to the moment. 'Sorry, miles away.'

'I said I was joking. I'm not going to report you to HR. They stopped taking calls about you anyway, your file was too full.'

'Ha ha. Funny woman. Let's get this done.'

Both of their smiles evaporated, and they entered.

The absence of the body did little to reduce the harrowing impact of the crime scene. Malkie glanced at Steph. Ever the stoic, she betrayed no outward reaction, but she'd gone paler than her usual wan complexion.

Malkie turned away; anything else he needed to know about the body and the carnage around it he'd get from the photos when they were uploaded.

Apart from an exsanguinated body, nothing out of the ordinary had stood out to either of them, nothing to suggest anything that might hint at the reason for the brutal, and specific, manner of Ferguson's death.

He and Steph shared a look. *Why kill someone like this if not to send a very specific message?* The upstairs rooms yielded nothing of note, nor the kitchen. Malkie checked the knives in a wooden block on the counter, but – as he'd expected – none were missing. He had to guess that whoever did this came prepared and had no need to improvise.

'It's an interesting word, isn't it. Premeditated.'

'Eh?' Steph lifted her head from peering into the cupboard beneath the sink.

'Premeditated. Very sterile word for what it implies. It doesn't even begin to describe how cold a person has to be, the hole they must have inside them, to kill like this.'

He sighed, his shoulders slumped. 'I don't think I'll ever understand it, Steph. How can one person care so little about another to be able to do this. I bet some abattoir workers care more about the cows they slaughter.'

He stopped, felt himself approach the brink of the huge, black, bottomless hole he used to fall into so easily, and had taken years – decades – to train himself to step back from.

Steph punched him on the arm. 'It's always going to be like this, mate. Because people will always be like this. At least we get a chance to catch the bastards and hope they make it to a jail cell for the rest of their filthy lives. That's all we can do, Malkie. Mourning for people like her is a luxury we can only allow ourselves once we've processed and collated and recorded and all the other shite we do.'

'Sheila. Her name was Sheila. Not *"her"*.'

'Malkie...'

'I know. I know. Stay detached.' *As if that ever makes it any easier.*

They continued their examination of the scene.

Old and threadbare sofa and a single armchair. Coffee table with – why wasn't he surprised – three copies of the *People's Friend* spread across it. A log-effect electric fire unplugged from the wall, and two cardigans on the floor beside her.

Malkie gazed around him, at threadbare patches in the carpet and grubby glass in the windows and a sofa that had seen better days decades ago. 'Poor old girl was probably too scared to turn the heating on. Her and half the pensioners in the country.'

The armchair seat cushion held an indent he guessed came from years of languishing in front of daytime TV. Beside the armchair, a knitting basket, full to the top with balls of wool, knitting needles and what looked like half-finished projects. Half a scarf. Half a woolly bobble hat. A pair of baby bootees, dusty and frayed. He turned to find Steph staring at them, her face white.

She swallowed, turned and walked out.

What have I done now? What's tearing her apart?

He tossed the bootees back in the knitting basket and followed her; seeing Steph distressed about anything was enough to shake him to his core.

Outside, he found her sitting on a low wall separating the perfectly maintained rose garden from the road, beyond which stretched the most beautiful view.

'You built yourself a lovely wee life here, didn't you, Sheila?'

He swallowed a lump in his throat and made yet another in a long line of rash promises to himself.

Fucker that did this is going away. If the courts and some slimeball of a lawyer get him off, I'll—

He stopped, had a word with himself. He couldn't afford to let cases get this personal. Would he never learn?

He sat beside Steph but said nothing. He was learning. She'd explained to him before that the last thing most women needed in times of distress was some well-intentioned but blunt and clumsy bloke climbing aboard a metaphorical trusty steed and charging at their problems, determined to 'fix' them. Very often, all women wanted was someone to listen without judging, and that was all. And a laugh, had to end with a laugh, she told him.

So, he waited, gave her all the time she needed to tell him as much as she could about what had so clearly been hurting her so much all week. It killed him, he itched to pile in and drag her thoughts out of her, but he cast his mind back to the department-mandated therapist they'd sent him to first time he went off the rails, and finally realised how damaging and counterproductive it could be to make demands on someone at the very time they needed space.

When she eventually spoke, her voice was flat and bleak.

'What was your mum's name, Malkie?'

He recovered quickly. This was one of those situations where *'not everything is about you, Malkie'* applied.

'Maureen.' He resisted the urge to follow up with 'Why?' He could do this. For her he could learn.

'And your dad's name?'

She knew his dad's name. Where was she taking this? 'Thomas. Tommy.'

She smiled, but it came nowhere near her eyes. Malkie's heart fractured in his chest to see Steph, of all people, laid bare like this.

Oh God, if she needs to build up to it, how bad can it be?

'What was your mum's name, Steph?' He knew the answer already.

'Joyce.'

He swallowed. The second question would release... what?

'And what was your dad's name?'

She paused, swallowed again, stared down at her hands clasped in her lap, so tight her fingers had turned white. Again, instincts he was working hard to develop told him to keep it shut, to wait. When it came, he wanted to die.

'I found out last week I was a rape baby, Malkie.'

He resisted an almost overwhelming urge to shout and swear and promise her he'd find and castrate the fucker, but only just.

He reached across and laid a hand on hers. She interlaced their fingers and squeezed. For such a skinny wee runt, he thought he might end the evening with broken fingers.

As slow as a sequoia toppling in an ancient forest, she leaned. Her cheek rested on his shoulder.

Still, he waited. Held her hand, but said nothing.

He heard her sniff and saw her wipe her nose on her jacket sleeve.

He rested his cheek, in turn, on the top of her head, but still said nothing.

When he saw tears spill down her cheek and onto their intertwined hands, he knew she'd found the release she needed.

For now, at least.

FORTY-ONE

By the time Steph finally lifted her head, wiped her hands, smiled sheepishly at Malkie and stood, he knew he needed to stop on his way home to his dad.

He dropped Steph off at the station. She said nothing more throughout the entire drive, then simply sighed and climbed out of the car. She turned before walking away, but Malkie spoke first.

'Do I need to worry about you, partner?'

She smiled, full of warmth and fondness. 'Stop stealing my lines, you old fart.' Then she was gone, headed for her own car.

Got to end on a laugh, she'd said.

Malkie drove up to the Houston North Road and checked the dashboard clock. Seven o'clock. He pushed a button to quick-dial his dad.

'Hello? Malkie? Can you hear me? Is this stupid thing on?'

Malkie smiled as familiar fondness warmed his heart.

'I can hear you, Dad. Listen, I'll be honest, I'm clocked off for the day but... I'd like to pay someone a visit, if you don't mind. Will the shepherd's pie keep?'

'Hah! Cheeky sod. You know damned well the shepherd's pie ended up getting thrown out the back of the cabin for the foxes. We need to get a proper gas supply in as soon as we can afford it. Can you stop at the Chinese on your way home? Are you going to be very late?'

Malkie smiled. 'Good idea, Dad. Wish I'd thought of that.'

'Liar. This someone you want to visit. Is it for their benefit or yours?'

'Bit of both, Dad, I hope.'

'Then take all the time you need. If you're not back here with – what was that red stuff we had on the boat? – by ten, I'll make myself some chilli and crackers. Just like Columbo liked. Remember that?' He chuckled.

'Chicken Chasni, Dad. I'll be back by nine.'

'Oh, Malkie, one more thing...'

'Yes, Dad?' But he knew what was coming.

Click.

Malkie imagined his dad chuckling and pleased with himself, and he smiled like he couldn't have hoped to after a day like today. He turned right on the Houston North Road and drove towards Edinburgh.

He arrived at the LESOC to find it in darkness.

He rolled the car windows down and closed his eyes, heard nothing but wind and tree branches whispering to each other.

He jumped when someone rapped on the roof of his car. He'd nodded off.

'Detective Sergeant McCulloch. How lovely to see you. Any particular reason for a visit at such a late hour?' Her words came out stern but even in the short time he'd known her he'd learned to see the mischievous twinkle in her eyes. For a rich and titled toff, she was a wee sweetie.

'No, Miss Reid. I was just—'

'I'm afraid Deborah always retires early. She watches rubbish on the TV for hours before she takes her meds, then they tend to knock her out until morning.'

Malkie glanced again at the front of the house. He felt a ridiculous urge to ask Miss Reid if any of the front-facing windows were hers, then he kicked his own arse mentally for such childish thinking.

What are you? Twelve years old?

He sighed, stared down at his hands in his lap.

Miss Reid placed a gentle hand on his shoulder. 'You are a good man, Mr McCulloch. And I've met a lot of bad men. Would you like me to tell her you dropped by?'

'No, but thanks, Miss Reid. I just needed a chat with someone who knows what a mess I can be.' He smiled, sheepish at his own self-effacement.

She chuckled. 'Mr McCulloch, we're all a mess. Good grief, you think I just sail through all of this like a perfect and untouchable little Miss Nightingale?'

Sadness filled her eyes. 'We're all broken, Malcolm. May I call you Malcolm?'

He smiled back at her. 'Yes. I'd like that. May I call you Helen?'

'No you bloody well may not, impudent pup. Now go home. When you wake up tomorrow, find time to visit her when she's up and about. I guarantee she'll be delighted to see you.' She winked at him then wandered off.

Idiot. Why do I do this to myself?

He called after her. 'Miss Reid. Yes, actually. Let her know I dropped by to say hello, would you?'

'I was planning to, anyway, Detective. Goodnight.'

Malkie chuckled to himself, then quick-dialled his dad.

'That was quick, Malcolm.'

'Aye, she's not in.'

'She?' Malkie heard the nosey smile in his dad's voice. He'd have some explaining to do over dinner.

'Chicken Chasni coming up, Dad.'

Despite his disappointment, he drove out of the LESOC grounds with a smile on his face.

FORTY-TWO

Paul Gaddon couldn't wait.

When that old cow walked through his door she was leaving again in pieces. He cracked open the barrel of his shotgun for probably the tenth time in an hour. Two gleaming brass firing caps nestled in the barrels. He looked forward to sending six hundred lead pellets blasting into her old guts. He could worry about cleaning up afterwards; nobody came up the rutted and axle-breaking track to his farm without a damned good reason.

He hadn't been surprised to hear she was coming after them. Difference between him and them was that he didn't give a shit.

She was never one to speak up for herself, and no one else spoke up to protect her. Not even that bloody stupid women's thing that started up in the late seventies. That, in his never at all humble opinion, had started the rot. After that it wasn't long before they were letting any flake in. Claudette Crawford had once got pissed and ranted for an hour in the basement bar of the old station that it was 'individuals' that caused the rot, and she'd looked right at him as she said it. But he'd been proven right: every police force in the country now had internal investigations and public enquiries coming out their ears. People forgot too quickly that they were the thin blue line, and all these idiotic 'initiatives' did was weaken the last layer of protection the idiot masses had against scumbags and dealers and traffickers and fuck knows what other deviants and lowlifes.

He glanced out the window. Somewhere in his mind he knew it was completely possible to approach the farmhouse from the back or sides, across the barley fields his dad, and his grand-dad, and his great-fucking-great-grand-dad had taken so much pride in. He'd sold off all but one of them, right behind the house. He'd set himself up for life from the proceeds, had a freehold on the land he kept and the farmhouse and still had ample money to live the life he liked. He could afford to fix the approach track a dozen times over, but why would he make it easier for arseholes and scroungers to get to him? Tesco delivered to a lock-box at the roadside and trekking down once a week to lug the bags back gave him all the exercise he needed.

He'd been fit, back in the day. Standards were laxer than today. So many of his police colleagues had been physical disgraces, but he always took care of himself. Now? He chuckled. Calling himself a wreck felt like a compliment. But no problem. A couple of twelve-bore shells from his favourite fox-control shooter was faster than she could be and would punch a hole in her – hopefully a huge fucking big hole – she couldn't stop if she tried.

He forced himself to relax. He was ready for her.

When he woke with a start, later, he had a second to realise he'd nodded off, before the distinctive smell of an ether-soaked cloth choked him and burned his airways and he lapsed back into a terrifying, irresistible darkness again. His finger spasmed and pulled on the trigger of his shotgun, blew a front window out and shredded the curtains. The explosion was deafening in the closed confines of the room. He slipped into blackness again before the ringing in his ears stopped.

When he came around again, he found himself strapped to a chair by his ankles, waist, chest, and wrist, and his woolly winter scarf wrapped around his eyes and over his head. He could only make out rough details through the weave of the wool. His attacker was taking no chances.

'Fuck you, Crosbie. Cut me loose, let me have a fair crack at you, you fucking useless old cow. I'll fucking destroy you, you fucking hag.'

Something sharp pricked the top of his scalp, and he froze. His bravado stuck in his throat, suddenly thick with fear.

'Shhhhhhh.'

Paul's blood ran cold and acid burned the back of his throat. He refused to throw up, refused to demean himself, considering she meant to do that in spades, anyway.

He heard her rummage in a kitchen cupboard then she returned to her position behind him. She placed something beside the chair. In her thin and bony fingers he glimpsed something a shade of pink he'd always hated: his dish-washing basin.

He flinched as a sharp scratch burned down the length of his forearm, then a hot trickle down to his wrist and his fingers, then syncopated drumming of thick liquid dropping onto plastic.

He knew now. 'Seriously? Still this shite? Is this supposed to send a message, you stupid old bag?'

Cold and leathery fingers reached around from behind his head and stroked his cheek, and he heard another 'Shhhh.'

He refused to beg, not to her. He'd had enough, anyway. All that money and the doctors could do fuck all about the cancer fifty years of smoking had planted in his throat. Fuck it, she was doing him a favour.

Shame he wouldn't get to see her fly backwards out his front door with a surprised look on her kisser and trying to hold her own guts in, though.

That would have made it all worthwhile.

FORTY-THREE

Fisher banged on her door. He'd been looking forward to seeing the look on her face since he'd decided he needed to pay her a visit.

He turned his back to her video doorbell, wanted to announce himself in style.

Her voice sounded, tinny and distant, from the speaker above the doorbell.

'Who are you? Step forward and turn around, please?'

Fisher did so, a huge smile on his face and his hands spread out to his sides, as if springing a surprise visit on an old friend.

He heard silence for a moment, then 'Fuck.'

He sighed, but his grin stayed in place. 'Cut the shite, Claudette, and open the door.'

More silence. He started rapping on the door, repeatedly, rhythmically, insistently. She buckled in seconds, and the door swung open.

'Hello, Claudette. Been a while.'

She stared past him, cast her eyes around the garden and the fields beyond. Like the others. As if every one of them wanted to hide from something. Just how many of them were party to Alice Garten's death?

'You going to invite me in? He barged past her into her hallway and pushed the door closed behind him. He nodded towards the inner rooms of the small cottage. She walked slowly, glancing behind her. When she headed for the kitchen, he grabbed her shoulder and steered her into her living room. 'I don't think so. Too many sharp, pointy things in a kitchen. Let's go where the scariest thing in the room is a comfy chair, shall we? No, no, not the comfy chair!' He chuckled, pleased with himself. She frowned at him, apparently not getting the joke.

He indicated the sofa. 'Sit.'

She sat, back straight, knees and feet together, hands clasped in her lap. If she meant to hide her trembling fingers from him, she failed. Fisher sat in an armchair opposite. He remembered genuine affection for her, still felt a remnant of it now. They'd got too close, back then. Claudette had taken a shine to him after he'd charmed her when she attended a callout at Fisher's favourite pub. He'd always wanted to fuck a Uniform, and got to tick one off his bucket list, but an initial mutual attraction had crumbled when they'd tried to do the relationship thing and she proved to be too high-maintenance for his tastes. She still looked lean and fit now, and she'd aged well. A layer around the middle didn't hide what looked like a compact core; she must still work out, as much as any woman in her sixties can. And she still had great skin, always did. A few fine lines around the mouth and eyes, but her complexion shone, smooth and pale. Still tasty, even at her age.

'Bit of a mess, isn't it, Claudette?'

Claudette said nothing. Her eyes betrayed her fear of him, even after so long.

'What do you want?'

Fisher feigned hurt feelings. 'Don't you trust me, Claudette?'

She deflated in front of him, all defiance bled from her. 'I don't know who to trust anymore.'

She took a moment, seemed to need to work up to her next statement. 'Is she coming for all of us, you think? For me?'

'Crosbie? Unless I can stop her, yes.'

Claudette leaned forward, her arms crossed in front of her as if to hold herself together. 'What can we do?'

'I'm trying to fix it. *You know who* called me out of nowhere and hired me to find her. To kill her.'

'Who?'

Fisher shrugged. 'Her. The voice on the phone, the one that dished all those tasty jobs out to you, me, and Paul via Mark Balfour. What happened to Mark anyway? He just disappeared, no word, no warning, he was just gone one day.'

'Nobody ever found out. Shaw interrogated all of us, said she always suspected Balfour was bent but she never found out how. All we could do was close ranks and deny all knowledge. If we'd told her we'd been in on Mark's side-jobs she'd have had us all off the Force and our pensions gone.'

'Did you ever talk to her? Her on the phone? The one with the jobs?' Even he heard the question come out sounding about as loaded as any question could.

Claudette leaned forward. 'You know who she was, don't you?'

'Is. Her name's Montrose. You know her?'

Claudette stared at him. He saw her mind working. 'No. Never met a Montrose, I don't think.'

Fisher saw no indicators to suggest she was telling anything but the truth. Not as smart as she always thought she was.

'So, is Crosbie after us because of that thing in '78?'

Claudette looked at him, surprised and disbelieving. 'Seriously? Yes. Crosbie has never forgiven us for closing ranks and hanging her out to dry for what she did to Alice Garten. You don't remember?'

Fisher shrugged. 'It wasn't a big deal to me, at the time. More for you lot and your precious careers. Right now, Crosbie's just an unfinished job for me and I need the money. What did happen, that night?' She didn't need to know he feared reprisals too, if he failed to finish the job.

'All I remember is that it was Shaw's turn to check on the girl, but she came back looking seriously pissed off and asked Crosbie for a word. They disappeared for an hour then they came back, both of them looking grim. I assumed Shaw gave Crosbie an arse-kicking and that would be the end of it. I didn't know it would all explode and Crosbie would be left to suffer so much fallout all by herself. The woman could barely say boo to a goose unless her back was up, then she was a vicious wee sod, but she took her punishment. Had to respect her for that. But it looks like she never did forget we did nothing and watched her go down for it. Shaw, me, all of us.'

'You and she were friends, weren't you? Besties?'

Claudette's eyes snapped up. 'We were friends. As much as she ever had friends. But that was then. I tried to keep in touch with her after she left the Force but after a couple of months I never heard from her again. Eventually I stopped trying, had other problems...'

Her eyes flicked to the mantelpiece above her fireplace. Only for a second, but it was enough. Fisher stood and wandered over to it. The surface was cluttered with all sorts of rubbish. Half-full ashtrays, cigarette packs, three disposable lighters, a vape pen and a box of canisters, still full. Keys, coins, various other rubbish. Then he found what she must have glanced at. Face down, a framed photo of some rain-greyed glen, looked like Glencoe.

'Is that where we... You know?'

'Aye. Only picture I took. On our way to the cottage.' Her face fell. 'I didn't feel like taking any more after...'

Memories came back to Fisher. Too much drink. Bad sex.

Embarrassing. His mood switching so suddenly. Her flinching from him.

'Not my finest moment, that weekend.' He couldn't hold her gaze, surprised to find himself still having some small capacity to regret his own past actions.

Claudette waved the moment away. 'It happened. I got over it, so you should too.'

Fisher felt his mind make the same switch, another uncontrollable mood swing like the one that spoiled that weekend in Glencoe, the only time he ever thought a woman might come to mean something to him. And she'd spoiled it. He remembered, now: she'd been needy. Needy and petulant.

Resentment flared at the thought of her still blaming him for his humiliation when she'd probably caused it herself in the first place. How could he have forgotten the most valuable lesson his dad had ever taught him: trust no one because people always turn on you. Always. Claudette had seen him exposed and vulnerable, and made no effort to spare his feelings. She never had been anything special, after all, had she? Cold indifference settled on him, insulated and comforted him, approved of his next course of action.

'Where's Crosbie, Claudette? I need to find her and finish the job, or...' He swallowed, couldn't bring himself to admit the woman he now knew to be called Montrose still scared him.

Claudette's face blanched. Her mouth opened and closed, but no words came out.

Fisher stood over her. 'What are you not telling me, Claudette? You know I'm not a man to allow nostalgia to cloud my present judgment.' He glanced at the photo, then back to her. 'So, please. Tell me what you know before I have to spoil our memories completely.'

Claudette lifted her face. Her eyes had turned stony and defiant. She looked up at him as if daring him to hurt her after what they'd nearly had together.

Her defiance bled from her as Fisher pulled his multitool from his pocket and unfolded a miniature pair of pliers. 'Where is she, Claudette? I know where to find the Montrose woman but where's Crosbie?' He fixed her with a gaze that he hoped said he thought no more of her than he would a joint of meat he intended to carve up.

Still she said nothing.

He didn't have time to coax the information from her. He grabbed his multitool as he propelled himself at her. She screamed, not the helpless scream of a defenceless wee thing but a scream of outrage. Did she think because they had history he would go easy on her? He didn't have that luxury, much as he regretted having to lower himself to physical inducement. She'd made a mistake crossing her arms and legs. In the second she took to unfold herself, he was on her. He straddled her lap, pushed one arm under his left leg and pushed her other arm against her chest. She wriggled, yelled her fury at him, but he was immovable.

He waited until her struggles stopped, until she sagged back into the sofa, breath heaving in and out of her, her eyes livid. He lifted his multitool and opened the pliers.

'Don't you fucking dare, Fisher. I know nothing. I knew where Lillian was living, but from what I hear she's gone on the run after you fucked up, so she could be bloody anywhere.'

He gripped the end of one fingernail in the jaws of the pliers and tugged. He only pulled for a split-second, not long enough to exert any real force, but her eyes widened. She bit her lip and it bled.

'Next one is for real, Claudette. You know me. I hate violence, always found it inelegant, lacking in style, nae finesse, like.'

She stared ice at him. Hot, livid, excoriating ice.

'Let's try again. What else do you know, and please don't make me work too hard for this, Claudette.'

'I. Know. Nothing. Except you scared her, set her running, now no one knows where the hell she is.'

He leaned in, yelled in her face, made her recoil. 'Don't fucking lie to me, Claudette. I know you have more.' He forced himself to calm down and studied her eyes. 'Aye, there's more. You were pals once and I think you're still pals. I can understand you wanting to protect a pal, but I need to find her and finish her.'

He gazed around him, grabbed a lace cover from the back of the sofa.

He balled it in his fist, rolled it up against his chest while his other hand stayed clamped on her wrist.

He stuffed it in her mouth. She tried to clamp her teeth shut but couldn't stop his hand from penetrating.

Her eyes were wild now. She thrashed under him, adrenaline pouring strength into her arms and legs and her core, which he was impressed to find felt as strong as he'd thought it would. 'Claudette. Babe. I'll do this all night if I have to.'

When she exhausted herself, he gripped her fingernail again and tugged on it, enough – he knew – to hurt like a bastard, but he stopped short of actually tearing it out. Only once before had he ever had to pull one all the way out, and he'd been disappointed in himself for needing to go that far.

She screeched like he wouldn't have thought she had any strength left for. Her scream turned to miserable and pleading sobs, muffled through the gag but enough to let him know losing a fingernail would not be necessary.

He checked the jaws of his pliers, wiped them on her cardigan, then folded them away and returned his multitool to his pocket.

'Now. Claudette. Let's not have to bring Mr Multitool out to play again, OK?'

He leaned in, his face inches from hers. 'Where is Crosbie? If you lie to me again, I'll need to assume even ten fingernails might not get you to talk and I might as well just finish you. Hang on, you have a nephew, don't you? Lives in Glasgow? Does he have fingernails, Claudette?' He chilled even himself. Desperation was forcing him to behave like the animal he'd always heard Michael was, but the instant he started to enjoy this he would lose himself.

He pulled the gag from her mouth. She spat more blood, stretched her jaw open. She laid her head back on the headrest of the sofa. As she closed her eyes, tears poured down her cheeks.

'There was a man. She didn't love him – I don't think she was ever capable of loving anyone – but she seemed to feel some affection for him. His name was Ben.'

'Hutchison?'

'You know him?'

'No, but someone else mentioned him to me, earlier today.'

'He disappeared, years ago, not long after... He had a sister, though. Lived in North Berwick back then.'

'Had?'

'I don't fucking know, do I? I told you: he disappeared soon after that night, but that was an age ago. None of us ever knew where he went. He just disappeared. I assumed...'

He raised an eyebrow. 'What? What did you assume, Claudette? That I was told to kill him? I didn't even know his name until today. I was never on the inside, remember? "*Need to know*" and all that shite. Maybe if I'd known a bit more than you fuckers thought I needed to know I could have helped clear this whole cluster fuck up back then, before it festered into this mess. Fuck's sake, you lot were so up yourselves you treated me like a bin man. Taking out your trash, usually with menaces.'

Fisher settled on her lap again, and gripped another finger-nail in his pliers. Claudette shook her head, sobbed and moaned, shock starting to take the edge off her fear.

'Claudette.' He slapped her. 'Claudette, listen to me.'

She stared at him, a pathetic glimmer of hope in her eyes, eager and desperate to comply.

'I'm not enjoying this, Claudette. I'm really not. You have more. I know you do.'

Tears poured from her eyes again as she shook her head. Not frantic now, but pleading and terrified. He tugged on her fingernail, and saw her break. She slumped, gently pulled her hand from his. He released the pliers but held them ready.

Fisher studied her. Waited.

'Alright. Yes. I have something. But I need it. For insurance. For when one of them comes for me, Fisher. If you take it, I've got nothing and I'm as good as dead.' She broke down, sobbed quietly.

'Let me have it. My need is greater than yours. Actually, that's not true, but my need matters more to me than yours.'

She looked away, ashamed and brutalised. Impotent, and she knew it. He sighed, as if disappointed in her. 'You've already told me about his sister, Claudette. I'm getting tired of your attitude now. What else do you have, and do not start pissing me about again.'

Something in his eyes, a certainty of an intention to finish the job if he had to, finally broke her.

'The photograph. Our rotten fucking weekend in Glencoe.'

Fisher stood and picked up the frame.

'She'll kill me. You know that, right?'

Fisher fumbled with the clips on the back of the frame. When the backing card came away, a folded sheet of paper fell into his hands. He opened it out. He took a moment to read it and realise the significance, then he gaped at her.

'Oh, Claudette. Baby. You've sat on this all those years?'

He stuffed the paper in the inside pocket of his jacket.

She didn't move, said nothing. Fisher heard her start to sob, quiet and miserable, and walked outside.

Claudette had so nearly been so much more to him, but he shed a pang of regret at what had been the same unwelcome encumbrance as every other emotional attachment in his life.

FORTY-FOUR

Dad had tried to make shepherd's pie on the portable gas burner but had burned it to a black crust on the bottom of a camping pot that he was sure he'd have to replace.

Malkie served up Chicken Chasni and chips on the bench and seating thing on the front patio of the cabin. It was always a shame that the cabin sat at the west end of Harperrig Reservoir, so the front porch faced east and missed the evening sun. Lovely on the few weekend mornings Malkie had ever managed to drag himself out of bed before lunchtime. Still, the view out across the water to the cluster of houses at the far end was spectacular. He promised himself the next Saturday morning he got to wake up in his own bunk in the cabin, he'd haul himself out to see the sun come up. Dad would make him coffee, install him in the best patio chair and wrap him in something warm. Malkie could sleep all he wanted with the sun on his face until the ugly side of the world intruded again. When was the last time he'd got through an entire weekend without a callout or stroppy call from management? He honestly couldn't remember.

They ate in silence. Companionable and comfortable.

When Malkie rose to clean up his dad waved him back into his chair.

'Sit, son. Relax while you can.'

Relax while he could. Did he ever? Should he learn to? Louisa 'Gucci' Gooch had told him he needed to take up yoga. He'd replied that him in Lycra would almost certainly break some public decency law. She had laughed, but he knew she'd been disappointed he didn't take her seriously. Maybe it was time to try something new. Not yoga, though. Walking. He kept promising himself he'd walk the ridge of the Pentlands again, but never actually made the effort. The old Drovers' Road led past the far end of the reservoir, up to the Cauldstane Slap and beyond to West Linton and Peebles. A public footpath led right to the Drovers' Road alongside the sheep fields that lined the north side of the water, so he had no excuse. He could suggest it to his dad, but that would make sure it would happen, and for reasons he feared to explore in himself, committing to anything gave him the shits these days.

Commitment? I'm a father, if Sandra was telling the truth.

Where had his fury come from? If he was honest with himself – something that didn't always come easy to him – he felt relief more than anything else. Dodged a bullet? Side-stepped another crisis?

What had he pompously told so many people before? *One cannot help what one thinks, only what one does with what one thinks*. He didn't want a child, never wanted kids. He'd make the worst possible father, couldn't hope to live up to his own dad's standards.

How much damage would he do without being able to commit himself as much as the hardest job in the world demanded? No, the kid would be better off without knowing a sad case like him was its father. Was that where his fury came from, her refusal to show him the respect of telling him? No, that would be the last thing she'd expect him to want to know, so for whatever reasons, selfishly or uncharacteristically considerate, she had done the best thing for all three of them.

It hit him, the reason the news had infuriated him beyond his ability to control.

They'd reconnected.

He'd avoided her and her rotten family ever since the days their relationship imploded with almost fatal consequences for him. He'd stuffed her in some dark corner of his mind with no light switch. He still heard whispers from that corner some nights, about his first and biggest real-life fuck-up, but he never acknowledged them.

And now, they were a thing together, again. They had made a person. A small, innocent person who, with the right parenting and education, may have grown up to exhibit none of the worst of the two of them and some of the best of them, if either of them could lay claim to possessing any redeeming qualities at all.

'Malcolm, you're doing that thing, again. Please don't.'

He roused himself. Dad had put out a couple of the strawberry tarts Malkie always asked for when they used to go out to garden centres for lunch, but his appetite had disappeared.

'I wasn't, Dad.'

The old man's expression told Malkie he was having none of it.

Malkie relented. 'What thing? There are so many, according to you and Steph.'

Dad chuckled, shook his head in mock exasperation. 'You're wallowing, or dragging stuff up. Both of them make you look the same. Which is it, this time?'

Malkie sighed, conceded defeat in the face of a man who was smarter and sharper and more emotionally switched-on than he could ever hope to be.

'Bit of both, I think. Stuff from the past setting me off and me not bothering to fight it. Own worst enemy, you know that.'

Dad took a forkful of his strawberry tart and chewed slowly. He swallowed and put his fork down, pacing himself, making the enjoyment last. 'Good God, that's good. Life still has some joys to keep us afloat, doesn't it, son?'

Malkie raised his eyebrows and stared at his dad. 'Really, Dad. A mouthful of strawberry tart can send any problem packing, can it?'

Dad wilted, shrugged his shoulders as if to say he was only trying to help.

Malkie decided he might just be the nastiest piece of shit in the whole of West Lothian. 'Ach, I'm sorry, Dad. Here, have mine too.' He pushed his plate across the table.

'It's something I can't talk to you about, Dad, not yet. But it's not something we need to worry about, I promise. I just have something ugly to process.'

Aye, myself.

'It'll work out. It always does. We just have to keep on doing what we can until it does, right?'

Dad smiled, but pushed his plate away now, too. 'Aye she was a wise old bird, your mum.'

They both turned their gazes out across the reservoir. Darkness had fallen, and all they could make out now was the soft glow of Edinburgh's streetlights that silhouetted the low rolling hills between them and the city. From the top of the Pentlands Edinburgh looked stunning, but Malkie knew the startling view masked a wealth of quiet desperation. A sprawling expanse of homes and workplaces and pubs full of people, and only some of them like him, reaching the ends of new tethers every day and tying a knot to hold on to.

He knew he was projecting, as Timothy called it. Seeing in others what he loathed in himself for no good reason he could think of other than the shame-dumping Timothy had begged him never to succumb to. He envied people, that was his trouble. Without any knowledge of them or frame of reference, he envied people and the grass that had to be greener than his. Stupid, stupid attitude but it was all he had.

'Malkie, stop it. Please. You're scaring me.'

Malkie jumped, again. 'Sorry, Dad. I'm at the start of a case that's already getting ugly and' – he asked himself how much of Steph's trouble he could tell his dad without betraying her confidence – 'Steph's got some stuff going on I can't seem to help her with. And that's frustrating, you know? After all the times she's been there for me, I can't help her now.'

'Aye, she's some girl. You two never thought about...'

It took a moment for Malkie's penny to drop. 'God, no. We'd kill each other in our first week together. And anyway, she has standards.'

'Stop that, or I'll never buy you strawberry tart again. And I wouldn't make a threat like that without meaning to back it up, boy.'

'OK, OK, old man. Message received.'

He found he wanted to tell him all about Deborah, but immediately imagined him as a youth, explaining to his stunned parents that, yes, he'd managed to get himself a girlfriend, and no she wasn't ready to come round for dinner yet and yes he had some condoms. Not that they had helped; Sandra had reminded him the hard way that they needed to be in his wallet and on his person, not stuffed in his bedside table drawer, to be of any use.

He remembered how his mother had to have 'the talk' with him, because his dad had been too embarrassed and out of his depth to explain what he himself had known his entire life but never talked about. Malkie had told his mum he'd learned all he needed to from Raymie Wilson's *Razzle* magazines and the little he listened to in sex education classes.

His mum had tried to laugh that off and failed, then proceeded to educate him, start to finish, on the kinds of trouble a man could get a girl into without 'taking precautions'.

Thoughts of his mum, as always, dragged ugly memories and painful questions to mind. Dad was already worried about him, more so because he had no idea why Malkie was struggling. Would now be a good time to try to engage him in a post-mortem of that evening?

As he considered this, he realised he was fast losing his temper, already. Not with his dad. Not even with himself, for a change. He'd had a bellyful of knowing he'd had something to do with his mum's death but never seeming to get any closer to remembering how. He owed it to himself, to his dad, to Steph, to clear the block in his mind, to get past it, deal with it, so he could focus on becoming the better man he always wanted to be and who Steph and his dad waited eagerly to help him become.

He needed to know. He needed his dad and him to fumble their way, together, towards an answer.

'Dad.'

Malkie's tone brought his dad's eyes up with alarm in them.

'Can we talk? About it? You know?'

Dad slumped back in his chair, closed his eyes, and sighed. 'Yes, Malcolm. There will never be a good time, so...'

Neither spoke for long seconds, until Malkie found the courage to put the first feeler out.

'Last time we spoke about it you said whatever we did that night might have contributed to what happened.'

'I think I said, "what we did or didn't do", but my point was we didn't start the fire. We just' – he swallowed, took a moment – 'we didn't save her.'

'What did you mean?'

Dad leaned forward, rested his elbows on his knees, stared at his slippers. 'You know what I think the biggest killer in most people's home is, Malcolm? Complacency. I think I know what I did and what you did that might – might, son– have made a difference, but I haven't wanted to tell you because—'

'Because you knew I'd start flogging myself with it like a penitent given a new scourge for his birthday, right?'

Dad said nothing, He didn't need to.

Malkie settled his mind, now reeling because his dad did believe they had contributed. That they were both responsible in their own ways. He needed to know and he was terrified to know. The fact that his dad seemed ready to talk about it as calmly as he did spoke volumes.

'You want me to go on, son? I'd like to, but it's going to hurt us both. I mean, *really* hurt. So, I need to know you'll do all you can to keep it in some kind of perspective. I need your solemn word on that, your promise beyond any possibility you'll even think about betraying my belief in you.'

Malkie let out a long, slow, profound breath, emptied his lungs and imagined all trace of his innate tendency to let himself and others down, drain from him. His dad needed his oath, and breaking that oath for any reason, ever, might break them forever.

'What did we do or not do, Dad? Tell me, and we'll work on dealing with it together.' He fixed his dad's eyes with his own and took his hands in his own. 'I swear it, Dad.'

Dad nodded, smiled as if he couldn't be prouder of his son. It took him what felt like an age to get the words out.

'You closed her bedroom door, son.'

Malkie reeled. He had. He remembered. On top of whatever cruel words he'd thrown over his shoulder at his mother, he'd slammed her door shut on her heartbroken apologies, her pleading for him to stay.

'And I forgot my duty of protection to her, son. I owed it to her to hear her screams, or to hear the door slamming. But I had those stupid, stupid, bloody earbud things in to listen to the rugby. I never heard anything, son, until I smelled the smoke and it was too late.

'Like I said before. Complacency, son. My sin was complacency. Neither of us knocked that candle onto the floor, but both of us contributed to her screams going unheard. Even if you'd left her door open, I still wouldn't have heard her calling out for me. Those bloody earbuds block everything else out. I would have heard nothing. So, if anyone is ultimately responsible...'

Dad's eyes filled and overspilled. Malkie's followed suit. They clutched each other's hands, leaned forward until their foreheads touched, and wept together.

FORTY-FIVE

Malkie jumped at the sound of his phone ringing. His work phone. He heard a bump as his dad sat up and bumped his head on the underside of Malkie's upper bunk.

'Ow! Dammit, I'll never get used to this. When we can we get the second bedroom waterproofed, son?'

'I'll put it to the top of the list, Dad. Go back to sleep, it's only...' He checked his watch. 'Fuck's sake, it's not even six.' He swung his legs over the side of the bunk and dropped to the floor. Dad laid back down, rubbing the top of his head, his thin grey hair standing up as if he'd been shocked.

On the freezing front porch, Malkie pressed the button to receive the call, even as he considered lobbing the damned thing into the loch and claiming later he'd lost it.

'Malkie.' Steph's voice, tired and pissed off.

'Steph, tell me you misdialled. Please.'

'We've got another one, Malkie.'

'What? Already? Who, this time?'

'Victim's name is Paul Gaddon. Lived out past Caldercruix. It's North Lanark but they called us because they linked it to the first murders. I think they were happy to dump it on us on the basis that it started in our patch.'

A heavy weight sank in Malkie's guts. 'What do you mean "started in our patch"?'

'Same MO.'

Malkie feared to voice the fact that Steph would already know. 'He's on Gucci's list.'

The sigh on Steph's end of the line told him she realised the significance, too. 'Aye. So, that's two out of five, not counting Crosbie herself. Two in two days.'

Malkie took a breath, let it out in a long, pained sigh. Crawford, Gaddon, Ferguson, Balfour, Crosbie, Shaw. Five constables, one detective sergeant. One dead girl. And now two dead ex-coppers. *Throw away the paddles, shit creek, here we come.* His dad called from the bedroom at the back of the cabin. 'Should I make coffee, son?'

'Text me the address, Steph. I'll be there as quick as I can. Bloody sun's not even up yet, and I wanted to see it.'

'What the hell are you talking about?'

'Nothing. Text me the address.' He hung up and yelled back into the cabin, 'No thanks, Dad. Go back to sleep. I just need to pop out for a wee while. Work.'

Dad appeared in the doorway, his face grim. 'I'll make coffee. You can take it with you.'

By the time Malkie reached Paul Gaddon's farmhouse, he feared his car's suspension would be knackered beyond repair. The bumps and potholes in the rutted track from the main road had spilled his coffee all over the passenger seat and clattered his teeth together more than once. By the time he pulled up outside the house he was ready to explode at someone, anyone, for anything. He calmed down when he saw Steph. She stood with her back against her car, her hands on her hips, her face down. Malkie's foul temper disappeared under a blanket of dread.

He approached Steph. She looked up, saw him, and shook her head. 'Same MO. Same sick, specific MO. This is meant to send a message, isn't it? Why does this make me feel like puking? I've seen worse, we both have.'

'Because the day we get used to seeing this stuff is the day something's died inside us, partner.'

She nodded. 'Come on, I've been in already but I'll wait at the door while you have a look.'

As they approached the farmhouse, Malkie ran through the usual questions. No other witnesses. Nobody else seen in or around the property. The body had been discovered by a milkman who saw lights on and the state of the front window from the foot of the track and walked up to have a look.

'Poor bastard. Is he OK?'

'Answering questions for Gucci, in the back of that patrol car.'

One front window in the farmhouse seemed to have exploded outward, but he saw no damage to the rest of the building. At the SOCO van, he found Sally on wardrobe duty again.

'Do you ever sleep, Sally?'

'Love of the job, Malkie. Love of the job.' She handed him a sealed bag. 'XL again, I assume?'

Malkie suited up and gave Steph a nod from inside the scene tape. He walked the footplates into a front room and stopped in the doorway, his gorge rising, despite having known what to expect.

Almost a mirror of the previous scene. This time a man, Paul Gaddon, ex constable in the Livingston Police Service in 1978, and another name on the list.

Two out of five. Management will go ballistic. A giant slab of a man rose to his feet from behind the chair the deceased sat in. Malkie had a swift word with himself: *don't call him 'Big Man'; he hates it.* Never a good idea to piss off a man who could take three days to complete your initial forensic report.

'Hiya, Bruce. That is you, isn't it, Bruce?'

'Don't start, Malkie.' He stepped to the side of the chair. 'Anything you want me to explain that isn't already obvious?' He sounded tired and depressed. It occurred to Malkie that no matter what coping mechanisms these people used, and how much they supported each other, seeing this kind of thing every day had to wear them down, didn't it?

'Nah, I'm good, mate. I'll get the photos later. I just came in to tick the box that says "*SIO has examined the locus*".'

Bruce returned to his work. Malkie stared at the basin full of blood, and the small pools that had formed where it had over-spilled.

'You guys can tell how long blood has been pooled, can't you, Bruce?'

Bruce straightened and sat back on his heels, twisted to glance at the blood on the floor. 'Usually, but when we arrived the central heating had gone into overdrive because of that smashed window, so we had cold air pushing in and hot air pushing back against it, so it's kind of difficult to be definitive. You know what I'm going to say next, don't you?'

'Wait for the report. I know.'

'That's right.'

Malkie allowed the man his point scored, figured he deserved it if Malkie had upset him during their last shout together.

He noticed something on the surface of the blood in the basin. A protrusion through the surface, barely there, and froth had collected on it, covering it over. He peered more closely to make sure he was seeing what he thought he was before daring to mention it.

'Bruce. Mate.'

Something in Malkie's tone brought Bruce to his feet immediately. 'What?'

Malkie pointed. 'Is there something in there?'

Bruce took an unopened pack of plastic tweezers from his kit on the floor beside him and bent over the bowl. Malkie forced himself to step forward, peered over Bruce's massive shoulder. He carefully pulled something from the blood, something bigger under the surface than its protruding part suggested. Bruce pulled it free of the tug of the surface skin and placed it in a plastic evidence bag with a pair of tweezers. He sealed the zip lock, scribbled his initials and the date and time and an evidence identification number on the white panels at the top, then held it up to the light.

Malkie squinted to make it out amidst the dark red mess, then wished he hadn't.

A tiny blue pompom. From a woolly hat.

And judging by the size of it, a child's woolly hat.

FORTY-SIX

'Malkie. Crosbie, Hutchison etc. Progress?' McLeish made it
clear he meant 'Any progress?' rather than 'What progress?'

The CID room hushed. McLeish folded his arms over his
chest and leaned back against a desk as if settling in for some
serious entertainment. Thompson had been dragged into
another meeting, so McLeish had another chance to rip into
Malkie.

Malkie sighed but stood. He'd come straight from Paul
Gaddon's crime scene and was dreading what he was about to
say. SOCOs had found hair with intact follicles at both scenes
but – as ever – the backlog in forensics was slowing everyone
down, and he'd been told to expect the DNA test results to take
the full published minimum lead time, which meant he had
nothing, right now.

He was about to give McLeish and his minion Pammy
Ballantyne and various other members of the Malkie
McFuckup anti-fan club enough material to feed their confirmation bias for months. And anyone who until now had held
out some hope for him might now join the club and bolster their
numbers.

'We now have two MisPers. Two MisPerses?' Malkie frowned, couldn't decide which was right.

McLeish growled at him. 'McCulloch.'

'Sorry. We now have the Billy Irvine stabbing which may have been self-defence, two MisPer cases plus' – he had to swallow and brace himself for the reaction he expected – 'two separate homicide cases. On consecutive days.'

An audible wave of disbelief swept the room, and McLeish had to cast his sternest frown across the gathered audience before they stopped sighing and tutting and muttering. Malkie had expected it but still struggled to bite down on an urge to tell them all to go fuck themselves.

'We're still looking for both Crosbie and Hutchison, can't find a trace of them other than one alleged sighting of Crosbie by DCS Shaw, which is odd given their ages and Hutchison's condition. The victims in the two homicide cases are ex-serving police officers based in the old Livi Police Station when it was still a going concern. Both are on the list that Lou Gooch managed to get us from the city archives – good work, Gucci.' She smiled from the back row, and he felt the *fuck them all* he thought she sent him in her brief look, although he'd yet to hear her use that kind of language. Probably Steph's influence.

'Both of the homicide victims were killed in their own homes. No struggle, but we don't yet know why. We've been through the personal effects gathered at the scenes and found nothing to indicate they'd been in touch with each other or Lillian Crosbie since all three resigned in '78. And no obvious link to our second MisPer, Ben Hutchison, either. CCTV camera searches are ongoing, nothing yet. No bites on the MisPer web page other than the original sighting of Lillian Crosbie at the shelter from where Ben Hutchison was – we assume – abducted. I think we're on *Crimewatch* tonight, aren't we, Steph?' She nodded. He had no doubt Thompson would do the talking on camera; his gob was rarely allowed within a mile of a microphone.

He hesitated before getting his next words out, struggled to believe they were true. 'Also, Detective Chief Superintendent Megan Shaw claims Lillian Crosbie attacked her at home.'

A collective groan. All present would realise how much pressure, how much heat, would now be piled onto Malkie, and many would fully expect him to let the whole of 'J' Division CID down in a spectacular fashion.

Malkie ignored them. 'That's what we have so far, except for the distinctive method of killing the victims.' He hesitated. Preparing his words, he suddenly realised just how explosive the connection was. He'd much prefer, now, to stop there, but he'd dropped a morsel to them, and backtracking now would sound even weaker than admitting the little they had.

He wondered who would sniff blood and want to nail him.

Pam Ballantyne spoke, to no one's surprise. 'And that is, DS McCulloch? You didn't say.'

'No, Pammy, I didn't.' He sat.

McLeish sighed. 'Malkie.'

He sighed, which was a mistake, as good as confirming Pammy's suspicions that he'd omitted the information for a good reason.

'Both victims were... exsanguinated.'

A buzz ran through the room, quashed by a look from McLeish.

'They were tied to chairs and bled to death.'

Malkie felt the mood in the room drop. Few coppers would wish a case like this on anyone. Content to follow from positions of safety on other teams, they'd all be happy not to be involved in something that could turn into a shit show of monumental and very public proportions. Few cases turned out to be anything other than violent and messy crimes of passion or cynical but simple hit jobs. Bleeding someone to death suggested a whole new level of psychopathy that might interest some more prurient members of the team, but would be given a wide berth by most.

Thompson spoke from the back of the room. No one had heard her arrive. 'An item of clothing was found in the victim's blood, which may only have been coincidental but we feel is worth checking out. We've asked forensics if anything similar was found at the first scene. It might just have been something random that fell into the basin but is otherwise unconnected. I've put in a request to expedite, but I don't know if management have approved it. I'll chase that up today.'

Ballantyne again. 'And what was that, ma'am?' She held her pen ready above her notebook as if to demonstrate good reason for digging further.

Malkie answered, refused to let Thompson let him off with too much of the unwelcome interest. 'It was a pompom, Pam. Anything else we can help you with?'

'OK, OK. Let's move on.' McLeish clapped his hands together, checked his notes, and looked for his next victim. Malkie heard none of what followed, zoned-out and miserable until Steph dug an elbow into his side and nodded for him to follow her.

She sat at her desk and waited for him to sit at his. 'Well, that could have gone better.'

'Don't I know it. We've got loads and we've got nothing.'

Steph turned to her screen and opened the case file, scanned it and turned back to him, her face as miserable as his. He realised she must need something to distract her as much as he did. He'd wait for her to mention her revelation again. He'd learned enough to give her the time and space to broach the subject herself, but he was watching out for her. He owed her that much.

'Malkie. Pay attention.'

'Yes, Steph. Sorry, Steph.'

'Grow up. I was saying there's one other avenue we could explore.'

They waited until mid-afternoon to broach the subject with Thompson, whose face fell. She must have been expecting it but them asking made it real.

'Oh God, what can I say? I can't refuse, can I?'

Steph shrugged. 'Not really, boss. Sorry.'

Thompson sighed again. And again. She played with a pen on her desk, spun it around in her fingers.

Malkie and Steph waited, knew how difficult this was for her. A career-limiting move, some would say.

'OK, both of you go. Tomorrow, though. She has surgery this afternoon, did a lot of damage tearing her wound open when she fell over. I don't want any conversation with her taking place when she can claim later she was dopey from her surgery. And, Malkie, I don't want to hurt your feelings, honestly, but Steph, you do most of the talking, OK?'

Malkie opened his mouth to protest, then thought it through, and shut it again. 'Makes sense, I suppose. You two still have careers worth protecting. I'll do the introductions, explain why we need to talk to her again in as little detail as I can, then explain that Steph is running the investigation operationally, so she's best placed to ask the questions. Fair enough?'

Thompson and Steph both appraised him, then shared a look of surprised approval. Malkie refused to rise to the bait and kept his gob shut.

'That sounds like an excellent approach, Malkie. Steph, you OK with that?'

'Yes, boss, as long as Malkie's OK with it and she believes us.'

'Fine. I'll behave, OK?'

They smiled at him, which he found not in the slightest bit patronising.

Thompson sat back in her chair. 'I'll call the hospital, see if she's fit to talk to you. Keep yourselves available all day, OK?' She opened a file on her desk and picked up her pen: they were dismissed.

Before Malkie could close her office door behind him, she spoke again. 'Malkie. Please. I'm begging you.' She looked up from her papers. 'You know, right?'

'Best behaviour, boss. Promise.'

Thompson's phone rang as Malkie and Steph rose to leave. Thompson pointed them back into their seats. She listened, closed her eyes, swallowed, thanked someone, then replaced her phone on the desk as if it might explode in her face.

She took long seconds to speak.

'Forensics. They say they sent an email already but I haven't seen it yet.'

Malkie and Steph shared a glance filled with mutual dread.

'Ferguson's blood did contain something. Wasn't noticed when they first poured it all into a sterile container.'

Her face blanched.

'A button. From clothing of some kind. A small blue button.'

FORTY-SEVEN

'Malkie, she's here again, the woman from the other day. She's waiting for you outside. Get yourself a bloody personal assistant, will you?' Bernie hung up.

Malkie crossed to the windows that looked out on the land-scaped lawns around the Civic Centre. Sandra Morton sat on a bench, leaning forward, her elbows on her knees, her head bowed. As he watched she seemed to have some kind of crisis or anxiety attack. She straightened up, heaved in long breaths, stood, paced backwards and forwards, she glanced towards the front entrance and seemed to deflate in front of him. She staggered backwards, sat heavily on the bench.

Despite himself, Malkie found himself grabbing his jacket and heading for the stairwell.

She looked up as he approached the bench. Her face lit up with desperate relief.

He sat beside her and took a long, deep steadying breath for himself.

She waited. She looked terrified of what his reaction would be to her reappearance.

I've got no clue what my reaction will be.

He stared ahead of him. Wondered if she'd speak before he mustered the courage to ask. The one time he – as a fully grown adult male – should have had questions he needed answered, and he couldn't decide if he even wanted to know.

What the hell was happening to him? She'd revealed he was a father. He felt sick, out of his depth and out of control.

How would an adult deal with this? Mature and reasoned acceptance? A considered and measured conversation about the reasons why she'd kept this from him for thirty years?

She waited, studied him, the dread and fear in her eyes giving way to a need to know the truth regardless of the answer. A need to find out where she stood. The kid had to be thirty by now, far too late to think about forming a relationship. And he felt so far beyond capable of handling such responsibility it was a joke.

Even in the privacy of his own mind, he choked on the words. Father. Dad. A role he doubted he'd ever feel capable of fulfilling.

Focus, man. If she's telling the truth, then regardless of what she did, you owe them both.

He opened his mouth but she spoke first.

'Yes.' Her voice small and weak, filled with dread. 'Yours. A girl.'

It all became even more real. He'd thought his guts couldn't sink any lower. He'd been wrong. He reeled. This was too much, more than he'd ever expected to have to bear. Until his mum died, that is. On balance, he'd done far more damage to his own parents in the past year than anything he'd ever done to Sandra. If she'd waited until now to tell him, she'd obviously coped, maybe even flourished as a mother.

Whatever she did or didn't deserve for her treatment of him so long ago, no child should have to pay for the mistakes of their parents.

He braced himself to learn more about a person that until a

few minutes ago he had no idea existed and couldn't want less to get to know.

You callous bastard. She's your daughter.

'What's her name? Does she know about me?'

Sandra stared at him, a gaze he found unreadable but one which he couldn't imagine promised anything he wanted to hear. 'Do you care, Malkie? No, don't get upset. I mean the question genuinely. I promise. Do you really care what I called her?'

Something in her tone introduced an itch he dreaded to scratch. He considered his words long and hard, not bothered about choosing words she'd approve of – he was long past caring about her opinion – but so he would later recall this conversation and not feel shame at his heartlessness, his callousness. He didn't want a daughter. He didn't want to be a father. He didn't want to know what school she went to or whether she went to university or whether she had a boyfriend or girlfriend or what bands she listened to. Most of all, he didn't want to know if she'd turned out as cruel as her mother's rotten family. He harboured no illusions he'd ever be the kind of man to want to know these things, so he clung to the consolation prize of at least not letting her know he was such a callous shit.

'Malkie? Do you really want to know? I mean, in your heart?'

His silence had already spoken for him. Her face set hard, her eyes bleak and desolate but accepting. 'I thought so. Don't worry. You won't have to learn to be a daddy, or pay for anything. You're off scot-free, Malkie.'

He opened his mouth to utter false protestations, to claim he cared more than he knew he ever could, but she held her hand up, cut him off.

She took a moment, studied his eyes, seemed to need to summon courage to cross some threshold.

'I miscarried, Malkie. I lost her.'

Malkie threw his head back and screamed to the heavens. Two words bellowed from his mouth, spittle flying, the sound of his fury echoing back from their surroundings as if to amplify them.

'Fuck's sake.'

Again, heads turned. He was heedless. Sandra's tears started again and she stood. She stared at him. If she hoped he'd experience some epiphany, some realisation of having lost what he thought he'd never fucking well had, she got nothing. He had nothing to give her. On some level he sympathised with the agony she must have endured. Alone. But he couldn't overcome his decades-long hatred of the woman to feel any more grief than he would for someone dying in hospital in the TV programmes his dad watched.

Sandra walked away. He tried to find words, anything that might be even nearly appropriate in such ugly circumstances, but none came. He watched her walk away. She seemed to weaken at one point, hesitated, seemed about to turn back, but then continued walking.

He kicked out at nothing, at freezing air, furious at his own messed-up excuse for grief. He waited until he could be certain Sandra had left the grounds of the Civic Centre, then stood and shambled back to the building, every step a painful refusal to buckle.

FORTY-EIGHT

Paul had been right on the money. Fisher could see why Hutchison's sister still lived in the same house: Georgian edifices like this tended to stay in families for decades. With only three other Hutchisons in North Berwick, it hadn't taken him long to decide this had to be the one. Wealthy, ostentatiously so. View out over the North Sea, several quiet beaches within a fifteen-minute drive. None of the neighbours within hearing distance of each other.

Oh yes, there was money here.

The boy who answered the doorbell scowled when he saw Fisher. 'Can I help you?'

'I'd like to talk to Rebecca Hutchison, please, if it's not too much trouble.'

'Are you from the police?'

Odd question. Had they been here already? He needed to up his game.

'Is Miss Hutchison available?' He fixed his eyes on the lad, poured all the threat he could into his look; he didn't have time for subtlety.

The youth wilted in front of him, his eyes bewildered; one

simply didn't expect to be menaced on one's own doorstep in a neighbourhood like this.

'I'll see if she's available.'

He started to push the door closed, but Fisher slapped a hand on it and pushed it open. 'Excellent, so she is at home then.'

He stepped forward, forced the lad to back up. Up close, he towered over him, and his broad shoulders must have eclipsed any daylight coming through the window in the door. The boy backed up, his eyes wide now. Fisher loomed over him and darkened his expression.

'Who else is in the house right now, and don't fucking lie to me.'

Tears welled in the lad's eyes and spilled down his cheeks. 'Nobody. Just Miss Hutchison and me.' His tone was plaintive, as if afraid Fisher wouldn't believe him and might hurt him.

Fisher pushed him ahead. 'Living room. Or reception room or whatever you toffs call it. Now.'

He led him into what had to be a sitting room.

'Sit.'

He did.

'What's your name?'

'Peter. I'm—'

'Call her.'

Peter froze. Fisher stood over him, pulled his multitool from his pocket and folded out the fixed blade. Peter flinched and shrank back into the massive leather sofa. He looked like a child on it.

'Grandma,' he called out, his voice weak and trembling.

Fisher wiggled the blade at him. 'Again. Louder.'

Peter called out again, just as fearful but louder.

A voice sounded from the back of the house. 'Yes? What is it, Peter?'

Fisher grinned and held a finger to his lips.

After a few moments, the lady of the house entered the sitting room. She recoiled at the sight of Fisher holding a knife over the terrified boy. She opened her mouth, but nothing came out.

'Sit down, Miss Hutchison.'

After a glance at a phone sitting six feet away, she sat next to Peter and took his hand.

Fisher sat opposite them. The sofa felt soft and luxurious under him and he wished he could lie back and sleep. He was so tired.

He folded his blade away and placed his multitool on the arm of the chair beside him.

'I need to find your brother, Miss Hutchison. Where is he?'

Her eyes widened, filled with fear, and Fisher feared they were about to do the *I don't know, I really don't* thing. He sighed, really couldn't be bothered today.

As if he was watching a bad TV cop programme, he heard the words he dreaded.

'I don't know.'

He stared at her, let his eyes communicate his displeasure. She seemed to shrink in front of him. Peter glanced from her to him and back again, and seemed to realise where this might go, too. He started crying.

'I promise you. I don't know. I haven't seen him or heard from him in years. That's the truth and hurting me will only force me to lie to you because I just don't know.'

Fisher studied her. He believed her but needed to be certain. He picked up his multitool and folded out the miniature pliers. Both of them seemed to shrink even smaller, if that were possible. They clung to each other.

He squeezed the plier jaws together a couple of times as if testing them.

'I'm going to ask again and if I don't like what I hear, I'm going to start pulling someone's fingernails out. Do you understand?'

The stared at him but no words came.

Fisher surged forward in his chair and bellowed at them like a man unhinged.

'Give me something that will help me find your brother, or God help me I'll make you suffer like you never thought possible. Do you fucking understand me?'

They screamed, drew their legs up and curled up, foetal, still hanging on to each other.

Fisher was pleased with himself. He'd played it perfectly. They'd be pushovers now, certainly with one of them expecting a fingernail to be ripped out.

He grabbed Peter by a wrist and yanked him to his feet. He screamed like a banshee and reached for his granny. She tried to hang on to him, to stop Fisher from pulling him from her grasp, but there could never be any competition.

Peter's legs buckled. Fisher let him collapse to his knees and followed him down. He kneeled with one arm wrapped around him from behind. He forced the boy to bend over the table, smacked his face down on the glass top. He grabbed one wrist and twisted it behind Peter's back. He screamed again but went still as Fisher eased off again but held his arm in place.

Hutchison sat forward. 'Please don't hurt him. He knows even less than I do. He never even met Ben, and I hardly talk about him. I promise you – he knows nothing.'

Fisher adopted an expression of intense thought, of careful consideration. 'I guessed that, but you see, hurting the subject of an interrogation just tends to unhinge them a bit and they'll say anything they think you want to hear to make the pain stop, because their little brains get fused by the agony and stop working. But...' He picked up his multitool again and pinched one of Peter's fingernails in the tips of the jaws. 'Watching someone else screaming and begging and knowing that you're the only one that can make it stop. Well, that works much better.'

Peter screeched even louder. The noise started to grate on Fisher. He slapped the boy on the back of the head. 'Shut up, you irritating little twat.'

He did shut up, except for whimpering and hyperventilating.

Fisher smiled at Hutchison again. 'Now, where were we?' He pulled on the multitool, on the fingernail, until Peter screamed and sobbed and fought to thrash himself out from under Fisher.

Hutchison surged forward, reached one hand towards Fisher as if to make some connection that would make him listen to her.

'Give me something I can use or I pull it right out.' Peter had lapsed into a shocked whimpering, but now he moaned, 'Please, no. Grandma?' and started crying again.

Fisher watched as she seemed to trawl her mind, desperate to find something, anything, she could give him to stop Peter's ordeal.

'I'm losing patience. Try harder.'

She bent forward at the waist, lowered her head to her lap, laced her fingers behind her head, and rocked, as if trying to shake something loose.

Fisher counted off thirty seconds. Hutchison rocked and moaned. Peter sobbed, quiet now he was both brutalised and exhausted.

'Not good enough. Sorry, wee man, looks like asking a friend was a waste of time.' He brought his pliers down to the same finger as before. Peter shrieked and thrashed and nearly managed to push off even Fisher's bulk.

'The phone!' She sat up straight, a pathetic gleam of hope in her eyes. 'He gave me a phone, years ago, shortly after he disappeared but while he was still calling me occasionally to let me know he was OK. I forgot all about it, it was so long ago.'

Fisher eased up his hold on Peter, who sighed and seemed to deflate under him, as if he sensed some hope of an end to his ordeal. Fisher hoped so too; he really couldn't be bothered with this undignified nonsense.

'He gave me a phone. It was an old thing, a flip phone with an aerial, and he said it was for him to contact me and I was never to use it. And not to tell anyone about it, ever.' Her eyes pleaded with his, and Fisher found himself believing her.

He stood, dragged Peter to his feet by his upper arm. The boy gripped his fingertip with his good hand and clutched it to his chest as if he could squeeze the agony from it. Fisher pushed him ahead, towards the hallway.

'After you.'

She stood, still terrified but eager now.

'It'll be in his study. I never changed anything. I always hoped he'd come home one day, so I—'

'Enough with the sentimental tripe, woman. Get it.'

'Yes. Of course. Just please don't hurt my grandson again.' She walked away down the hallway and opened a door on the left. Fisher pushed Peter into the room.

A study. Huge green leather-topped mahogany desk in the middle of the room facing a massive bay window with a view out across the clifftops to the sea. Bookshelves on every wall, filled with more dusty old books than Fisher had seen in any one place outside of a library. Dust everywhere, coating everything, floating in the sunbeams streaming in through the windows. When she said she'd not touched the place she wasn't exaggerating.

She crossed to the desk, pulled the bottom drawer open, rummaged, and produced an old phone. She held it out to him as if in payment for a hostage's release.

Fisher took it from her. He didn't bother trying the power

button and wondered if he'd even be able to get the damned
thing charged, let alone working. He knew someone who could
get some juice into this, might even have an original charger.
Fisher knew lots of people who knew stuff.

'Nothing else? Be very sure, woman.'

She cast a long, probing gaze around the study, seemed to
genuinely rack her terrified and addled brains for anything else
she could offer him to get him to leave them alone. She probably
wondered if she was bartering for both of their lives. She
couldn't know that Fisher found any useless waste of life inelegant, an admission of failure to resolve matters via other
methods.

'Big house, this? Old, aye?'

They stared at him, confusion pushing fear from their eyes.

'Does it have a big fuck-off pantry in the kitchen? I bet it
does. Show me.' He indicated with the phone in his hand for
them to move through to the kitchen.

Fisher took one look in the pantry and smiled. 'Perfect. Bit
small but it'll do. In you both go.'

They did so, but stared at him, confused. He sighed as if
disappointed to have to explain.

'No outside windows. Plenty of food.' He scanned the
shelves and nodded. 'Yep, plenty of bottled water. Hang on.' He
glanced into a utility room, found a bucket, and placed it in the
corner of the pantry. 'Perfect. It's been a pleasure meeting you
both.' He smiled, tapped his fingers to his forehead in the
absence of a hat to doff, and closed the door.

He remembered the other thing he'd wanted to ask them.
He opened the door again and they cowered back against the
shelving.

'Did your brother ever mention someone called Montrose?'

Hutchison shook her head, her eyes terrified.

'A man called Michael?' Another wild shake of her head.

'I believe you, this time.' He closed the door on them again, noticed it opened out into the kitchen rather than inwards into the cramped pantry. A huge American-style double fridge-freezer toppled onto its side ensured they'd not get out quickly.

He pulled his phone from his pocket and dialled a number.

'Davina, you old tart. Got a job for you.'

FORTY-NINE

[CC] [18:32]

She called me. Crosbie. Just like her, she couldn't get any actual words out, she just breathed down the phone at me. Actually, she sounded a bit ragged, injured maybe, we can hope.

[18:33]

Is anyone fucking listening? I'm pished and I need one of you bastards to talk to.

[AF] [18:33]

I'm here Claudette.

[CC] [18:33]

Ah, Fisher. You fucker. Last night, well out of order.

[AF] [18:33]

You forced my hand, Claudette, lied to me, gave me no choice. That hurt my feelings, so it did.

[CC] [18:34]

You know what? I hope she comes for me
soon. I'm going to drink myself stupid every
day until she does and hope I sleep through it.
And then I hope she comes for you right
after me.

Hah! Listen to me. Ready. I'm not ready. I'm
bloody petrified, but I'd rather she finished me
sooner rather than keep me hanging on, know
what I mean?

I always wondered if you were saveable. Until
you threatened to pull my fingernail out. Anyone
else still on here, don't trust him. He's a fucking
psycho.

[AF] [18:35]

Claudette?

Claudette, fucking answer me.

Claudette?

FIFTY

Malkie sat at the bar, his head perched on one hand pushing his cheek up into his ear, his other hand braced on the bar. His phone lay on the sticky and grimy wood. He eyed it as if it might jump up and bite him on the arse. The recording that lurked inside the thing might yet.

'Strawberries.'

Monty nodded and widened his grin even more than Malkie thought he could.

'Strawberries.'

'Would I lie to you?'

'If this is disgusting, I'm killing you then arresting you, understood?'

Monty reached for the shot glass. 'If you're going to get stroppy about it, then I'm not taking the chance, mate.'

Malkie stopped him and picked up the glass. Lorraine, somehow always perched on the stool next to Malkie's no matter which one he chose, turned to watch him.

'What do you think, Lorraine? You think this might be the one?'

'You never know, Malkie. You never know.'

Malkie swallowed it in one go, the way Lorraine had taught him. He felt a shot of strawberry hit his tongue before the same underlying taste of alcohol he always dreaded hit the back of his throat and burned down into his stomach.

He managed three seconds without reacting, then coughed and spluttered and gulped a mouthful from the glass of mineral water he'd had ready.

Lorraine shook her head. 'Ach well, Malkie. Keep trying, son.'

Monty's raised eyebrows asked Malkie the inevitable question.

'One more. That was OK until it hit my throat. Maybe given enough time...'

Monty poured him another with a triumphant flourish and placed the open bottle beside Malkie's glass.

Ready for it this time, Malkie was able to enjoy the sweet taste of strawberries before the alcohol warmed his throat, but this time he found he could handle it.

Monty leaned his elbows on the bar and studied Malkie's face. 'Ladies and gentlemen, I think we have a breakthrough.' Lorraine and the two other regular spectators of Malkie's thus-far futile attempt to find an alcoholic beverage he could actually enjoy, applauded him with single hand slaps on their tables.

Malkie slumped on his stool, sank into himself, and Lorraine patted his arm. Lorraine had lost her two children in a drink-related car accident years previously and seemed intent on drinking herself to death to go and join them.

Tommy had been a plumber, shafted by his own bank for the sake of some suit's annual bonus, and had never recovered enough self-respect to do anything other than drink his way through the proceeds from the bank selling his business out from under him.

Steven, Malkie's third booze buddy, sat at his usual table, but face down, his hand clamped to a half-finished pint.

'What's wrong with Stevie tonight?'

Monty sighed. 'His dad finally died. Last week.'

'Ach, poor sod, is he grieving?'

Monty snorted. 'Grieving, my arse. He's celebrating. Tommy's a free man at last, and the world is now his crustacean.'

'Mollusc.'

'Eh?'

'Nothing. Forget it.'

Malkie necked the remainder of the sickly-sweet liqueur in his shot glass, and – in honour of Stevie – necked another one from the bottle.

'Ach, Malkie, now I have to charge you for the whole bottle.'

The door opened. Malkie turned and his heart sank.

Steph sat on the stool beside his. 'You must be Monty. Can I have a G&T, please. Good stuff, if you have it.'

Monty feigned offence but turned to the rack of optics to find his decent gin.

Malkie scowled at her. 'How did you find me? I made a point of never telling you about this place.'

'Your dad mentioned Monty's name that night on the boat after the Callahan case. Easy enough to do a search on publicans within staggering distance of your previous digs.'

'Ah Callahan. Not my finest work, that.' He poured himself another measure of medicine and necked it. He was pleased to find it slid down more enjoyably than previously. This one might have some potential.

'Oh, stop that. You did what you could. We all did.'

Steph reached for the bottle, stoppered it and handed it to Monty. 'Put this somewhere safe, please, would you?'

Monty took the bottle, glanced at Malkie who nodded, and put Steph's G&T on the bar in front of her. She picked it up, but before taking a sip she scowled and rubbed the bottom of her hand. 'Good grief, Monty. Do you ever clean this bar?'

'Every year, whether it needs it or not, doll.'

Steph fixed him with a look that promised imminent castration. 'My name is Stephanie Lang. Steph to my friends. You can call me Detective Constable Lang, Monty.'

Monty grabbed a damp cloth and started wiping the bar. Steph tugged on Malkie's jacket sleeve and indicated one of several free tables; Malkie had never seen the place even half-full.

'We've got CCTV operators looking for that Anton Fisher guy. Megan Shaw has uniforms guarding her room twenty-four seven.'

She sipped her G&T and grimaced. 'Bloody tonic's flat. Why do you drink in a dump like this?'

Malkie gazed around at the pub. Grubby, peeling wallpaper, a tartan carpet worn through to the floorboards; only the lights above the bar did anything to brighten the place.

'I feel it reflects the man I aspire to be, Steph, if I'm not being over-ambitious.'

Steph turned on him but had the decency to keep her voice down. 'Now, you stop this shite, right now. I know about your Dog, mate, and I hate the bastard, but you have to rise above it.'

She sagged and the fury drained from her face. 'We need you, Malkie. Thompson needs your unique investigative talents. Damn it, *I* need you.' She stared down into her lap, and Malkie felt shame sluice through him. What had he told himself less than a week ago? Time to be there for her. He stood and crossed to the bar, picked up his unfinished glass of mineral water, and returned to sit beside her.

'Sorry, Steph. I'm here, now. I promise.'

He saw tears spill down her cheeks. She sniffed, quiet and miserable. Malkie took her hand in his and held it. She squeezed his fingers so hard he thought they might break.

He waited, could wait all night if he had to. As much as it

ripped his heart out to see Steph, of all people, laid bare and broken like this, he could wait as long as she needed him to.

'I know who he is.'

Malkie waited.

'My biological dad.'

Still, he waited.

'My Uncle Terry. Not a blood relative: a mate of my real uncle. A guy I knew from my infancy. He damned near brought me up whenever Mum was inside.' She looked up at him now, her eyes glassy and red-rimmed, bewildered and appalled. 'He raped his own best mate's sister. I used to fall asleep in his lap in front of the Saturday football on TV. Fuck's sake, I feel sick.'

She looked lost and bewildered. Both of them were only too aware of how low humans could sink, but this was her own family, her own childhood memories he was watching go sour and crumble inside her.

She looked into his eyes, desperate for him to make sense of it. 'Who does that, Malkie?'

'Only an animal, Steph. Only an animal.'

He turned in his seat to shield her from the view of the others and pulled her towards him. Monty raised a remote control and a TV hanging in one corner started playing some music channel. Malkie nodded to Monty over Steph's head, acknowledged the man's capacity for sensitivity when it mattered. Steph leaned into his chest and huddled there, clasped her arms between them as if holding herself together. And still, Malkie waited.

After long, long, seconds, she spoke again in a small and miserable voice.

'Malkie?'

'Yes, Steph?'

'I've got snot all down your shirt.'

'Disgusting,' he said.

She punched him on the arm, her 'go to' gesture for

disarming awkward moments. She managed a smile, but it was weak and didn't reach her eyes.

'You want to talk about it? Or not talk about it? Whatever you want. Just say, Steph. I'm happy to—'

'Oh, shut up, you old tart.' She laughed, a genuine laugh this time. 'Just be you, Malkie. That's what I need.' She considered for a moment. 'But maybe keep it shut for a while, aye?'

'Not sure I can do that, but I can steer clear of touchy-feely stuff, is that enough?'

She laughed again, and it warmed his heart.

They sat in silence and watched music videos, until the thought that had been rolling around inside his head all evening wouldn't wait any longer. 'There is one thing... You won't like it but I promise it'll distract you, I'm pretty sure of that. Something we need to discuss before we go to re-interview Shaw tomorrow.'

She looked curious and filled with dread at the same time. She necked the rest of her G&T and grimaced. 'Go for it.'

'While you were sending our Fearless Leader that photo of Fisher, I wandered back in to sit with Shaw for a minute.'

Steph's eyes flared.

'No, don't worry. She was out of it. 'But...' He stumbled, unsure of how to tell her about Shaw's cryptic mumblings.

He placed his phone on the table, lowered the volume, and played the audio clip.

Steph stared at the phone and pinched her lower lip with her fingers, something she always did when she needed to reach a safe and correct conclusion.

Eventually, she looked up at him. 'That's definitely her. No doubt about it?'

'It's her. I recorded it in her hospital room while you were away.'

'Why didn't you tell me about it, then?'

Malkie floundered. Steph was the last person on the planet

he ever expected to be fragile. How could he tell her he wasn't convinced she could handle this ugly development?

Steph's penny dropped. She squeezed his arm. 'Ah. Patronising but well-intentioned, as ever. Never mind. That is some bloody distraction, right enough. What the hell do we do with this?'

Malkie shrugged. 'That's why I'm sharing it with you. I don't trust myself to pass this on to Thompson. Maybe together we can...' He faltered as he saw the expression she turned on him.

'No way, mate. I'll stand beside you but I'm not playing her that. I love you more than you deserve but not that much. Sorry, no.'

He slumped. 'Fine. I'll tell her first thing in the morning. You stay at your desk. I don't want you getting dragged into this mess with me.'

He groaned. *How the hell is she going to react?* He could hear the conversation play out in his head. 'Sorry, boss, but the woman who's about to become an area commander as good as admitted she was responsible for Alice Garten's death.' The 'as good as' would nail him right after 'Are you certain that's what you heard?' and 'Hang on, you said she was sedated at the time?'

How bad could it go?

FIFTY-ONE

Uber geek Davina Tilson had never failed to disappoint Fisher, and she didn't this time.

Unlike Joey, who Fisher couldn't fear if he came after him out of his head with a machete, Davina was one woman he'd never piss off. She might not hurt you physically, but she'd empty your bank accounts and cancel your credit cards in a second. Her speciality was blackmailing people she considered to be the pond-life of society. Anyone who made their money by screwing others out of theirs, anyone who stole from old ladies or overcharged for resealing their driveways with nothing more than soap and water, and especially those she considered the worst of the worst: any politician.

Fisher himself had been on the receiving end of countless 'I see what you do when your wife is out' emails, and he'd ignored them all. The difference with Davina was that she really did have video footage of people enjoying the best of the internet and she really would publish given half an excuse. Unlike the Eastern European gangs that ran thriving industries on scaremongering the innocent and guilty alike into handing over huge sums of Bitcoins 'just in case', she always sent her targets a thirty-second clip of their orgasm faces to make sure the funds were sent, usually within minutes. She and Fisher used to watch them over pizzas and beers and piss themselves.

The other thing about Davina was that she hoarded. Every bedroom in her flat was stuffed full of shelving units stacked with electrical devices and cables and chargers and old PCs and games consoles and PDAs. She had always been the epitome of the phrase 'early adopter' and never, ever threw anything away. With only the briefest glance at the Nokia Fisher held out to her and a quick check that the battery hadn't leaked, she disappeared into one of the rooms and reappeared with a charger. She plugged it in, and Fisher was relieved to see the display – chunky white pixels against a black background – inform them it was charging.

Fisher had brought pizza and beers, but Davina finished a cheese sandwich and two chocolate fingers before starting on the pizza.

Fisher pointed at them. 'Is my pizza not good enough for you?'

'Habit,' she replied, without inflection. She turned her head to the other room and whistled. Before Fisher could ask why, he heard a thump followed by claws on a floor and a three-legged dog walked into the room looking old and grey and sleepy. The dog wandered up to her, she gave it a couple of slices of ham from the pizza, then the dog wandered off again.

'When did you get a dog? Does that even count as a dog, that skinny wee thing?'

Davina tutted, turned a disapproving look on him. 'He's my guard whippet. Don't laugh. He's fast and mean for his age. You, of all people, should appreciate that.'

'What's his name?'

She grinned. 'Gimpy.'

Before Fisher could ask why, the phone beeped. Davina

stopped the video just in time to save them from seeing another victim gurn and grunt his way onto her list.

She turned on the phone and waited an age for it to boot. It flashed 'No network' and wouldn't respond to any button press.

Davina took it from him. 'Expected but it's always worth a try. Come through to my inner sanctum, old man.' She led him to what had to be her workshop, her centre of operations. She opened the back of the phone and pulled the SIM card out, a huge, old thing, twice the size of the ones used nowadays. She rummaged in a pile of what Fisher took to be junk until she pulled a plastic box out wrapped in gaffer tape, with a dozen wires hanging out of one end and a single one hanging out the other. He recognised the single cable as a modern USB-C, but the others were like nothing he'd ever seen.

'Made this myself. It's a bit like you, Fisher.'

He scowled at her. 'Continue.'

'Ancient and a bit rough to look at but still got it where it matters.' She grinned at him. She knew just how dangerous he could be, but they both knew she was too useful to ever fear him.

She selected one of the dozen wires and pushed the SIM card into a socket on the end of it, then plugged the single plug into a laptop. She started up some piece of software that looked nothing like what he was used to seeing on a computer. No high-resolution, colourful icons or graphics and no windows, just simple green text on a black background. Her fingers flew across her keyboard, stopping occasionally to wait for the screen to update. Strings of letters and numbers and other symbols flew past, and he managed to make no sense of any of it.

'OK, what do you need?'

Fisher stared at her, shrugged. He had no idea.

'No idea. What's on there?'

She smiled at him, tolerant and patronising. He often felt an urge to give her a slap but he'd managed to resist, so far.

She entered some more gibberish and a load of text scrolled down her screen. She waited for it to stop, then grabbed her mouse and flicked a wheel on top of it. The text rolled up again, faster than he could follow, then she reversed direction and scrolled back again slowly.

'OK, we have... nothing. It's empty. No messages. No contacts. Nothing. Nowt.'

'Fuck it. I needed to find something. Fuck it. Is there no memory card? Nothing?'

'No. SD memory cards weren't introduced until 1999. It's a dead phone, Fisher. Empty as Gimpy's head.' She shrugged, her face suggesting *Don't shoot the messenger*.

Fisher threw the remains of a pizza slice down, sat back, closed his eyes, and swore under his breath more times than he could count. When he opened his eyes, Davina was admiring the phone. 'This is in really good nick. Been looked after. I might get a few notes for this on eBay. Can I keep it?

Fisher waved his hand at her. Least he could do: Davina never charged him for her services.

She smiled, polished the casing on her sleeve. She removed the battery from the back and flipped it over.

They both saw it.

A folded sheet of the thinnest paper Fisher could ever remember seeing. Sellotaped to the back of the battery.

They looked at each other, eyebrows raised. Both leaned in, their curiosity piqued.

She peeled the paper off and unfolded it.

Photographs. Seven of them. Labelled Crawford, Gaddon, Balfour, Ferguson, Crosbie, Shaw. And Fisher.

It took Fisher a few seconds to get his words out. The face labelled 'Shaw' was her. Montrose.

'Davina, get one of those search things up and look for "Megan Shaw" and "Montrose".'

Davina's fingers flew across the keyboard and a web page

appeared, some kind of corporate networking thing, a photo of Montrose top-right and a bio. Fisher scanned it. When he found what he'd thought he would, he swore under his breath at his own stupidity. She'd got a divorce only a few years ago. She had reverted to her maiden name but her son had stayed a Montrose, of course.

He took the sheet of paper from Claudette's Glencoe photo from his pocket and scanned the table of initialled details, and suddenly everything made perfect, hilarious sense.

FIFTY-TWO

When Malkie arrived at the station for morning briefing, the Major Investigation Team had landed.

He was surprised they'd taken so long to appear, and he had to wonder why the stabbing of one junkie and the fatal exsanguination of two victims hadn't been enough to pull them from other cases. He suspected the stabbing of someone as far up the command structure as Shaw – even though superficial and not fatal – had accelerated their response, while the deaths of three others before and after, hadn't.

When he arrived, Malkie saw them through the window in the door to Interview Room 2. McLeish and Thompson sat with them, Thompson attentive and taking notes, McLeish leaning forward, elbows on the table, engrossed in one of the MIT officer's words and nodding, sombre and appreciative of some pearl of professional wisdom.

He found Steph at her desk, reviewing the case file, and looking like nothing was jumping off the screen at her. 'We've got nothing, Malkie. Nothing.' She swivelled her chair to face him.

'SOCOs have found DNA at both murder scenes, but as

usual there's a backlog. They hope to get something to us this afternoon. Not one sighting of Crosbie. It's as if she's a seventy-something-year-old ninja granny. Where she lives, out in the sticks, there are very few cameras, but you'd think she'd show up on a bus camera or something. Or a supermarket. Even a hit from a corner shop would be something. Where the hell is she and what's she doing?'

She shook her head, as clueless as he was. 'No sighting of Ben Hutchison either,' said Steph. 'Bearing in mind the state he was in when I saw him, and Lizzie Taylor's assurances that he barely functioned unless told what to do, I can't imagine him escaping wherever he is, assuming he was abducted. I wonder if that Fisher guy has him? Is he behind these killings? Was Crosbie just the first in a set he was intent on cleaning up, only he massively underestimated her? And if that's the case, there are' – she counted off the names on Gucci's list – 'two names unaccounted for. Where are they?'

She threw her pen at her desk, laid her head on the back of her chair, and sighed. 'We've got nothing, old man. Nothing. And now MIT will want us to go over every door-to-door, every interview, every shred of the scant intelligence we've managed to gather.'

The door to Interview Room 2 opened and Thompson appeared first. She cast Malkie and Steph a resigned look as she passed them on her way to the front of the CID room. Two MIT officers appeared next, with McLeish close behind them, gesturing towards the CID room.

The male officer was of medium height with thinning fair hair, wearing a sensible suit and tie and expensive-looking wire-frame glasses. The other was female, black pencil skirt and plain white blouse, minimal make-up and dark hair swept severely back from her forehead and gathered into a bright purple scrunchie. She smiled at Malkie and Steph as she passed their desks. Neither returned it.

Thompson sighed and settled back in a chair. McLeish stood to attention at the front of class.

'We have been joined today by two officers from MIT. That's the Major Investigation Team, Malkie.' Cue sniggers from around the room and a stony stare from Malkie.

'They regret they couldn't join us earlier, but they're here now to offer their full support, see if we can make some progress on our double MisPers and our double murders.' Thompson shot him a glare from behind, not quite subtle enough to escape the notice of the gathered officers.

'I'd like to introduce to you DCI Martin McGowan and DI Donna Campbell.' McLeish stepped to one side and gestured for the MIT pair to step forward. The obsequiousness came off him in waves.

McGowan spoke first. 'Good morning, all. As DI McLeish has already said we can only apologise for our late arrival. Normally we should be assigned at the first sign of a homicide, but operational matters delayed us getting freed up to be reassigned.'

Malkie closed his eyes to stop his reaction earning him another kicking from Thompson. *Aye, like finding out a DCS might get dragged into it.*

He looked around the room. 'Can DS Malcolm McCulloch identify himself, please?'

A buzz went around the room, bottoms were shuffled on chairs.

Malkie raised his hand. 'That's me, sir.'

McGowan smiled at him. 'Can you and DC Lang, and DI Thompson, join me in Interview Room 1 immediately after morning briefing, please, and we'll get cracking right away, aye?' His smile seemed genuine and Malkie decided to withhold judgment for now.

McGowan continued. 'Those of you not directly involved in DS McCulloch's case, we'll try our damnedest not to disrupt the smooth running of your cases, but we may – with the permission of acting DCI McLeish and DI Thompson – ask for occasional assistance with investigative actions. On a priority basis, of course.' He glanced at McLeish, who nodded and opened his mouth, but McGowan continued.

'I'd like to be out of here by the end of next week, before the Scotland v Italy game at Murrayfield. I think we can go all the way this year, and I'd like to be able to enjoy it. With that, I'll hand you back to acting DCI McLeish. I look forward to working with you all.'

He backed up to stand beside DI Campbell, who had remained reactionless throughout and continued to do so.

McLeish reclaimed his rightful spot in the limelight. The remainder of the briefing was conducted much as usual, although McLeish couldn't help but comment on the fact that Malkie's case on the agenda would be skipped in deference to the MIT.

Back at their desks, Malkie and Steph stared at each other. Malkie went first.

'Are we better off now, or not? I can't decide.'

Steph sighed. 'Well, we have a proper DCI on board now, unlike McLeish just playing at being one. That might help expedite operational matters, but I suspect we're about to come under a huge amount of pressure to deliver, above and beyond the usual, I mean.'

'Fuck.'

'Indeed.'

McGowan appeared at their desks. 'DS McCulloch and DC Lang, shall we start?' He walked off towards the interview room. Malkie and Steph followed, and Thompson hurried out of her office, presumably loath to let Malkie's mouth start without checks and balances in place.

DI Campbell closed the door behind them. Thompson, Malkie and Steph sat on one side of the table, Campbell and

McGowan on the other. McGowan pulled a manila file from a briefcase he'd left beside the table earlier. He opened it and made them wait while he studied the first three pages. Eventually he spoke without lifting his eyes from the papers.

'Bit of a shit show, isn't it?' He looked up and smiled. Malkie's hackles rose but settled again; the man seemed almost genuine, for Management.

McGowan closed the file and sat up straight. He interlaced his fingers on the table in front of him.

'OK, I've read the file and I've reviewed the case notes so far, and here's how I see things. Please correct me if I'm wrong.'

Thompson shuffled in her chair. As uncomfortable as Malkie was finding this and he imagined Steph was, too, it would be nothing compared to the pressure on her.

'We have three homicides, one possibly self-defence. One civilian and two ex-Uniform. All victims identified. Offender IDs suspected but not confirmed. Two related MisPers. And homicide risks identified against two further individuals, both ex-Uniform. Is that all correct?'

Thompson nodded. 'Sir.'

'For the moment, DI Campbell here will co-lead as your liaison with MIT and all the benefits our specialism can bring, but I'll be backing her up with necessary approvals and authorisations, OK? I'm too swamped to take active lead at the moment, but I was asked to show my face because of DCS Shaw's attack. Isn't politics great?'

Malkie glanced at Thompson, who looked as surprised as he felt.

McGowan grinned. 'We get a lot of friction from CID officers sometimes, would you believe? Locals see us as clueless and interfering nuisances. I know, it's hard to believe, isn't it?'

He grinned again. Even Campbell managed a small, wry smile.

'Nothing could be further from the truth. If our experience

and separate perspective might spot something you folk didn't then we will, of course, discuss it with you, but otherwise we're here to work alongside you and grease any wheels we can to expedite your investigation.'

He delinked his fingers and placed his hands palms-down on the table. 'And that's it. I'm going to bugger off back to our office and leave you in the capable hands of DI Campbell. DCI has attended, box ticked, I shall now leave you to it.'

He stood. 'Now, does that sound good to all concerned?'

Malkie and Steph looked to Thompson, who nodded but looked uncomfortable doing so. 'Yes, sir. Er, thank you.'

McGowan put his overcoat on, packed his manila file in his briefcase, smiled once more at them, and left.

Malkie and Steph and Thompson stared at each other, as if all wondering what the hell had just happened.

Campbell leaned forward. 'He's magnificent, isn't he?' She stared at them, waited for a response. None came. She laughed, slapped her hand on the table. 'Oh, good God. Lighten up.'

She settled back in her chair, still chuckling to herself, and opened her own manila file.

'It looks to me like you guys have done everything the Murder Investigation Manual dictates and more – door-to-doors, CCTV and other passive data opportunities checked, interviews recorded and cross-referenced, ID established on both of your MisPers and your murder victims. SOCO reports inconclusive from the scenes of both Crosbie and Hutchison's disappearances, and still to arrive from the murder scenes. I believe no computers or mobile phones were found at Crosbie's or Hutchison's residences. That's odd, in this day and age, but I gather both MisPers were solitary and reclusive individuals. So, no digital strategy required, so far. I'm guessing financial checks and ID verification have taken place?'

Thompson nodded again. 'All done by the book. ID was verbal in both cases initially but verified formally soon afterwards. We're having trouble finding out where Lillian Crosbie banked because we didn't find a single item of paperwork in her entire home except one photograph which appears to link Crosbie to Hutchison, many years ago. No bills, bank statements, insurance policies, pension statements. Nothing. Mr Hutchison's sister pointed us to a firm of solicitors in Edinburgh. We believed we had insufficient cause to seek a warrant to see their files on Mr Hutchison's affairs but we've escalated that given the fact he appears to have been abducted from his room at the shelter he's lived at for the past forty-five years, and also given our murder cases. We haven't found any trace of Mr Hutchison or Miss Crosbie. Absolutely none, which is exceedingly strange given how difficult it is to disappear off-grid, these days.'

Thompson took a breath. 'However, on Wednesday we obtained new information that has proved to be highly significant.'

Campbell looked at her, interested; Shaw's photograph of Fisher might not have been uploaded before she took her copy of the file.

Thompson opened her file and produced a copy of the photograph Shaw had given them. 'This is Anton Fisher. DCS Shaw told us he's been in touch with her and is threatening to derail her forthcoming promotion by telling all who will listen that Shaw conducted a cover-up in 1978 to protect Lillian Crosbie from the consequences of her actions. She doesn't know whether he hopes to blackmail her or what other motive he might have. Detective Sergeant McCulloch has positively identified Fisher as the man he saw in Crosbie's home the night Billy Irvine was killed and Crosbie went missing.

'Of course, we also have Shaw's stabbing by Lillian Crosbie. We were all a little confused by how seventy-something-year-old Crosbie managed to enter Shaw's home despite heightened security since a recent break-in, but Shaw assures us there's no chance she was mistaken. Lillian Crosbie tried to kill her. Again, motive unclear at the moment. We've asked forensics to expedite the blood and other DNA analysis from the murder scenes, but we don't have a DNA sample from Fisher, so we'll need to keep that for later, hopefully after we apprehend him.'

Campbell listened to every word in silence, then blew her lips out and raised her eyebrows. 'Excellent case summary, DI Thompson. And as my boss said, what a shit show, eh?'

Thompson sighed. 'You're not bloody kidding.'

After a surprised second, all smiled and Malkie felt some of the tension bleed away. Campbell seemed OK, and deserving of a chance.

Campbell held her hands out in invitation. 'This is primarily your case, so please tell me what your next investigative actions will be and how I can help. I can ask DCI McGowan to have a word with forensics, see if he can hurry along the reports, for a start.'

Thompson nodded. 'That would be a great help. Thanks. We're currently devoting all our efforts to confirming Fisher's identity and trying to locate him. Apart from the fact that all the usual procedures have turned up absolutely nothing of use so far, he's the only person other than our MisPers and murder victims we can definitively say is up to his neck in this, somehow.'

Campbell smiled. 'I know that feeling. Doing all you can and nothing's happening. And with Shaw's attack and whatever involvement she had in poor Alice Garten's death all these years ago – yes, I pulled those files, too – the pressure on this one is going to be an absolute pig, right?'

She turned to Malkie and Steph. 'I've heard good things about you, DC Lang.'

Steph nodded, gracious.

'And I've heard mixed reports about you, DS McCulloch.'

Malkie smiled and shrugged. 'I can be a tad accident-prone, DI Campbell.'

Thompson snorted. 'It's your gob we always have to worry about, Malkie. But I can attest' – She turned back to Campbell – 'Malkie's instincts are among the very best, and no one can ever question his dedication and his commitment. I'll vouch for him, gladly, whatever you've heard.'

Campbell studied Malkie, then cracked a broad grin. 'Good. I hate drones. OK, is there anything else any of you feel I should be aware of for now?'

Malkie and Steph shared a glance. Steph answered, 'No, nothing else for now.'

Thompson stared at Steph – one eyebrow raised – for a few seconds, but Steph didn't elaborate.

Campbell stood. 'DI Thompson, is there a desk I can use?'

'Yes, of course.' Thompson stood and opened the interview room door.

Campbell turned back to Malkie and Steph. 'Did you get around to checking out the quote on that photo you found in Crosbie's bedroom? "*Time and silence*"?'

Malkie and Steph glanced at each other. Malkie spoke first, didn't want Steph to take any flak that might be coming. 'Not yet. DC Rab, sorry Robert, Lundy was meant to check it out but he never got back to us.'

Campbell feigned disappointment. 'Shame.' She walked through and Thompson glanced at Malkie and Steph. She scowled a question at them, then followed Campbell.

Steph gaped at Malkie. 'Accident-prone? Seriously?'

Malkie shrugged. 'What else would you call me?'

Steph stood and walked out. She called over her shoulder, 'A well-intentioned disaster zone is what you are, mate.'

She disappeared down the hallway towards the CID room. He heard her calling, 'Rab? Where are you, Rab?'

FIFTY-THREE

'I'm ready for you, Crosbie. Come and get me. I'm hammered enough, now. Christ, there's still a quarter bottle left. That won't do.'

Claudette necked most of the remainder of the vodka without stopping for breath. Something in her, some fundamental, lizard-brain survival instinct tried to make her throw up, to purge the lethal levels of alcohol from her blood, but she refused it. When acid burned up her throat and demanded to be released, she swallowed it back down with more vodka and kept drinking.

She'd wanted to lose all consciousness and never wake again, but all those years of drinking now made her wonder if any amount of booze would be enough to black her out completely.

She turned to scan the room. Everything swam. She threw up anyway, her stubborn death wish losing a battle with her physiological self-preservation mechanisms.

Physiological self-preservation mechanisms. How the hell am I capable of coming out with plummy shite like that in this state?

She stood, with more difficulty than she expected – so why was she still conscious? She staggered to the kitchen, rummaged in the cupboard under the sink. Bottles of cleaning product tumbled out as her hands swept everything out in careless, flailing swings of arms she barely retained any control of.

No booze. No more bottles. And she wasn't where she wanted to be, yet.

She crawled back through to her armchair. She'd sat in the one with its back to the front door, and left the door unlocked. She didn't even want to see Crosbie. She just wanted it done. Some part of her still quailed at the thought of pain and violence and whatever punishment Crosbie would consider fitting for her betrayal.

Claudette had harboured her doubts since the night it all happened. Crosbie was never the kind of officer to show much initiative at anything. Superb at following process and protocol, shite at thinking on her feet or taking action without leadership. If she had pushed that poor girl out into the cold on a shitty night like that, someone had to have put her up to it. Shaw? No, she had too much to lose. All that female empowerment stuff and her on posters in every station in Scotland. It was ridiculous. But Shaw took it seriously. No, if Shaw did anything wrong, it was trying to cover up for Crosbie. She should have cut her loose and let her answer for her own actions. It could have been that pathetic idiot Ferguson. She was a sour-faced wee sulk at the best of times, but she couldn't hear Crosbie's name for years afterwards without going off on one. Did Ferguson tell Crosbie to throw the girl out the door, that night?

Claudette heard the front door open, the metal insulation strip scraping on the threshold. Who would have thought a bit of neglected DIY would turn out to be the first sign Claudette's days were about to end?

She upended the last vodka bottle and was pleased to feel a few cool drops land on her tongue. She dropped the bottle and held her arms out. She remembered her phone, the text she'd typed in earlier. She managed to hit the send button with her thumb after a couple of attempts, then she dropped it to the floor. It didn't matter if Crosbie read it, as long as Fisher did. He was a sadistic bastard but he could be relied on to see something through.

'Come and get me, Lillian. Do your worst. I think I'm pissed enough I won't feel anything.'

She waited. She closed her eyes but that made her head swim even more and threatened to bring up the remainder of the vodka in her stomach.

A hand, cold and wrinkled and knotty, rested on her shoulder. She raised one of her own and placed it on top. 'Your hand is freezing, old girl. You need to wrap up better. Not good to go wandering about in the snow, Lillian.' She laughed, and while she laughed she marvelled at the ability of so much alcohol to render even her own imminent death a thing to be laughed at, rather than the terrifying and desperate ordeal some cowering scrap of her rational mind feared.

The hand on her shoulder lifted to her cheek, and Claudette leaned her head sideways into it, nestled her face into the cold and leathery fingers.

'I'm sorry, Lillian. That's the truth.'

'Shhhhhh,' a voice whispered, comforting and calm, and Claudette smiled: this was right, this was just. This was no murder about to take place. This was a settling of old accounts, the honourable payment of debts due. A balancing of past sins and restoration of justice. The woman had been wronged and they all deserved to pay penance to her. Now it was Claudette's turn, and she embraced it like a sinner given one last chance to do good, to get something, anything, in their credit column.

The fingers pulled gently from Claudette's and rested on her arm, slid the sleeve of her cardigan up her forearm. Claudette watched in fascination, all fear dulled by the blessed numbing and mental dislocating effects of so much vodka. Her executioner reached around from behind to hold the arm while the other hand drew a blade down its length. Blood seeped, then ran, down to her wrist. Both hands let go of her arm, and she lifted it to watch the blood – so much blood, her blood – pour back down to her elbow. The hands from behind pushed her arm gently back down to hang towards the floor. Only now, she noticed someone had put her washing-up basin from the kitchen sink on the floor.

'Ah good. I love this rug.' She waved her fingers and watched her blood trace patterns on the plastic before too much had drained and all was one dark, red surface.

'This makes sense, Lillian. This seems right. Appropriate. We reap what we sow, right?'

A hand stroked her hair and the voice said 'Shhhhh' again.

Claudette closed her eyes. Something about the finality of what she could still just barely understand was happening settled her. She felt a new kind of numbness and light-headedness sweep through her to add to the effects of the alcohol.

'We let you down, Lillian. All of us. We should have... You know... Sorry...'

She gazed around and up and wished she hadn't.

'Who the hell are you?'

FIFTY-FOUR

Malkie returned to his desk with a stinking headache. Thompson had nailed both him and Steph for the look they'd shared and they'd had to tell her everything.

Four murders, one just the wrong idiot in the wrong place at the wrong time and three they'd had on a list but who'd dropped off the radar so effectively that Malkie's team had failed to get to them before Crosbie did.

He stopped his own train of thought. Was he still believing a seventy-something-year-old woman could do all of this? And if she did, simply to settle such an old score? Because Shaw had told the entire country that Crosbie had let an innocent girl die, so long ago? It made no sense. Unless it was Fisher who was committing all the murders, after all. But then Crosbie knew everyone on the list whereas there was no indication that Fisher knew any of the officers on the list in the late seventies. And Shaw had said Fisher had threatened to blackmail her, nothing about suspecting him of having killed anyone else.

All of which dragged him inexorably back to Shaw's mutterings. Thompson's reaction had matched what both Malkie and Steph had predicted. She had started on at Malkie for such an egregious breach of protocol, recording a senior – damned near executive – Police Scotland officer while she lay unconscious and addled with sedatives, without her knowledge or permission. The inadmissibility of the recording came nowhere close to being the salient issue, though, and they all knew it.

'What the bloody hell were you thinking, Malkie? Even by your standards, this is off the stupid scale. Can you imagine the depth of shite you'll land us all in if she ever finds out?'

'Ma'am?'

Thompson held up a finger, the same way Steph did to Malkie so often. He wondered if she found it as bloody irritating as he always did.

'Malkie?'

His temper broke. 'Do you want to hear it? Or do you want me to delete it? Then we can all pretend we never heard the damned thing?' He pulled his phone from his pocket and started pushing buttons. 'And we can all go back to having fuck-all and try to forget that Detective Chief Superintendent Megan fucking Shaw as good as admitted to...' He couldn't get the words out.

Thompson finished for him. 'Admitted to some level of responsibility in the death of Alice Garten beyond that previously thought to be the case.'

Malkie slumped in his chair, dropped his phone on the desk. They all stared at it. Malkie could swear he saw Thompson's brain working, weighing up her curiosity to hear Shaw's words for herself against the much wiser course of action: plausible deniability.

Steph stood. 'With all due respect, bosses, this is way above my pay grade. I'll be at my desk, wallowing in despair.'

Thompson sat back in her chair. 'Oh sit down, Steph. We all need to talk about this. No, don't worry, I'll make sure none of this falls on you. Malkie and I are on the hook for this one.'

Steph sat again but looked about as unhappy doing so as

anyone could. She pushed her chair back from the table, as if to put at least some symbolic distance between her and whatever was going to be discussed.

Thompson stretched her arms above her head, grimaced as she tried to work what must be unbearable tension from her shoulders. 'I'm at a loss, guys. What we're all thinking is that Megan Shaw was far more responsible for Alice Garten's death than she claims she was. But without any kind of evidence – actionable evidence, I mean – what the hell can we do? I'm not even comfortable logging this as inadmissible intel. Actually, I don't want this anywhere within a million miles of the case file.'

Malkie twirled his phone on the desk. 'I could just ask her about it.'

Both women shook their heads, as if stunned even he would suggest something so stupid.

'Think about it. Whether she's guilty of what we think she might be guilty of, she'll deny all involvement, that's a given. What if I say I heard her say it, but I don't tell her I recorded it? Just to see her reaction?'

Thompson and Steph shared a long look. Steph shrugged but said nothing.

'You realise if she comes to me with a formal complaint, I'm going to have to tell her I expressly ordered you to say nothing about what you claimed you heard, right? I mean, I'll have to hang you out to dry. Your pension might not survive what she could do to you. Are you really prepared to risk that?'

Malkie shrugged. 'She can't hurt me for asking. Last I checked, investigating intel from any source wasn't against protocol whether that intel turned into actionable evidence or not. Worst I can see happening from asking is another black mark, and if we're honest with ourselves, what's one more of them on my record, right?'

Thompson shrugged as if to concede the point.

All sat in silence for a while. Thompson would be weighing

up the pros and cons of setting Malkie's gob loose on such a senior officer. Steph would be wondering if she felt like accompanying him, for all the good that would do if his mouth got carried away.

Malkie just wanted to crack on.

As they waited, a knock sounded on Thompson's door, and Rab Lundy's face appeared. 'You were looking for me, Steph?'

'Yes. Where the hell have you been? Did you manage to identify that quote from Crosbie's photo?'

'Aye, I did. Sorry, did I not pass that on? It's from some old book called *The Count of Monte Cristo*, by some guy called Alexander Dumbass.' He grinned, proud of his literary wit, then strutted away back to the CID room.

Malkie groaned and slumped back in his chair. He banged the heel of one hand against his forehead. 'No, no, no. Damn it, no.'

Thompson's patience broke first. 'What?'

Malkie opened his eyes and looked around the room as if contemplating a dash for escape rather than say any more. '*The Count of Monte Cristo.* I never read it but I think it's about a man wrongly accused of a crime who then exacts his revenge years later.'

Thompson blanched. Steph threw her head back and groaned. 'Did Rab never think to bring this to us immediately? Certainly shines a whole new light on this case.'

'And on Shaw's half-conscious ramblings.' Malkie tried to keep the I-told-you-so from his face but Thompson's warning glare told him he'd failed.

She came to a decision. 'Oh, good grief. Malkie, go. Steph, I'm ordering you specifically not to go with him. Are we clear? All of us?'

Steph nodded, more emphatically than necessary. 'Yes, boss. I have no intention at this time of going anywhere near Glasgow tonight, boss.'

'Crystal, Susan. I absolutely am going back to bloody Glasgow despite you ordering me specifically not to, and I have no intention at this time of requesting Detective Constable Lang to accompany me.'

After a long pause, Thompson stepped over a line Malkie never, in a million years, thought she would. She nodded with a look of dread at Malkie's phone.

'God help us all. Play the damned thing.'

FIFTY-FIVE

[CC] [17:46]

It's me. Claudette. I've been waiting for her,
made it easy for her. I've had enough. If I've
sent this, then she's here and I haven't drunk
enough and I'm still awake. Christ, I hope it
doesn't hurt too much. Well, bye all. It's been a
pleasure knowing some of you. Oh, and the
bitch on Mark Balfour's phone we were all so
scared of. I think that was Shaw, all along.

[17:47]

Detective Chief Superintendent Megan fucking
Shaw.

FIFTY-SIX

As Malkie was about to leave for Glasgow a knock at Thompson's door preceded Gucci's hesitant face, peering through the gap. 'Sorry, boss. Courier just delivered something I think you need to see. Label says "FAO SIO Lillian Crosbie case – urgent".' She held an envelope to Malkie. He reached for it but Thompson took it from Gucci's hand. Gucci fled, looked relieved to back out the door and close it on whatever awkward conversation she'd interrupted.

Thompson opened the envelope, scanned it, then dropped it on her desk, lunged for her phone and quick-dialled a number. 'Bernie, DI Thompson here. The courier who delivered this envelope for me. Did he show you any ID?' A pause. 'Damn it. OK, Bernie, can you line up the CCTV for the foyer and the car park, please? Aye, urgent. I'll be there in a minute.' She disappeared out into the corridor but said, 'Look but don't touch,' over her shoulder as she left.

Malkie and Steph craned their necks to read the paper.

The paper looked old, stiff and dry, and the ink had faded. An ancient police Custody Record sheet dated December 31st 1977. A table with three columns, filled from the top to halfway down the page. It looked to have been torn from a book. On the last few lines they saw four entries with the same name in the leftmost column: Alice Garten. First, Garten's initial booking-in, signed 'MS'. Then two entries that looked to be regular hourly checks, both signed 'LC'. Finally, an entry stating that Garten had been released on her own recognisance.

It was initialled 'MS'.

By the time Malkie and Steph reached the office behind the front reception desk, Bernie Stevenson and Thompson were already watching the recorded CCTV footage.

Thompson saw them arrive and beckoned them over. 'Can you start that one again please, Bernie?'

Bernie clicked an earlier point on the video timeline at the bottom of the screen, and the video jumped back. A man, big, powerful-looking, balding, leather jacket and jeans, walked through the front door and up to the front desk. He made no effort to hide his face.

Anton Fisher handed an envelope to Bernie, then nodded at the camera, turned, and walked away while Bernie held the deliveries book up and called after him.

Malkie sprinted for the front door. He didn't expect to find Fisher waiting for him but had to try. He stood outside the huge glass doors and cast his eyes across the landscaped lawns that surrounded the Livingston Civic Centre, that housed, amongst other admin and legal functions, West Lothian's Police Scotland headquarters.

He scanned the darkness, the shadows of bushes and trees on the far side of the lawns, the lighted walkway that led to a footbridge over the River Almond towards the twin shopping centres. Would Fisher have the balls to watch him from some shadows, somewhere? He knew Thompson would be moving on to check the Automatic Number Plate Recognition cameras at the entrance to the car park. Trouble was, unless Fisher was a very stupid man, he wouldn't have driven his car anywhere near the station for just that reason. No, he had to have fled on foot.

Malkie took one last look around the perimeter of the grounds, then returned inside.

Steph was waiting for him. 'No hits from the car park ANPR. Was that him? You sure it was him?'

'Bloody right, it was him. Bastard. What the hell is he playing at?'

They returned to Thompson's office. She'd procured an evidence bag and sat studying the sheet, safely isolated in plastic, on her desk.

When Malkie and Steph walked in, Thompson looked up at them. 'Take a photo of this and get it off to Forensics right away. After you've talked to Shaw again, get out there and bloody well find Lillian Crosbie. I'm going to ask Donna Campbell to ask her boss to kick some arse at Forensics and get us those scene reports tonight.

'And send Rab back to Fisher's address. He already checked it after he got it from the electoral roll, said it looked like Fisher's been home and packed in a hurry, but check again, anyway. I'll get on to Tech Forensics, ask if there have been any hits on Crosbie or Fisher or Hutchison on CCTV anywhere. Wouldn't be the first time they'd found something but taken an age to get it to us.'

FIFTY-SEVEN

In the secure car park, Malkie headed for his own car. He always dumped the driving on Steph, but officially she wasn't coming with him this time, was she?

Steph climbed into the passenger side and looked out the windscreen. 'I'm not here. You ain't seen me, right?' She tapped her nose and smiled. Another joke, another cultural reference that had bypassed Malkie's whole life. Like PC Misha Howarth's 'gonna need a bigger crime scene'. What the hell was that about?

He pulled his phone and dialled the nurses' station at Glasgow Hospital.

'Ward seven. Can I help you?'

'Hi. This is Detective Sergeant Malcolm McCulloch from West Lothian CID. I just wanted to clear an out-of-hours visit to DCS Megan Shaw. It's related to official police business, and it's imperative we—'

'Ms Shaw discharged herself earlier today, Detective McCulloch. She dismissed the constable that was on duty outside her room when a couple of large gentlemen in suits arrived. Her own private security, she said. The constable seemed reluctant to let her go but I believe Ms Shaw is a pretty senior officer? Did no one tell you?'

Malkie sighed. So much for joined-up Police Scotland. 'No, nobody told me. Thank you. I'll catch DCS Shaw at home.' He hung up.

Steph scowled at him. 'Nobody told you what?'

'Shaw discharged herself. But you didn't hear that from me because you're not here, right?'

'Damned right. She must have gone home.' She looked in her phone and typed Shaw's Edinburgh address into Malkie's dashboard satnav.

When the route map appeared, Malkie decided a brief detour was called for.

'Can we stop somewhere on the way, Steph? Just for ten minutes?'

'Where?'

He hesitated. She'd also been there before, during their last major investigation together, and he hadn't covered himself in glory.

'The LESOC.'

She turned to stare at him. 'Callahan or Fleming?'

He kept his eyes on the road, couldn't look at her. 'Fleming. Deborah. I visited Callahan's grave a couple of days ago and she came out to see me.'

They drove in silence for a while.

'I'll only need ten minutes.'

Silence for several seconds, then, 'Will she want to see you again, you think?'

Now he looked at her, waited for her to look back. 'She said she would.'

She thought for a few seconds before answering. 'Good luck, mate. Whatever it is, good luck with it.'

'Thanks, partner.'

At the LESOC, Steph got out and started walking back towards the entrance gate. 'Going to stretch my legs. Pick me up at the entrance when you're done. I know you'll realise this already, but this is pushing our luck. We need to get to Shaw sharpish, mate, aye?'

Malkie smiled at her back: he would never deserve her.

Dame Helen Reid smiled as he appeared in her doorway. 'I saw you pull up. Was that Ms Lang I saw, too? Deborah's on her way down, already. I called her.' Mischief glinted in her eyes. As Malkie turned to go, she said, 'I think you two might just be good for each other Detective McCulloch. I hope so. Be a good friend to her would you, please?'

Malkie expected to feel pressure, an expectation of taking on another responsibility he could screw up like so many before. But he didn't and smiled inside. When an elevator door opened and she trundled into the hallway in a motorised wheelchair, the smile reached his face.

'Detective Dirty Old Man, hello.' Malkie laughed, and her face beamed back at him despite her scars. He found himself lost for words. From the first instant he met Deborah, during his failed attempt to bring tormented ex-soldier Walter Callahan home safely, he had known he would always find strength and inspiration in this woman's stubborn refusal to let even the worst of injuries break her. He realised he felt a depth of fondness for her already, after only a few short meetings, a fondness he couldn't remember feeling for any other woman he'd met. More, the depth of his affection didn't frighten him, and it didn't scare the hell out of him that he might hurt her.

Deborah trundled out the front door and down the ramp, and Malkie followed her. They crossed the circular drive to the duck pond where they'd first met. Malkie took a seat on the same bench.

Deborah stared at him, her hands resting in her lap, one hand gloved in leathery burn scars and twisted inward. He noticed for the first time that she was missing two fingers on that hand. He lifted his gaze to her face, similarly scarred and striated, one eye filmed over, the other clear and bright, and her teeth... When she smiled, only half her face lifted, but her teeth gleamed. Somehow the helicopter crash that had wrecked so much of her had left her perfect, beautiful teeth unmarked. Malkie thought, not for the first time, that he might never see a more heart-warming smile.

'So, is this a social call or are you working undercover again? You look less scruffy than last time I saw you.' Her lopsided grin widened and her eyes twinkled.

'I was just passing and thought I'd say hello.'

'To make up for calling too late last night, you mean?' Her grin widened even further and her eyes shone with glee.

Malkie felt warmth in his cheeks. He smiled, found himself less sorry to have been busted than he should.

'Dame Helen?'

Deborah laughed. 'Yes. She told me all about it over breakfast. She said you were quite put out that I'd gone to bed already.'

'Ah. Very funny. Silly old fart making a fool of himself, right?'

Her grin faded but a warm smile remained. 'I suspect you're no fool. Dirty Old Man, obviously. But no fool.'

They sat in silence for a few minutes. He found himself comfortable saying nothing. Normally, saying nothing, for him, was a defence mechanism, a way to minimise the damage his mouth seemed to have a particular talent for getting him into. But this was different. Deborah seemed to accept everything at face value. She'd asked him nothing about his life, about his family, or his job, and yet he felt certain that came from a willingness to wait, to get to know him as quickly or as slowly as he felt comfortable with. She had to be at least five years younger than he was, but she showed more maturity and confidence in herself than most people he knew ever achieved. Possibly a result of recovering from near-fatal injuries to find herself cut loose and left to find her own way back to whatever kind of life she could make for herself.

Malkie found himself staring at her. She'd closed her eyes and her chest rose and fell, slow and steady. At one point he feared she'd stopped breathing and was about to reach for her when she started again with a huge inhalation, followed by a long and languid exhalation and a contented sigh.

'How do you do it, Deborah?'

She opened her eyes, looked surprised. 'Do what?'

Malkie realised he had no idea how to answer. 'How do you... keep going? You've had it so rough. Some people would give up, but you... you keep going.'

She thought for a moment. 'There was this guy stayed here for a while. Geoff something. He came in with only minor injuries, really, but he'd also been diagnosed with multiple sclerosis.' She gazed off to the distance as if searching for the rest of a memory. 'He did nothing but moan and bleat and whine about the rotten hand life had dealt him. All day, every day. Complete victim mentality. Nice enough guy but every day he woke up he surrendered to his bitterness without even thinking about fighting, you know?'

Malkie watched her, realised he'd be happy to listen to her all evening, if he could.

'That poor man went downhill so fast it was horrible to see. We watched him fade away in front of us. One night his heart just stopped.'

She paused, dropped her gaze to her hands in her lap.

'I think I decided to hang on to the fact that once they'd told me I was out of danger, that I wouldn't die on an operating table again, I realised that this' – She held up her left hand, scarred and broken and missing two fingers – 'This and the state of the rest of me was as bad as it was going to get. Am I making sense? That poor sod's condition was progressive and he just accelerated it. Maybe he just didn't want it to take years to kill him.'

She stopped again, considered her next words. 'I don't know. Whatever years are left to me, I want them. They're mine, you know? Dame Helen always says *"Don't count the days. Make the days count."*'

She looked at him, grinned, sheepish and embarrassed. 'I do talk a lot of tripe sometimes, you know. I should have warned you about that.' She laughed.

Malkie had to choke back tears.

Before he could think of a response worthy of her courage and her clarity of sight, footsteps in the gravel driveway made him turn. Steph approached. She stopped by the car, leaned back against it, and fiddled with her phone.

Deborah's smile faded. 'Work?'

Malkie's mind crashed back to ugly reality. 'Aye, I'm afraid so. I have to go and talk to someone who should scare the shite out of me but doesn't, and that might be why I really shouldn't be the one to talk to her. But it's a conversation only I can have. Did that make sense?'

'Not to me, but as long as it makes sense to you. If it's the right thing to do, the smart thing, then go get her, Detective.'

He considered her words. 'Smart, no. Right? Hell yeah.'

He stood. After a moment's awkwardness, he leaned down and kissed her cheek. Not the smooth, undamaged side, but the scarred and leathery skin of her other cheek, the side that proved what a survivor Deborah Fleming had decided she was going to be.

She glanced at him, surprised, then her eyes brimmed. She took his hand.

'Visit me again soon, Detective Dirty Old Man, and that's an order.'

He smiled, then turned to go before his own eyes welled up.

Steph saw him approach and climbed into the passenger side. Malkie climbed into the driver's seat. He stared out the windscreen and let loose one small sigh.

Steph said nothing, but he thought he felt fond approval coming off her in waves.

FIFTY-EIGHT

Malkie and Steph found lights on in Shaw's home at The Grange in Edinburgh. He asked Steph to wait in the car. Should any difficult questions hit her later, she was to claim Malkie asked her to accompany him but made her stay in the car and didn't say why. She'd asked what the hell she was there for if all she was to do was wait. Malkie had been able to find no good reason except that he wanted her there to discuss whatever was said between him and Shaw. After a hand on his arm and a reminder of what he might be risking – not just his own future, but his dad's too – she let him leave the car.

He paced the pavement outside Shaw's garden gate as he agonised over how – or even whether – to enter the house and broach the subject. Of all the ways this could go, none promised to end well for him. If he was lucky, he'd get another huge black mark on his otherwise shocking disciplinary record. If unlucky, goodbye job and pension and any hope he had of salvaging a decent life for himself and his dad. He had to admit the future he hoped to build for them would seem idyllic and privileged to many people. The cabin, once renovated, would be cosy and peaceful, the view across Harperrig Reservoir and down the hulking line of the Pentlands on the southern skyline, even their financial situation would improve once his dad's charred plot of ashes was sold. With no mortgage outstanding on the cabin or the land it sat on, they could be comfortable for life. Even his dad's boat *The Droopy Goose* might be brought back into a fit state to embark on the cruising holidays they'd always dreamed of.

Was he really about to risk it all just to call out one possibly – he reminded himself – corrupt cop with a shameful past? Bringing her down would do him no good except scratch his chronic self-righteous need to kick the shit out of injustice anywhere he found it. In the increasingly corporatised world of modern policing, hanging someone as senior as Shaw out to dry might even fuck *his* so-called career beyond repair. Doing the right thing often clashed directly with doing the political thing. Trust in the police was a fragile thing these days, and the last thing senior management would welcome was another stain on their upper echelons.

He'd been here before, driven to gamble everything on evidence no one could refute, but which could blow up in his face and end up biting him on the arse anyway. At what level did a Police Scotland executive become untouchable? It probably depended on what shite people tried to stick onto them, but Malkie would bet his pension a forty-five-year-old error by a PC in Shaw's charge would slide off her fairly easily.

But that was where he struggled. 'I'm sorry, Lillian. They made me...' she'd said. Who? And made her do what? In all the research he'd done into that event so long ago, he'd seen nothing but statements corroborating Shaw's version of what happened that night. Alice Garten was arrested for public order offences and dumped in a cell to cool off. Shaw decided to go easy on the girl, omit any paperwork, give her a bed for the night, then drive her home. But Lillian Crosbie had – against character by some accounts – thrown the girl out in the snow at an ungodly hour and into the icy embrace of a West Lothian winter.

Shaw had claimed she'd thrown the book at Crosbie, brought the full weight of what disciplinary procedures they actually paid attention to back then, but now she was claiming Fisher was concocting some story about Shaw having covered it all up to protect Crosbie. If Shaw had claimed Fisher had stabbed her that might have made sense, but why would Crosbie try to kill Shaw and go after the other officers on duty that night? Because they didn't protect her from the fallout of her own mistake?

They made me...

The words rattled around his brain, wouldn't come into any kind of clarity, any kind of explanation that made sense.

He stopped. As so often before, his brain presented him with the worst possible explanation.

Shaw had turfed Alice Garten out, and blamed Crosbie.

But why? The answer to that came as quickly and as sickeningly. The women in policing thing. Shaw had been their poster girl, their shining example of how women could flourish in the Scottish Police Force. Malkie could imagine the boys' club of Scottish policing in the seventies and eighties would be just desperate to see women in uniform crash and burn and take their unwelcome ideas about women on the beat with them.

If Shaw did have more to do with Alice Garten's death, then wouldn't the powers that be have gladly sacrificed Crosbie – quiet, timid, ineffectual Lillian Crosbie – to save their poster girl from going down in ignominy?

It all made more sense to Malkie than he wished it did. He yearned for some other theory to pop into his frantic mind, some other explanation that didn't involve his career self-destructing.

But nothing came. It all made sense. Crosbie had been thrown under a bus to protect Shaw and her glittering rise through the ranks. And now, what? Crosbie was taking her revenge? But why now, after so many years? A thought tickled at the back of Malkie's mind. He pulled his mobile phone from his pocket. He recalled the video of Shaw's press conference a few weeks ago, the one he didn't get to watch to the end before interviewing her the first time. Some reporter asked loaded questions about cover-ups and whitewashing in the police force. He entered 'Shaw' and 'promotion' and 'cover-up' into a search engine. Top of the list of hits was a news piece about the announcement of Shaw's imminent promotion to Area Commander. Malkie held his breath as he clicked on the video.

The same video appeared. Shaw stood at a lectern, camera flashes going off all over her, taking questions. He watched her fend off a few inane queries about women in the police force and juggling motherhood with such a stellar career. Then he found it, and he remembered. A reporter from one of the red tops.

'Is it true, DCS Shaw, that you were based at the old Livingston Police Station on the night of Hogmanay 1977, when a young girl, Alice Garten, was released prematurely from custody and died of exposure on her way home?'

Shaw's jaw muscles bunched, but only for a second. Malkie didn't doubt she had an answer prepared.

'A most unfortunate incident. The young lady, Miss Garten, was brought to the station for her own protection. She had been acting violently towards some youths in the city centre and was showing no signs of relenting, so for her own safety, we put her in a cell with some warm blankets and some hot tea. She calmed down and we assured her we'd take her home first thing in the morning. Unfortunately, one of my officers, for reasons we never managed to fully determine, released the girl prematurely, as you say. Miss Garten seemed to have gotten lost and died of exposure while trying to walk home.'

Shaw paused, seemed to take a moment to gather herself.

Malkie couldn't know if anyone present at the press conference had been convinced, but from what Malkie had seen of her, needing to take a moment in such a public situation didn't match the woman he'd met.

'The officer in question was reprimanded to the full extent of disciplinary procedures at that time. She served for a few more years, I believe, then left the Force.'

The journalist puffed up, obviously ready to go for his killer question. 'And can you comment on persistent rumours about a cover-up to protect Constable Crosbie from the fallout from her actions? I believe you were the ranking officer on duty that night, correct?'

Shaw hesitated, then seemed to come to some kind of decision. 'The officer in question was Police Constable Lillian Crosbie. Had we known how unreliable she was we would have taken steps to retrain her, but her actions came as a complete surprise to all of us on duty that night. The poor woman was unfit for the job and should never have been in the uniform in the first place. What she did was shocking and negligent and I'm sure she's carried the terrible impact of her actions on Alice Garten and on her fellow officers with her for the rest of her life. But as to rumours of a cover-up, I can assure you that by unanimous agreement of all on duty that night, Lillian Crosbie was subjected to full disciplinary action, and no concessions were made to her being a member of the Force. Now, would anyone else—'

Malkie stopped the video. He'd heard enough.

'They made me...'

If the unanimous testimony was that Crosbie had released the girl, then what else could Shaw have been pressured to blame on her?

Shaw had been the one who threw Alice Garten out in the middle of winter. Shaw was responsible for her death. Lillian Crosbie had taken the fall for it. No wonder the old girl was now going after Shaw. Her and the other officers who did nothing to stand up for her. If Shaw hadn't gone on to hang Crosbie out to dry so brutally to the country's press, might this whole mess have simply never happened? Was that the trigger? Crosbie had seemed, if not happy, then at least content to let it lie. Had Shaw's lies about that night been the thing that pushed Crosbie from a decades-long isolation into a need for retribution?

The words on the photo came to mind. '*Time and silence*'. They perfectly described Crosbie's self-imposed hermetic existence. Until Shaw pushed her beyond her tolerance.

Did Fisher find out that Crosbie was on the warpath and saw an opportunity to score some points – and some easy cash – from Shaw? But Billy Irvine failed to kill her and she escaped. But why kill Crosbie? Especially with a huge promotion imminent?

Enough. Get in there and get the answers.

He stomped up to the door and knocked, then braced himself, his heart in his mouth. She opened the door and studied him, imperious and disapproving, a half-full crystal whisky tumbler in her hand. On the floor of the hallway behind her he saw three suitcases and an overnight bag. Before he could ask about them, she spoke over him.

'You haven't found Fisher, I take it?'

'No. Not yet.'

She shook her head, disgust written plainly on her face. 'And Ben Hutchison? Have you found him?'

Malkie felt a lead weight of dread land in his guts. 'No. No, ma'am.'

'Thank you, DS McCulloch. Now, have you found Lillian Crosbie?'

'No, ma'am.'

'Any promising lines of investigation in either of the murders she's committed?'

Malkie shook his head, but something tickled his mind. 'You mean the murders we *believe* Crosbie committed, ma'am?' He knew he was reaching, but her certainty about Crosbie's guilt smacked a little too much of an opinion based less on evidence and more on... on what? Why would a senior police officer state such an assumption so confidently without evidence? Police investigations were a structured process designed to gather and collate intel and evidence. They had it hammered into them as detectives that premature assumptions led to confirmation bias, and so even assumptions based on overwhelming observations had to be tempered in the absence of verifiable facts.

Shaw took a moment to answer. 'Who else, DS McCulloch?'

Malkie's bullshit detector blew itself off the scale. Something in her eyes. Non-verbal communication they called it at Tulliallan, but Malkie had been an expert at reading people for far longer ago than his cadet days. Long years trying to read people and for the most part failing miserably had at least taught him how to spot the telltale signs that he was not welcome in company, or that he'd just put his foot in it again. Or that someone had just said something they'd really rather they hadn't.

'Forgive me for being a tad slow on the uptake, ma'am. It's just that you said you clearly identified Crosbie as the person who stabbed you, but as yet we have no positive forensic evidence of Crosbie's presence at any of the crime scenes. I'm just not used to an SIO making such sweeping assumptions without verified evidence, that's all.'

The look Shaw held on him could have curdled milk, but he held her gaze. She glanced over his shoulder and around the upper windows of the houses across the street. She stepped aside, opened the door wider. 'Inside, please, if you're actually going to be stupid enough to do this.'

Malkie entered. She closed the door, walked past him

without a word, and sat in one of a dozen chairs around a huge mahogany dining table in a room off the hallway to the right. Malkie took another chair at the same end of the table, adjacent but offset from hers.

Shaw crossed her legs at the ankles, placed her whisky glass on the polished mahogany, and nestled both hands in her lap, every inch of her exuding the kind of entitlement and arrogance Malkie found it so easy to loathe. 'Given that you've found neither of them, why are you here, DS McCulloch?'

Malkie returned her gaze. He doubted he could be formally disciplined for a mere suggestion of professional disrespect, but she could ruin him in other ways.

'In the hospital, when you had your fall and needed to be sedated, I sat with you for a while, ma'am.'

Shaw waited.

'I thought I heard you say something as the sedatives were taking effect. Something that troubled me, and I feel it only fair to make sure I'm in full possession of all possible information in case you were trying to communicate something to me.'

Shaw stiffened.

'The thought that you said something to me you have no recollection of. That bothers you, does it?

'What is it you think I said, McCulloch?'

Malkie braced himself. He harboured no doubt he stood on the edge of a precipice. He could still back off, find some way to change what she said to take the sting out of it, but he knew he wouldn't. Something stank, and he couldn't stop it from offending his over-developed loathing of any possibility of privilege and position shielding people from justice. If there was something here, something she should be held to account for, he wanted it exposed. Even if only ever to himself. He needed to know.

'I got the impression you said something about being made to blame her for something. Crosbie, I mean. You said her name.

Actually, you said "Lillian". Can you explain that, please? Put my mind at ease? Ma'am?'

Shaw stared at him for an age. The longer she took to answer, the more Malkie knew she had more to do with Alice Garten's death than she claimed. Either that or she was holding her temper so she could inform him that his career was over without losing her temper and her dignity.

'You must have misheard me, DS McCulloch. I can imagine no reason why, even under the effects of sedation, I might say anything like that.'

'Then it's fortunate we don't need to rely only on my old memory, isn't it.' He pulled his phone from his pocket and placed it on the table in front of him.

Shaw glanced at it, then something seemed to break in her. She lunged forward and made a grab for Malkie's phone, her face suddenly furious; he'd touched a very sensitive nerve, and he felt a momentary rush of hope. He snatched the phone back before she could reach it. She collapsed back in her chair. Malkie sat back in his own chair with his mobile in his fingertips and prominently perched on his side of the table.

Shaw's eyes shot pure venom at him. Even Malkie was surprised at the change in her, at her sudden and complete loss of self-control.

'What the fuck are you playing at, McCulloch? Is that' – she nodded at the phone – 'meant to be some kind of threat? Were you stupid enough to record me under sedation? Am I supposed to be afraid you're recording me now? Are you really so stupid you don't realise that even if I did say something like that in some semi-conscious state, it would be so inadmissible as evidence any judge would throw it out in a second. Can you really be that stupid?'

Malkie sat through her rant, more convinced with every sentence that he had her rattled. He had one more card to play, one more chance to break her and get the confession he wanted.

'Can you shed any light on some items of clothing we found at Sheila Ferguson's and Paul Gaddon's murder scenes, ma'am? And when I say *"found at the scene"* I mean submerged in several pints of their blood?'

Her face turned white.

You already know they were baby clothes, don't you? You're up to your neck in this. Crosbie never did kill Alice Garten, did she?

Malkie stood, picked up his phone. 'I apologise for upsetting you, ma'am. I simply wanted to give you every opportunity to admit, even if only to little old me, what a fucking disgrace it was what you did to that poor woman. All so you wouldn't lose your precious place on the greasy pole. I can barely look at you.' He turned to leave, knew he'd just thrown everything away. He wished he could feel it had been worth it, but he felt nothing but regret that he'd failed to ignore a foregone conclusion to save his career and his pension and what happiness he ever thought he could secure for himself and his battered and heart-broken dad.

As he turned to leave, her whisky glass arced over his shoulder and smashed against a wall, and she hissed at him, 'You little prick. In a few weeks' time I'll be a mile up the food chain from you, and when that happens, you're fucked. Career, pension, any future job prospects, all fucked, you little shit.'

Malkie took a deep breath, but it didn't stop his temper from over-topping. He turned on her.

'Even if the entire fucking executive of Police Scotland closes ranks and shuts me out, I mean to make sure people hear what you did and what a filthy, disgusting, repellent excuse for a human being you are. Ma'am.'

Even Shaw looked stunned, probably hadn't had a Police Scotland officer as much as raise their voice to her in fifteen years.

'You can try, McCulloch. You can try.' The venom in her

eyes could have turned a weaker man than Malkie to a quivering, apologetic wreck.

He raised one finger to his forehead in mock salute. 'Yes, ma'am. I can.'

Back in the car, Steph opened her mouth to say something but Malkie held up one hand.

'Oh, Malkie. How bad was it? Actually, don't tell me. I'll wait for the edited highlights in front of Thompson.'

Malkie closed his eyes. Bile burned the back of his throat. He'd gone too far. Again. Would he never learn?

'Whatever happens to me, you were never here, OK? You were nowhere near me tonight, you didn't hear from me all evening, and you had zero knowledge of my intentions. Got that?'

She nodded, a resigned look on her face. She'd be there for him but couldn't hope to pick up all the pieces he expected his life to crumble into.

Malkie slapped his hands on his thighs, forced himself back into moving forward. 'Anyway, what were you about to say?'

Steph looked like she'd rather have her teeth pulled out than answer.

'Claudette Crawford.' She didn't need to say any more.

Malkie leaned his head on the car window and closed his eyes. 'Stop the world...'

'We want to get off?' Steph finished for him.

FIFTY-NINE

Fisher found crime-scene tape sealing his front door shut when he reached his flat. He sliced through it with his multitool; if this evening went as he expected, maybe even hoped, it would make no difference.

He poured himself a half glass of Glenmorangie and settled into his favourite chair. He dialled the number Michael had given him. Michael answered in a second.

'Where are you, Fisher? We need to talk.'

'I'm at home. You prick.' He hung up.

He sipped his whisky, savoured it in case it turned out to be the last glass of the stuff he ever got to enjoy. He was tired. Shaw would never leave him alone, now. She had too much to lose. Police Scotland wouldn't let her allow this mess to tarnish their already battered reputation if at all possible without dragging any other executive officers down with her. His only remaining hope was that he could help make that happen. If the coppers made good use of the page torn from the custody book from that night, she might yet go down. He had no doubt the torn page wouldn't survive long as credible evidence. After forty... How many years was it? Anyway, after so long he guessed no forensic lab could definitively prove those initials were written by her. Any decent brief would argue that Crosbie herself could have written 'MS' against Garten's release. Motive would be secondary; burden of proof lay on the prosecution, always. Particularly so when the reputation of an executive officer and – by association – the Force, could be hammered.

The passing of time gave him too much space to ponder just how monumentally he'd fucked this all up. First, giving any job from her, of all, people, to a moron like Billy Irvine: what was he thinking? Did he blame laziness? Complacency? Cowardice, even? All three. He should have done the job himself. Crosbie had got the better of him just that once, but he'd been on the back foot, scunnered by Billy's abject failure. That, and the appearance in Crosbie's hallway of what could only be a copper. No, if he'd gone in there calm and prepared and with his thinking straight, the old cow would have gone down easily and none of this shite would have happened.

How many people had died in just a week because of his unprofessionalism? Ferguson. Gaddon. Crawford.

He regretted what Claudette had forced him to do to her. They'd been an item for all of three days, all those years ago, but it still ranked as the nearest thing he'd ever found to feel nostalgic about. That could have been more, if she'd been able to see past his one isolated – he'd assured her – loss of control, and that one slap. She'd been intractable, despite his protestations that anyone could slip up once. Besides, he hadn't even bruised her, so why she'd had to build such a big deal out of it, he'd never worked out.

He'd done all he could to remain detached when he tortured her, told himself he was on a job and all he could do for her was hurt her as much as he could as quickly as he could, so as to at least minimise the length of her ordeal. But if he was honest with himself, he'd felt no different to when he'd questioned Ferguson and that stupid Hutchison boy, Peter. His hand had been forced on each occasion, and only their own stupidity and stubbornness had necessitated their suffering.

He closed his eyes. He'd downed three glasses of Glenmorangie in fifteen minutes and sleep called to him. Falling asleep, even for a few minutes, was the worst thing he could do with Michael on his way. But he'd taught himself over many years how to set some kind of internal alarm.

As he dozed, it occurred to him – was this the kind of complacency he'd despised in so many others? No, he knew himself, knew his limits and his capabilities. When Michael arrived, he'd hear him and he'd be ready for him. It had just been so long since he'd slept through a whole night.

He felt himself lean towards blessed and seductive darkness and shook himself awake again.

Was he giving up? Telling himself he'd fight on while tacitly capitulating? He'd always liked that word, even as he despised seeing other people – weak and spineless people – indulge in it. Capitulation. It had a ring about it.

Just a few minutes, so he'd be fresh to handle that fucker Michael if he dared to show his face.

He was so damned tired.

SIXTY

Both Malkie and Steph hesitated before they could approach Claudette Crawford's house. The same MO, the third victim. On top of having been bled dry, she looked to have had a fingernail loosened, too. With some kind of tool. Did this mean her death was more personal?

Malkie recognised none of the SOCOs, which suited him: he had no appetite for banter. They signed the scene access log and suited up without a word to the SOCOs or each other.

Inside, a feeling of déjà vu sickened Malkie to his stomach.

Claudette Crawford sat in an armchair, one arm hanging down to a basin on the floor full of her own blood. Malkie noticed she hadn't been tied down like Ferguson and Gaddon, but three empty vodka bottles on the floor might explain why it hadn't been necessary.

When they'd gone through the routine checks of the body and surroundings, Malkie turned to the basin on the floor. The blood was fresher this time.

He turned to a SOCO. 'When did this happen? I know, I know, it'll be in the report, but give me some idea? Last couple of hours? Longer than that?'

The SOCO thought for a second. 'I believe a neighbour reported raised voices, then what sounded like scuffles and muffled screams. She was too scared to look out the window but she dialled 999 immediately. So, the best I can offer you is three hours ago. But—'

'Aye, OK. I won't quote you on it. Thanks.'

The SOCO stared at him for a few seconds then turned back to her work.

He turned to Steph, and they both glanced at the basin.

'Sorry, me again. Has anyone looked in the basin?'

The SOCO sighed and stood, looked perplexed, as much as she could with only her eyes visible. 'For what?'

'That's a "no" then. Can you do that, please? Like, now?'

The SOCO opened her kit case and pulled out a plastic evidence bag and a sealed packet of tweezers. She opened them with a long-suffering sigh and approached the basin. After giving Malkie one more look that said '*Really?*', she bent down to the basin and poked around with the tweezers. Malkie and Steph both saw her hand stop, and she looked up at them, the expression in her eyes unreadable.

Malkie leaned over. Steph didn't. The SOCO pulled the tweezers from the blood. A small mass came out, too soaked in blood to identify, but obviously fabric of some kind.

Malkie's guts sank. Steph leaned in.

The SOCO held the tweezers as blood dripped, slow and sticky, back into the basin and the shape of the object revealed itself.

A baby's bootee.

SIXTY-ONE

She's not giving up. Not surprising, I suppose. Do they all deserve what they're getting? Do I?

Yes. I probably do.

What else could we have done but close ranks? What other choice did I give them?

And that idiot, Fisher. What was he thinking using a boy who was so out of his depth?

Sheila Ferguson dead. Paul Gaddon dead. And from the sounds of her last message, Claudette Crawford, too. How could they never work out I hijacked Mark Balfour's login to that stupid chat of theirs before I had him disposed of? Stupid man, trying to blackmail me.

Crawford didn't deserve any of this. She was the only one who wanted to defend Crosbie. I couldn't blame her for taking so much persuading not to.

Gaddon: disgusting, venal excuse for a man, always was. No one will mourn him.

And Ferguson? Weak. The most basic of threats had been enough to stop her from stepping up and revealing the truth. Loathsome and despicable, and she knew it. If ever there had been a case for medicinal alcoholism, Ferguson had been it. I wonder if the poor old cow ever learned to drink, after all. If anyone had enough to want to forget...

If memory served not one of them lasted more than another year in service, all quit during '78.

I've made myself recall the whole sordid story so many times, and I always come back to the same conclusion. What happened, happened. When I saw what I saw in her cell, I had no choice. We had to scrub and mop and sterilise that cell. How could so little blood cause such a mess?

Why hadn't she told us? Stupid, stupid, girl. We could have got her to a hospital. If only she'd said. What was it Crosbie called me while we were cleaning that cell? 'An empathy-free zone.' Was I? I made my decision based on everyone's best inter-ests, didn't I? Alice Garten needed to get home to her family, and without them asking difficult questions about a police escort home. Did her family even know the condition she was in? I might have forced a family crisis just showing up on her mother's doorstep. I had no right to force the poor girl into that, did I?

No, I did the best thing for the girl. For everyone.

And I kept the others out of it as much as I could, didn't I? Dealt with it myself. When the blame fell as it did, what could I do? I had responsibilities, people depending on me.

Yes, my hands were tied. For everyone else's sakes if not my own.

If only I hadn't signed that damned custody sheet before going in there. I always signed it after a check, never before. Why did I get it wrong that night, of all nights?

No. I'm not at fault here. My hands were tied. I had no other realistic choice. I had to let her take the fall.

It was my fault Alice Garten died that night.

Her and her baby.

But they won't let me go down for it, now. Not me. Not their poster-girl. I tried to be sorry, Lillian. I really did.

SIXTY-TWO

Neighbours complained about the smell coming out of Crosbie's home in the early hours of an otherwise bright and fresh morning.

Malkie and Steph stepped out of the car in silence, an air of dread and sick realisation thick between them. Malkie spotted a mass of flies swarming outside her bedroom window, and understood with a sickening shock where Crosbie had been all this time.

The smell hit them as soon as they opened the front door. Malkie choked on a mixture of revulsion and fury; from the strength of the odour, he feared she had to have been dead for days which meant not one of the killings of the past week had been down to her. He knew what waited for him upstairs, and as much as he feared it might break him, he owed it to her to be the first to find her. He needed her to be treated with the compassion and dignity he now knew she deserved and had deserved all through the past awful decades but had been ripped from her by Shaw's weakness. Steph stayed outside to call the city mortuary to come and get her, but she'd know what he needed first was a moment alone.

He found her laid out on her bed. Someone had brushed her hair and arranged her in a peaceful, funereal repose, her hands crossed on her chest. The little suitcase she'd been clutching the first time Malkie saw her sat on the floor against a wall, unopened.

On one side, low on her back, he saw a dark stain on her blouse, where he'd seen Fisher land a blow on her with his blade. So now he knew how she'd died, and could safely assume it had been the day after he first met her. How she'd made it to Ben's shelter and then back home without bleeding out testified to massive strength and willpower.

In her fingers, she clutched a copy of the same photograph they'd found the first night they attended her home as a crime scene. Crosbie and – he now recognised – Ben Hutchison, both young and full of ambition but ignorant of the hell ahead of them. He noted how the love in Hutchison's adoring gaze at Crosbie was absent from her face. He gazed, rapt, at her, but she looked forward, into the camera, only the smallest of smiles barely touching her lips. Was that the happiest time she ever knew? He could believe it had been.

The second photo had to have been Hutchison's, which meant he'd found her and done what he could to preserve her dignity in death. He must have faked his own abduction. To stop Shaw or Fisher from looking for him? He recalled Rebecca Hutchison's words and the admission that had tested Phillip Truscott's professional boundaries – did Ben Hutchison rip himself from one lonely hell into even deeper solitude, all to protect a woman he loved but who never quite loved him back?

She also held an envelope, unsealed but folded over, which Malkie would need to wait for a SOCO to open out for him. Malkie lifted the photo with a pen, enough to see the back, and found what he expected. '*Time and Silence. Love, Ben*'. Since he'd looked up the meaning of the quote from *The Count of*

Monte Cristo he thought it might just haunt him for the rest of his days.

Didn't work for you, did it, Lillian? Time and silence were no cure for the evils done to you, were they?

On a bedside table, a plastic carrier bag lay on a sheet of notepaper. Inside the bag, a single, tiny, blue baby bootee – the twin of the one found at Claudette Crawford's murder scene – along with envelopes and postage stamps. On the paper, in weak and spidery handwriting, every name on the list of officers on duty the night Alice Garten took her own life, four of them ticked off. Had Crosbie planned to send baby clothes to every person on the list? Was that what triggered Shaw, assuming it was her, to send Fisher to kill her? Had Hutchison found the list and possibly more items as yet unsent, and left them at each scene? For what purpose? To make sure the police realised what Garten knew and Shaw had covered up: that Alice Garten was pregnant when she was pushed out into a freezing Hogmanay night to die?

Malkie knew, now, whose DNA they would identify from all four crime scenes. Hutchison had never been abducted. He'd staged it himself, to throw them all off, and they'd swallowed it without serious scrutiny. On finding Crosbie dead, the woman he'd deserted for her own safety, he'd also found the list and put together what Crosbie had planned to do. He'd finished the job for her. Had Crosbie started the whole thing? Had Shaw's comments at the press conference been one insult too many and awakened Crosbie's bitterness and fury with such violent consequences? Without being able to search Shaw's home, he'd never know.

Had Hutchison hidden himself away for decades so Shaw or her thugs could never again torture him again to find Crosbie? Until her bedside appearance at the shelter pulled him from his unimaginable, self-imposed loneliness. There could be no doubt Fisher had sent Billy Irvine to kill Crosbie, but had Hutchison killed the others? Ferguson, Gaddon, Craw-ford? Had Fisher been hunting for Crosbie or Hutchison or both? Or did Shaw send Fisher after Crosbie, then after the others?

Whatever Shaw's involvement had been, nothing would stick to her, and her part in Alice Garten's death would remain untold. He'd failed to nail her, and he'd have to live with that for the rest of his life.

He stumbled from the room, couldn't breathe. Guilt flooded him. Had he done all he could? Was going up against such a senior Police Scotland executive only ever going to end one way: her reputation tarnished but free and unconvictable, and him lucky to keep his job? Had he risked his dad's happiness because he couldn't let go, couldn't allow the inevitable injus-tice to take its course? What was that old saying? '*You can't fight city hall*'?

Steph took his arm. 'Is she there?'

'Aye, she's there. I'm fine. No, that's a lie. We both know I'm not. But I will be. I have to be. Dad needs me. That'll keep me going. The DNA the SOCOs found at the murder scenes is all going to come back as Hutchison. What Fisher's involvement was – if any – is anyone's guess. I'm buggered if I can say.'

Steph leaned back against her car. 'Oh, this is sick. She never killed anyone except possibly Billy Irvine and if so, that was almost certainly in self-defence. Not Alice Garten and not one of the people on the 1978 list. Oh, I called this into Thompson and she told me Rab finally got around to checking out Fisher's flat again. Throat cut. So, we have to assume Hutchison?'

Malkie took a vicious kick at the garden gate and knocked it off its only remaining hinge. He took a second to swallow his rage.

'Fisher must have hurt her that night, after all. She must have broken back into her own home the day after we sealed it, after seeing the state Hutchison was in. None of us thought to look here again and she died alone.'

A new thought slammed into him and nearly floored him. 'Crosbie must have known all along where Ben was but respected his wishes to stay away, to make his sacrifice, his enforced solitude, worthwhile. And Ben must have known all along where Crosbie had been living and stayed away for fear of leading Shaw to her. Fuck's sake, the two of them gave up everything that mattered to them because they feared reprisals. How skewed was their thinking to have imagined Shaw would come after them after so long?'

'Only she did, didn't she?'

Malkie had forgotten Steph was standing beside him. 'Aye, but only after Crosbie pushed her buttons.' He glanced at the bag containing the remaining baby bootee. 'Silly old mare. But still, we – I – let her down. She was old and frightened and hurting and I let her die on her own.'

After a second, Steph spoke, quiet and gentle. 'Malkie, don't go there. This is different. You never had the slightest chance of saving Crosbie. No chance at all.'

He swallowed, breathed. 'All true. But you know I won't see that.'

'I know, but I'll keep trying. Watch my back and I'll watch yours. Deal?'

'Deal. We need to find Hutchison, now we know he wasn't abducted and he killed all of them. For her. Sneaky old bastard.'

She punched his arm. Steph chuckled. 'The world needs sneaky old bastards, old man.'

Malkie sighed and walked back to Steph's car. 'Oh, by the way. There's something in her hand for the SOCOs to retrieve. A photo like the one we found in her room that first night, and something in an envelope.'

'I'll deal with it.'

SIXTY-THREE

Saturday morning, and in the CID room Thompson, Steph, Malkie, and Campbell sat in miserable silence.

No one fiddled with phones. No one studied case notes. No one looked at each other.

The envelope found in Lillian Crosbie's hands had contained one last kick in the teeth for all concerned, one last sad and sordid secret to round off a sickening case.

Decades-old paper, faded and crumpled but legible. Alice Garten's original autopsy report and her death certificate. How the hell Crosbie had got a hold of them was anyone's guess, but she'd hung on to them for all these years, presumably to nail Shaw with one day, but one day never came.

Alice Garten had taken her own life. She'd miscarried in a police station cell then been turned out into a biting-cold winter night. Shaw must have foreseen an end to her glittering career as a poster girl for women in policing and possible reprisals from people far up the food chain from her. She had thrown the poor, distraught girl out in the cold to find her own way home.

She'd made Crosbie help her clean up the mess, then she'd let Crosbie take the fall for the whole horrific incident.

The autopsy report also revealed that Garten had died because she'd opened her wrists on the park bench beside the River Almond. Malkie couldn't stop himself picturing her, dying alone, tears pouring from her eyes and blood pouring from her arms into the fresh snow of a new year. The whole thing sickened him, and from the looks of the other faces around Thompson's desk, he wasn't alone.

Garten's official death certificate only said that she'd died of exposure. Accidental death. At least now they understood why Hutchison had killed them the way he did: bled out, long and slow and miserable, like poor Alice Garten.

And why all of them? Shaw caused the girl's death, but they all let Crosbie take the blame and ruined her life in the process. The limit of Crosbie's culpability was to obey the orders of a superior officer in the days when a career was not to be gambled with and women had so much to prove to the misogynistic ranks of the Police Force in the seventies. She'd helped mop up the cell and cover up their duty of care, but she had nothing to do with Shaw turfing the girl out into the cold to die.

Repercussions would follow, but no one present gave a damn about that for now. What hurt, what would haunt them all for months, was how for all their efforts, for all their work, they had achieved nothing.

Every detective and Uniform in Police Scotland dealt in their own way with the frustration of toiling for weeks or months to build a case that the Procurator Fiscal then decided had 'no reasonable prospect of a conviction'. It happened too often, the police and the Fiscal hamstrung by too many idiotic Home Office legal safety precautions and a Criminal Justice System on its knees. But they all knew this wouldn't even make it to the Fiscal. Though Thompson probably yearned to nail Shaw as much as he did, she'd know better than present the Fiscal with a case against a future Police Scotland area commander based on evidence even the worst of defence briefs would rip to shreds without breaking a sweat.

They had nothing. A page supposedly torn from a forty-five-year-old custody book that could probably not now be reliably authenticated. Items of baby clothes at every murder scene with only Crosbie's and Hutchison's DNA. Any decent solicitor would have the copy Hutchison placed in Crosbie's hand ruled unreliable, too easily faked even in the seventies.

The whole thing stank, but every person present knew it might never meet the evidentiary threshold for the Procurator Fiscal to reopen Garten's original accidental death verdict.

Phillip Truscott, Ben Hutchison's lawyer, had called asking if a warrant had been obtained to release the man's safety deposit box, and had sounded disappointed when told no. He'd also expressed concern about repeated failure to contact Hutchison's sister, Rebecca. East Lothian Uniforms had visited and found her and her grandson locked up in a pantry, dehydrated and filthy and the lad traumatised by his torture, but both alive.

Despite some apparent, but outdated, skill in avoiding forensic detection, SOCOs had confirmed Fisher's presence at Claudette Crawford's murder scene, but blood spatter suggested that Fisher had been responsible only for her torture before Hutchison later murdered her. Hutchison seemed to have made no effort to cover his tracks.

Fisher's murder was proved to have been at Hutchison's hands, too. No slow bleeding of him, though. A single slash to the throat, deep behind the jugular and out. Brutal but quick.

Not one scrap of solid, verifiable evidence linked Shaw to either Alice Garten's death forty-five years ago, or the more recent murders of Sheila Ferguson, Paul Gaddon, Claudette Crawford or Anton Fisher over the last week. A burner phone had been found in Fisher's flat. Calls had been traced to masts near Shaw's Edinburgh property, but with no Sheriff Court judge willing to issue a warrant to search Detective Chief Superintendent – soon to be Area Commander North East – Shaw's home on decades-old evidence, no one could confirm if the calls had been to Shaw, or to Hutchison, or Crosbie, or any one of the other people whose names had been on the 1978 list.

Donna Campbell had taken over the manhunt for Hutchison with Thompson's blessing, Thompson happy to support as co-SIO.

Shaw had announced that she'd found a camera hidden in her bedroom which showed Fisher sneaking around her room then standing over her as she slept and taking a photograph of her. She had presented the camera as evidence of a threat to her life, no doubt after verifying for herself that the memory card contained nothing that might incriminate her. Digital Forensics had started examining it, but immediately reported that the free memory space on the SD card had been erased with low-level formatting and so would prove irretrievable.

When confronted with the fact that Crosbie had been dead since before Shaw claimed to have been stabbed by her, she said it had been dark and she had been tired from long hours at Tulliallan. No one who listened to her believed a word, and she made no secret of the fact that she didn't give a damn for their scepticism.

Any realistic prospect of bringing a feasible case against Shaw disappeared into the vast gulf between overwhelming circumstantial evidence and what the Fiscal claimed was legally actionable.

Shaw would never answer for her actions. Apart from her undoubted – albeit indirect – murder of Alice Garten, too long ago to have any chance of prosecution now, she seemed to have no verifiable direct involvement in any of the violence of the past week, and without Ben Hutchison in an interview room and willing to talk, no one could see any definitive way to link her to Hutchison's or Fisher's actions.

The injustice of it all would choke all of those who'd heard Shaw's damning but inadmissible confession, but nothing any of them could do would ever see Shaw held to account.

SIXTY-FOUR

The moon shone down on Harperrig Reservoir, slivers of silver dancing on the black water. Not a single cloud marred a vast and clear cupola of stars that stretched from horizon to horizon and beyond the shadowy, black mass of the Pentland Hills that rose up to the south.

Malkie and his dad, Deborah, and Dame Helen, sat around the rickety table on the deck of the cabin, clutching mugs of hot chocolate. Deborah sat in her motorised chair, encased in layers of thermals. A woolly hat with a ridiculously huge pompom bobbed about whenever she turned her head. Dad looked miserable, like the cold was slicing through his puffer jacket and ravaging his old body. Helen Reid sat straight in her chair looking stoic and implacable, as Malkie would expect.

They sat in silence. A huge dinner had left them all stuffed and lazy. Deborah had been beyond excited to get away from the LESOC for an evening, and Dame Helen had glowed with delight to see her come alive.

Eventually, Dame Helen sighed and stood. 'We should get back, Deborah. You need your meds. And your sleep.'

Deborah pouted. 'Yes, Mum.'

Dame Helen tutted and headed for the LESOC minibus to lower the boarding ramp.

Deborah drove up the ramp in one smooth, confident attempt, and smiled sadly at Malkie as Helen strapped her chair into the mounting points on the floor. 'Thanks, Malkie. I had a wonderful evening. Can I come again?'

Malkie gave her a hard stare. 'I'm disappointed you have to ask me that, Deborah.'

She grinned, her eyes gleeful. She waved past Malkie. 'Goodnight, Mr McCulloch. It was lovely to meet you. I hope I'll see you again.'

Malkie's dad stood and shivered but waved back.

When Dame Helen had closed the doors and sat herself in the driver's seat, she smiled at Malkie. 'Thank you for a very pleasant evening, Malkie. This is a truly beautiful spot and you're lucky, you and your father, to get to call it home.' She thought for a second. 'I may not take too much persuasion to drive us out here again, some evening.' She gazed out across the silver-speckled water. 'I have a feeling this place is good for the soul, don't you?'

'We think so, Miss Reid.' Without realising he was about to, he squeezed her arm. She glanced at his hand but smiled.

When the sound of the minibus's old diesel engine had faded away up the A70 towards Edinburgh, Malkie returned to the deck. Dad stood and shuffled inside. 'I'm going to bed. I've been dying out here for the past hour but I didn't want to be rude. See you in the morning, son.'

Malkie chuckled. 'G'night, Dad.'

He walked down to the water's edge, sat on his favourite rock, and gathered his jacket around his neck. His breath puffed out in long, languid clouds of silver.

He'd never been a spiritual man, and had, in fact, often wished he could believe in God so he could have faith that people like Shaw would find themselves hurled into the depths of hell for their sins.

Spiritual. Whatever the word meant, he chose to believe that he and his dad and his mum had spent so many precious evenings here, and his parents had put so much love and effort into building the place in the first place, there had to be something of her here. In the trees and the water and the breezes that blew, always from the west, down the length of the Pentlands and across the water.

'Miss you, Mum.'

He chose to believe he heard her sigh of contentment in the wind.

SIXTY-FIVE

Something woke Shaw.

She knew this cottage, had slept in this room all through her childhood and into her teens. She knew every creak and sigh and grumble this old house ever voiced as it settled into the cold dark hours, but some noise had sounded wrong.

She told herself it was the stress of the past week making her fear trouble from every direction, and that it would pass.

She'd had confirmation from the Fiscal. No further action, no reasonable prospect of a conviction.

Her reputation amongst the executive had taken a battering, but she'd survive that. Senior appointments were never reversed, not in the corporate world of big business and not in the increasingly corporatised world of Police Scotland. It had been made clear to her, though, that Area Commander of the North East Division would be the pinnacle of her career: no further risks would be taken in supporting any further steps up the greasy pole.

She would have to live with that. Natural justice could only be served by crucifying that prick of a man McCulloch, but she was smart enough to see that going after him could only lead to more scrutiny, more suspicion, more digging into a past she should never have disturbed in the first place.

Had it been that damned press conference? Had Crosbie kept her mouth shut about it all those years, only to snap on hearing herself named and shamed and described as the flaky weakest link in the 1978 West Lothian police department?

Should she have let sleeping dogs lie?

She sat up in bed. Moonlight shone bright through the sash windows at the front of the property. She glanced at the clock. Dawn soon, and right enough, a faint glow had appeared in the distance, a soft border between the dark of the North Sea and the nascent red-golden light of a new day as it crept towards her. She rose and dressed. It had been years since she'd welcomed a new day in the cold, fresh country air. She'd missed the view of the sun as it crested the horizon and started to burn away the gossamer clouds of haar on the water.

She made herself a coffee and ventured out into the freezing Aberdeenshire air. In the garden, she checked that the package Crosbie had sent her had burned completely away. She'd watched the flames devour the weave of the tiny, woolly, blue mittens that should have adorned Alice Garten's baby boy.

Why did Crosbie feel a need to rake it all up again after so long?

The press conference.

She couldn't remember exactly what she'd said about Crosbie that day, and she'd never watch it again, but it must have been enough to reopen wounds inflicted so long ago. Which begged a question Shaw knew might haunt the rest of her days: if she had let it go, refused to bad-mouth her, might Crosbie have remained in her miserable little life? Should none of this have happened at all? But there had never been any question of risking that. Not after all she'd done to reach that position.

Beyond the gate in the drystone wall that demarked the

original croft boundary, moonlight painted the grasses and hummocks of the cliff top with dancing, swaying, lazy slivers of silver. Pink-tinged clouds scudded directly above but the sky above the sea ahead of her remained clear, the night's cupola of stars slowly fading as the sky took on the low glow of dawn.

She huddled down inside her coat and sipped from her coffee mug.

McCulloch looked likely to escape serious sanction and would keep his pension, but his retirement would be nothing compared to what she had planned. A Police Scotland executive pension promised to set her up for many comfortable and peaceful Autumn years, time enough to allow her – one day – to forget her mistakes, long past and more recent, and find some peace.

She heaved in a huge breath of icy air and let it out, imagined her cares drifting away on the thinning haar, out to sea. All her current troubles would pass, and she could think of far worse retirements to look forward to.

'Hello, Megan.'

She jumped and turned around.

'Michael. How did you find me? I suppose you want paid? I shouldn't give you a penny: you were only supposed to give me a shallow flesh wound, not nearly kill me, you idiot.'

She waited for an answer, but got a considered, appraising stare instead.

He stepped up beside her. 'You really don't recognise me, do you? Forty-five years can really change a man, can't it?'

'What are you talking about? Of course I recognise you. We talked just a couple of weeks ago at my son's house.' Her tone indicated a creeping dread, confusion and fear of where this was going.

'Does this jog your memory?' Michael raised one wrist and pulled his sleeve back to reveal long, straight, damning scars.

Ice filled her veins. It couldn't be.

'But we met before, Megan, long ago. You, me, and three big brutes in the back of a van. Don't you remember leaving me for dead on Granton Beach?

'How about these, Megan?' He unzipped his jacket and ripped his shirt open, buttons flying. She looked and she remembered, couldn't believe she'd inflicted so much damage on the man, but the evidence damned her.

'Do you remember doing these? Do you remember asking me a hundred times to give her up and I spat in your face every time? Do you remember that?'

She felt blood drain from her face and bile burn the back of her throat.

'Hu–' She swallowed and tried again. 'Hutchison? You were... Him? Michael? All that time?'

'We both hid behind other names, Megan. I disappeared for a reason. I abandoned her for a reason. To stop you from finding her. But you pushed her too far. You lied to the whole damned world about her and she saw it. You humiliated her. That was too much. You should have let it lie. She wouldn't have taken it any further; she only meant to send you a message, so you'd never forget what you did."

Shaw stammered, couldn't think of a convincing response, let alone put anything into words. "Wh – Why didn't you kill me when you had the chance?"

'It was too soon. She only sent those packages to remind you what you all did to her. But you went after her – you stupid, stupid, woman – and after you forced her hand I think she'd have made you wait. You had to be the last.'

She swallowed, her tongue suddenly thick and dry. 'The last to what?'

Tears welled in his eyes.

'Lillian's dead, Megan. And I never stopped loving her. I wanted you to know that. Do you know what that feels like? To be loved?'

She held her hands out, pleaded without words with the man whose life she'd now ruined twice, forty-five years apart.

'This is for Lillian.'

A shove in her chest and she tumbled backwards. It took five seconds for her to plummet and slam into the wave-battered rocks below, and another minute to die, pummelled and broken, her screams of rage drowned in bitter, choking brine.

A LETTER FROM THE AUTHOR

I hope you enjoyed this, my second book, and I hope you found yourself rooting, again, for Malkie's constant fight to seek redemption for everyone, himself included. If you want to join other readers in hearing all about my new releases and bonus content, you can sign up here.

www.stormpublishing.co/doug-sinclair

Can I ask you to be kind enough to leave a review of this book online? Let me know what you liked and what you didn't like, what resonated with you and what really didn't. I need to know so I can grow as a writer and help Malkie be a better man.

Book three will see Malkie have to face up to his biggest personal challenge yet, fatal fire-gutted homes that threaten to derail his ongoing mental recovery from his mother's death, as well as revealing shocking new facts that turn all he believes about her death upside-down.

A word about the 'procedural' aspects of the police procedural genre. I never wanted to write a police procedural in the traditional sense. I wanted to write about the impacts of terrible acts inflicted by one ordinary human being on others, but not only from the point of view of the perpetrators and the victims. Modern policing is such a stressful job. I'm in awe of all good, decent, police officers who look where most of us couldn't and put themselves in harm's way both from the people they hunt as well as from the psychological and emotional brutality that must batter them so often. I've conducted a fair amount of research into Police Scotland structure, policy, procedure, etc., but only to ease my constant fear of insulting these fine women and men by getting stuff too wrong. I'm sure to have been inaccurate on some facts, but my desire was always to write stories about people who get damaged and need to seek redemption and recovery of their own, who just happen to be police officers. My intention was never to be fully authentic or to show off how much research I did, but to write stories about people whom I admire and whom I feel deserve to be cared about.

And yes, I know, now, that chloroform takes minutes to render a person unconscious, not seconds, but I needed it to work more quickly to serve the story.

Please check out my website at www.dougsinclair.co.uk for information on coming books and some free short stories, some of which were written decades ago and languished in a drawer until I dusted them off and decided to believe in them. I write an occasional blog, too, where you can get to know me a wee bit better.

You can connect with me on Facebook, or Twitter, and I'd love to hear your comments. The more 'honest', the better.

facebook.com/doug.sinclair.12382
x.com/DougASinclair

ACKNOWLEDGMENTS

My amazing wife, Maaike, is by far the primary reason that my first book, *Blood Runs Deep*, ever saw the light of day. It's also only thanks to her unwavering faith in me that I managed to finish my 'troublesome second book' to a standard I felt willing to put 'out there'. Maaike is the reason I realised my dreams despite myself and never fell by the wayside.

So, again, my first thanks go to my wife, Maaike, and my mum, both of whom believed in me when I couldn't, and to Donna, my ever-supportive sister-in-law and beta reader.

Thanks, again, to Gordon Brown who got my book into the hands of Kevin Pocklington at The North Literary Agency, who then found it a home with the superb Storm Publishing. I'm as grateful as ever to Oliver Rhodes and Claire Bord for taking a punt on me, and to all at Storm – Kate Smith (aka 'Super Ed') for helping make my book 'sing', Alex Holmes and Shirley Khan and Laurence Cole for steering me gently but firmly through the later editing stages, Anna McKerrow for doing such a grand job of publicising me and putting me 'out there', and to Naomi Knox for supporting me through the run-up to my first ever book launch. Finally, thanks to the talented Angus King for bringing my characters to life so vividly in the audiobook.

Thanks, also, to all who supported and advised me, and kicked my arse when I needed it. Craig Robertson, Caro Ramsay, Douglas Skelton, Lin Anderson, Mark Leggatt, Neil Broadfoot, Gordon Brown, Michael Malone, Carla Kovach, Zoe Sharp, Alex Gray, Graham Smith, Alison Belsham, Noelle

Holten, Sharon Bairden, Jacky Collins, Kelly Lacey, Suze Bickerton, Pam Fox, Gail Williams – thank you for repeatedly reminding me I *can* do this writing lark.

The Twisted Sisters of Dumfries – Irene, Fiona, Linda, Ann, Jackie, Hayley – and the rest of the Crime & Publishment gang – Les, David, June, Angi, Steve and Karen – thank you for letting me join your gang and being there for me.

Andy and Al, Rich, Dave T, Meesh, Wendy – thank you for, well, you know.

Eleanor, Fergus, Rosie, Lorne, Kathy, Helen, Colin – thank you for turning up, mob-handed, to my launch and for not humiliating me as much as we all know you could have.

If I've missed anyone I really shouldn't have missed, please feel free to get me at playtime.